Away from Promise Cove

by

Casey Dawes

Mountain Vines Publishing

Copyright 2024 by Casey Dawes LLC.

All rights reserved.

No part of this book may be reproduced in any form or by any electronic or mechanical means, including information storage and retrieval systems, without permission in writing from the publisher, except by reviewers, who may quote brief passages in a review.

Some characters and events in this book are fictitious. Any similarity to real persons, living or dead, is coincidental and not intended by the author.

Book cover design by GetCovers

Edited by Amy Ewing

Published by Mountain Vines Publishing

Missoula, MT

Chapter One

The humid air slapped Elaine in the face as soon as she stepped off the airplane and onto the air bridge to the Louis Armstrong International Terminal. As she lugged her wheeled carry-on behind her, she wondered—not for the first time—what had possessed her to go to New Orleans for the winter.

Snow and cold, she reminded herself. The feet of white crystals that covered the lakeshore of Promise Cove from fall to spring was pretty, but difficult to deal with. Now that she was in her seventies, cold seeped into her bones as soon as the temperatures dropped below freezing and never left until well after the first day of spring.

She followed the signs leading to baggage claim. The few years she'd gone to Paris during the winter, the city had been just as cold and even damper than Montana, but then she'd had a lover to keep her warm. Well, she'd had him until he fell for someone else. She couldn't begrudge him, though. The woman actually lived in Paris full time, whereas Promise Cove called Elaine home as soon as it stopped snowing on the lower elevations.

That was never going to change.

Reaching the carousel for her flight, she wiggled forward until she could get a glimpse of the gray metal conveyer belt. People milled around her, adding to the heat and discomfort she was feeling.

At least she'd been able to stow her puffy winter jacket in her carry-on during her layover in Denver.

The buzzer sounded, and the belt shuddered into life. A few minutes later, she caught a glimpse of the first bag to make it off the plane.

It wasn't hers. Nor was the second.

About midway through the pile, she spotted hers, but couldn't shove her way through to get it in time. By the time it made another round, she'd been able to push herself forward to grab the back. A sturdy middle-aged man next to her helped her yank it over the edge and onto the floor.

"You pack everythin' you own?" he asked, a faint trace of the south coloring his words.

"Just about," she said. "Thank you."

"No problem helpin' out a pretty lady like you." There was a bit of flirtatiousness in his smile. "You enjoy New Orleans, now."

"I will, thank you." She wheeled her two bags toward the door where a line of yellow cabs waited.

If all the men were as charming as that one, she was going to enjoy New Orleans.

About fifteen minutes later her luggage was loaded, and she was seated in a yellow cab speeding down the major highway that ran through the city. Like the train that went from Orly to Paris, the scenery was constantly in flux, from poorer neighborhoods that had never quite recovered from the disaster of Katrina, to large, well-kept homes she could barely glimpse beyond massive foliage.

It was lush down here.

She longed to wash the sweat from her face. Did things ever completely dry off?

After about a half hour, the taxi exited the highway and whipped through some narrow streets to the place she was staying for the winter. Once she paid him, the driver dropped her bags on the sidewalk and tore off to find his next fare.

The outside of the building was done in a well-kept French Quarter style, with wrought-iron balconies and decorative pieces. Shutters embraced every tall window. The windows on the ground floor also had grillwork, probably as much for safety as for architectural enhancement. The front door was likewise embellished, the modern-day keypad striking a discordant note.

Elaine punched in the numbers the rental agency had sent her, and the door gave a comforting buzz. Hauling her stuff past the heavy door and into the lobby required a struggle. This time there were no obliging men to help her. The corner of the door rapped against her ankles more than once. She'd have bruises for sure.

Relieved to find there was a working elevator instead of the narrow steps she'd had to climb to her temporary abode in Paris, Elaine shoved her luggage into the car, pressed two and watched the doors as they meandered shut. Without a jolt, the elevator rose the single flight, and the doors opened with the same lack of enthusiasm.

Hauling her luggage back out, she oriented herself and walked down the hall to her apartment, once again guarded by a keypad. Another struggle with bags and door and she was home. All without seeing or speaking to another human being.

This new world of the internet and keyless entries was eerie. She missed the scolding voice of the concierge from her building in Paris. Was it possible she'd spend her entire time in New Orleans without meeting her neighbors? After decades in the small town of Promise Cove, it would be a strange occurrence.

Suddenly exhausted, she sank into the stuffed couch and shut her eyes. Somewhere in her temples, a headache had started to form. Tomorrow would be soon enough for exploring. Tonight she'd eat one of the meals Henry had thrust upon her as she'd left Promise Cove and fall into bed early.

THE BED WASN'T HERS. That was the first thing she'd realized when she'd woken up.

Her second thought was there was no coffee in the apartment.

But that would have to wait.

A shower in the delightful bathroom would come first. Like everything else in the furnished apartment, the bathroom was compact, well-appointed, and efficient. Linens had been provided. She stepped into the combination shower-bathtub and let the warm water sluice over her sweat-stained skin.

Heaven. When she lathered up with the soap she'd brought, the difference in the water was apparent. There were substantially more suds than in her bathroom at home. Shampooing reminded her of ads from her childhood: children sculpting their hair into stiff wigs of suds.

She smiled.

It was going to be okay.

Once dressed, she didn't even linger to sort out what she needed in her apartment. Nothing was happening until she got some coffee in her.

Still seeing no one, she made it outside to the street. Mentally flipping a coin, she turned left. She took in everything as she walked, including the Halloween decorations that draped every building, sometimes covering the entire front. Cobwebs draped latticework, and ghosts of all stripes stood on balconies or hung from overhangs. There were skeletons and pumpkins, but the décor leaned more toward those souls still lingering in some form on earth.

It reminded her of the Halloween decorations Sal Rivas put up at this time of year in Promise Cove to embrace his heritage's celebration of Day of the Dead.

She was concentrating so much on the decorations she almost missed the espresso shop taking up the corner spot of a cross street. Not her normal beverage, but why not? She was here to embrace the atmosphere of New Orleans and let it inspire her paintings.

It would be good to rediscover the joy she'd found painting in Paris, itself an unearthing of desires she hadn't experienced since before her marriage decades ago. Her husband had been gone for many years now, but there had always been something to do: keep the general store afloat, care for her child, and eventually help raise her beautiful grandchild.

The Envie Espresso Bar was definitely New Orleans inspired from the architecture to the aroma of fresh bread and spice-infused breakfast. Once she obtained her coffee, she settled into a chair by the window and indulged in people-watching while she debated what to have for breakfast.

As she would expect in a tourist area like the French Quarter, the music of voices contained many different accents and languages. The crowd was mostly young, but she did catch a man about her age staring at her over the top of his newspaper.

She smiled at him.

He immediately raised his paper.

With a laugh, she went back to contemplating breakfast. Spending time in New Orleans was going to be an adventure. The one thing this adventure could not contain, however, was romance. She'd had her fling in Paris, and the pain had been sharp when the affair ended. No, her time in the Big Easy was going to be man-free.

ONCE SHE WAS FULLY caffeinated and fed, she made a list of groceries she needed and located the nearest grocery store, which looked to be a more crammed version of the general store she'd run for decades.

The food was totally different.

There were all types of beans and greens in cans. Beans also came in bags; greens in bundles. How was she supposed to shop without familiar ingredients?

Stop it, she scolded herself. It was no different from Paris, and at least here the labels were in English, and the currency was in dollars and cents. She pulled together enough for a few meals. At the end, she threw in a local cookbook that promised New Orleans cooking on a budget.

She spent the rest of the day becoming acquainted with her new abode, taking another nap, reading, and talking with her daughter, Maggie. As daylight faded, she opened a bottle of wine, poured a glass, and took it and a small notebook out to the balcony that ran the width of the building. Lights came on, accenting the New Orleans architecture and the spooky Halloween decorations. The streets became more populated as people came home from work or started out for an evening's entertainment.

A little way down the balcony, a couple came out of their apartment. Once they settled into their chairs and clinked their glasses, the woman noticed Elaine. She gave a friendly wave, and Elaine waved back.

She should go over and say hello, maybe make some temporary friends. But the visual interest around her was too compelling. Instead of being neighborly, she opened her notebook and began to sketch.

Chapter Two

I t was the magic time, the moment when the first important guests arrived at Fontenot's Fish House for the evening, and the room began to buzz. It wasn't the same time every night, but Lance Fontenot was always aware when it arrived.

Today it was the mayor, his wife, and a couple of unfamiliar young faces. The young women were probably new members of the city council, and the mayor had brought them here to explain to them who they were really working for.

Not that the mayor was corrupt ... well, no more than any of the others had been. Graft and bribery had been an art form in the Big Easy since its founding. Even after the disaster named Katrina, Mayor Nagin had found ways to line his pockets.

Lance played nice with the politicians and cops who came to his restaurant. He had no say over what they did, so he may as well take their money. But he always listened to the conversations. Who knew when they may come in handy?

It was a tactic that had worked well for him in his former business career.

He greeted the mayor with a big smile and was introduced to Whitney Goodwin, a new city council member who was the new chair of the budget committee. The old one needed to be replaced after his recent incarceration for stabbing his wife in a fit of jealousy one night.

The wife had survived. The marriage and his position on the council had not.

The other person, a young man with a name that failed to stick in Lance's mind, had a position on the zoning board. He'd need to ask the mayor later who the person was. Zoning boards were always important.

"We have an amazing new dish tonight that I think you and your wife would enjoy," Lance said confidently to the mayor. "I know you love oysters, and tonight we have baked them under a topping of blended spinach and other greens, onion, garlic, Parmesan and Herbsaint."

"It sounds delicious," the mayor said. "Of course I will have it."

His wife, not an oyster lover, demurred as Lance knew she would. "Trout almandine?" he suggested.

She beamed. "Sounds wonderful," she said, exactly as she did every time he suggested it.

"You must try the oysters," the mayor said to the two young people. "No city council member can get away with not eating oysters." He leaned forward. "Our best decisions are made after a meal of oysters."

Lance laughed. The mayor often outdid himself with a character who oozed Southern charm and corniness, but too many people had underestimated his canniness when it came to getting what he wanted. After a few more remarks, Lance moved on to other tables.

This was the part of owning a restaurant he loved the most: greeting people and talking with them about the food he'd created, urging them to try new things. The patrons were usually a mix of tourists and locals, a ratio he cultivated for his own interest. Tourists came from everywhere and were happy to tell him about their origins. It was like traveling without ever leaving his roots.

When he got done with his first round, he leaned against the bar and sipped the glass of pinot noir the bartender had immediately poured him.

"Good crowd tonight," the bartender, a middle-aged man named Prosper, said.

"It is," Lance replied. He was fond of Prosper, a man he'd given a second chance after the convicted felon had served many years for committing armed robbery in his late teens. In return, Prosper was as dedicated and loyal an employee as Lance could ever wish to have. The man was intelligent and kind, even though he refused to change the speech patterns of his Cajun youth.

Lance respected that. Language was a powerful way to hang on to one's culture.

His eyes scanned the room as he sipped. He was more content than he would have imagined he would be when he retired from his position at the Port of New Orleans. The only thing missing was the woman he'd hoped to have at his side, greeting diners with the smile he'd fallen in love with in his early twenties.

But Camille had wanted no part of the restaurant business. After he'd proposed his plan, she'd told him she'd leave if he put it into practice. He hadn't believed her.

As a result, he'd been shocked when she moved with a retired physician to a villa on the water in Florida.

A group of cops came in with their usual swagger, some still in uniform. Those men and women had probably been identified as likely candidates to play nicely with the shadow cop system. Lance hadn't ever seen evidence of corruption in his restaurant, but there were frequent enough stories to let him know it existed.

Leaving his glass on the bar, he went to greet them warmly, even Vince Landry, a man he didn't trust any more than he would a crocodile snuggling up next to his grandmother. He'd gotten them settled and talked them into fried catfish when his gaze snagged on the tall young man coming indoors, a young girl in his arms.

His son, Xavier with his daughter, Avery.

As soon as the little girl saw Lance, she squirmed from her father's arms and ran across the restaurant to her grandfather, her brown curls dancing, and the blinking lights in her sneakers flashing with each step.

"Gran-papa!" she exclaimed with a large grin as he scooped her up.

"Hello, ma chou," he said, planting a big kiss on her plump cheek.

"Adorable," one of the female cops said.

There were murmurs from around the table.

"She'll be a beauty when she grows up," Vince said.

Lance cut him a glance, but reined in his desire to describe exactly what he'd do if a man like him came near his precious granddaughter.

"Hey, Dad," Xavier said.

"Hello. It's good to see you." Also, unusual. His son was usually too busy trying to save his marriage to come to the restaurant often. He turned to the cops. "Enjoy your catfish," he said, then walked back to the bar.

Prosper topped off Lance's glass of wine as he displayed a wide grin to Avery. "A Shirley Temple for you?" he asked.

Avery nodded. "Yes, please, Mister Prosper," she said in a perfect imitation of her mother, a woman who tried to pretend it was the 1950s, not the 2020s.

"No need to call me Mister," Prosper said as he prepared the drink. "We be friends, right?"

Once again Avery nodded, but her expression was solemn as if trying to figure out if it was okay to be friends with Prosper.

"Hey, Prosper," Xavier said. "It's good to see you. Things going well?"

Her father's warm attitude thawed Avery, and she gave Prosper a smile.

Lance's shoulders relaxed a bit. In spite of his daughter-in-law's outdated views, Avery needed to grow up to understand all people needed to be treated with respect ... unless they proved otherwise.

"It goes," Prosper said, pushing the sweet soft drink concoction toward Avery.

Lance put her down on a stool so she could reach it.

"Still enjoying the business, Dad?" Xavier asked, picking up the wine glass Prosper had filled for him.

"Absolutely." Lance said. What did Xavier want? He could tell by the tension in Xavier's shoulders there was something on his son's mind. "How are things going between you and ...?" He nodded in Avery's direction.

"I think I'm about done with that effort," Xavier confessed.

"Oh?"

"No matter what I do, things aren't changing. I got a promotion at work with more money, but it's not enough to get the house she wants. I don't exercise enough, do enough things with ..." Xavier gestured at his daughter. "Even my clothes are wrong."

"Sounds like she's looking for a way out," Lance said. "I'm sorry."

"Yeah ... well." Xavier sipped his drink, turned around, and leaned with his back on the bar as he scanned the large room.

Almost every table was full. Lights in the ceiling provided enough glow for diners to enjoy themselves, but not be in a glare. Tempting aromas filled the air, and soft music dimmed the clatter of plates and cutlery.

Xavier turned to Lance. "I'm miserable in my job."

Ah. Now they were getting to it. The marriage breakup had been inevitable from Lance's point of view. The pair were mismatched.

He planted a kiss on his granddaughter's head.

They had, however, produced a beautiful child.

But the business? That was new.

"Go on." Lance slid onto a stool of his own while his son took the one on the other side of his daughter.

"The oil business," Xavier said. "It stinks. Literally."

Lance chuckled.

"It's a dying industry," Xavier said. He stroked his daughter's hair. "At least I hope it is. We can't leave a boiling, burning planet to the little ones."

Lance kept quiet. While New Orleans had been built on cotton and its attendant slave trade, oil had certainly muscled in as the dominant industry. They drilled in the gulf, and brought it down from the tar sands of the Dakotas. Many people's livings were built on that industry. They wouldn't pivot easily.

But Xavier was right. They needed to do something to protect the little ones. It was a problem with no simple answers, no matter that politicians and those with a vested interest in one side succeeding or failing tried to feed an easy solution to the public.

"Go on," he said.

"I want to stay in NOLO," Xavier said. "I need to." He nodded at Avery. "That limits my choices."

"There's always the port," Lance said.

Xavier shook his head. "If I'm changing careers, I want to do something I'm passionate about." He stared at Lance and took a deep breath. "I love to cook, Dad. Just like you. I've got the business degree. Let me come into the business with you. I'd love that."

Xavier must be mad.

"No," Lance said. "Absolutely not."

Chapter Three

She must have been crazy.

When Elaine had applied for a permit to set up an easel in Jackson Square months ago, it had seemed like a romantic, wonderful idea. Her paintings would magically appear beneath her fingers, tourists would ooh and ahh, and the canvases would be quickly snapped up by rich passers-by.

The reality was totally the opposite.

Her permit was for a limited time and a particular spot. The spot was in a low traffic area, and she was forbidden to paint on Friday, weekends, or holidays. The area was close enough to walk to, so she didn't need to take a cab, but lugging her equipment through the muggy air made her feel limp and bedraggled.

She set up her easel and folding chair, then sat for a moment and stared at the coffee shop on the corner. It called to her, but how was she supposed to get coffee when her stuff was already spread out? She'd come back, and everything would be gone.

In Promise Cove she could leave anything anywhere.

But this was the big, bad city. Why, oh, why had she decided to come?

People around her were greeting each other, laughing as they set up and began to paint. A man brought a tray of coffee to one group, and Elaine's gaze followed longingly. Not far away, musicians and performance artists set up their props, including hats or open cases to receive money from generous tourists.

An oddly dressed person carrying an umbrella walked down the long sidewalk to the statue of Andrew Jackson on his horse. Each step was taken in slow motion, like he was dragging his legs through molasses.

New Orleans was like no place she'd ever been.

It was crazy to paint mountains at six feet above sea level. Surrounded by levees, refineries, and steam wheelers providing gambling halls, the Mississippi

River didn't seem like the right subject, either. Flower-bedecked horses pulling carriages of tourists didn't sit still long enough for her to sketch them.

Finally, she focused on a bed of flowers somewhat close by and started on them. It took a while, but the magic of her art slowly took over, and the voices around her became background noise.

When she'd last painted in Paris, she'd used oils at Henri's insistence, but she'd wanted a clean break and brought watercolors with her to New Orleans. It was a medium she'd used a long time ago, when she'd dreamed of becoming a famous artist with paintings shown in all the prestigious galleries in major cities.

Heady plans for a girl from Nebraska.

Instead, she'd married a local boy with a dream of owning a general store in Big Sky Country.

Mixing a little blue in with the crimson she'd used for several of the petals, she laid in shadows on the flower before repeating the process with the other colors she'd used, and finally darkening a green for the stems and leaves.

Satisfied, she cleaned off her brushes and relaxed, once again looking longingly at the coffee shop for a few seconds before pulling out her sandwich and determinedly biting down. As she ate, she went back to people watching.

A few other artists looked her way, but their expressions weren't welcoming.

Elaine smiled at the tourists, and a few smiled back, but many kept walking.

Really, if she stayed here much longer, she was going to get an inferiority complex.

She caught a man she half-recognized staring at her, but as soon as he realized he'd been caught, he scurried off.

Oh, yes! The man with the newspaper.

After finishing her sandwich, she checked to see if the paint was dry enough to add in details. May as well get it done and be on her way. She'd definitely have to come up with a different strategy or this was going to be a very difficult winter.

"You're facing the wrong way," a male voice said.

"What?" She had to shade her eyes to look up at him, and even then she couldn't make out his features very well.

The one thing she could guarantee was that he, like far too many men, was a know-it-all.

"Look around you," he continued. "None of the other artists are facing the street directly like you are."

She glanced around. He was right.

"People don't want eye contact; it makes them uncomfortable. They want a glimpse of what you are doing." He shifted around to position himself where he could see her canvas. "Which is very nice, if without passion."

Now he was insulting her?

"Are you an art critic?" she asked, standing.

"No, a restauranteur. I own Fontenot's Fish House."

Now that he was out of the sun, she could make him out. He was a good-looking man—and probably knew it—with dark curly hair, a sharp nose slightly bent at the end, and broad lips. His eyes were such a deep brown they were almost black, an exclamation point in the middle of his lush, dark, eyelashes.

In another time, he would make the perfect pirate.

"So," she began, "in New Orleans, owning a fish restaurant qualifies you as an art critic. I did not know that."

His grin revealed teeth that were neither perfect nor white. He shrugged.

"This is a town that thrives on intrigue and passion. We are born with an innate desire for both. I suspect you must be from the Midwest somewhere ... or maybe New England ... but you don't have that horrible accent. Places where people have convinced themselves that desire needs to be repressed."

"You have a lot of opinions," she said.

A whiff from someone's coffee container caused her to look across at the shop. But now there was another reason for her desire to walk across the street and into the café's open arms. A reason that was starting to make her very uncomfortable.

"Would you like a cup of coffee? I would love to get it for you ... as an apology for my opinions." He studied her. "Or perhaps you would like to get one for yourself? I could stay here to watch your stuff, if that is your worry."

"And steal me half blind?" she scoffed. "You could be anyone. You only say you own a restaurant."

The man turned to the artist next to her, a woman in a flamboyant red blouse who had steadily ignored Elaine the entire time she'd been there.

"Delilah, would you please tell this nice woman from the middle of nowhere who I am?"

The artist looked at Elaine with disdain. "He is Lance. He owns a fish market. But I don't go there because he charges too much money for fish my grandfather can catch from the dock. He can be trusted ... maybe."

"Delilah, you cut me to the quick," Lance said, slapping a hand to his heart.

"I'm only telling the truth," she said. With another glance at Elaine, she added, "I'll watch the man watching your stuff. You can trust me."

It was all very bewildering. Elaine felt like she'd been caught up in a play where everyone knew their lines except her. But necessity demanded she play some part.

"Thanks," she said as she grabbed her purse and half ran across the street to the shop and into its dark recesses. Fortunately, there was no line at the ladies restroom.

When she emerged a few minutes later, she stared at the dizzying array of coffee choices, before getting three black coffees and stuffing plastic milk containers, sugar packets, and fake sugar packets into her handbag.

On her return trip, she took her time crossing the road, very aware of the man who watched every step she made. Her body was very aware of his gaze. Most of the time, she was invisible to men ... to anyone really ... in the way older women so often are.

But being seventy didn't mean she wasn't still alive. Quite the contrary.

"Thank you," she said as she handed the coffee to her artist neighbor.

"He behaved," the woman said as she accepted the sugar but declined the milk. "I made sure of that." She leaned closer. "But he is still a thief with his fish prices."

"I'll be aware of that," Elaine said with a smile.

Lance was staring at the picture she was working on.

"You only paint flowers?" he asked.

"Usually I paint mountains," she said. She'd gone through a period of modern art when she'd traveled to Paris, but like everything else associated with those trips, she'd moved on to another style. She could do adequate landscapes, but they'd never quite satisfied her.

"Mountains?" he asked as he stood.

"I'm from a small town in Montana."

"Far away," he said. "I'd love to see the state. Is it as wild as they show on television? Cowboys and Indians?"

She laughed.

"So, no," he said.

"Not in the way they're shown," she said. "Promise Cove is a quiet, small town on a lake. That's where I'm from."

"Promise Cove. It's a pretty name," he said, moving out of her way. "I'd really like to see one of your mountain paintings."

"I don't have any with me." She turned to keep him in front of her.

"Perhaps you could paint one for me and bring it to my restaurant." He gestured to the other artists. "I have plenty of paintings of New Orleans."

"I'd look pretty silly sitting in this beautiful place painting pictures of something that isn't here."

"You would look unique." Lance nodded to the figure with the umbrella slowly walking back from Jackson's statue. "We appreciate differences in New Orleans." He reached into his back pocket and pulled out a card. "Bring me a painting, and I will give you a discount on the fish."

When she took the card, he kissed the air beside her cheek, waved, and walked away.

"Be careful," the woman next to her said. "He is one of the most eligible men in NOLO. Women will scratch your eyes out if they think he is interested."

Then she shrugged. "But he probably won't be for long. He is far too young for you."

Chapter Four

Lance glanced at the Halloween decorations lingering on the streets of New Orleans as he made his way to the seafood market. Skeletons would slowly morph into Santas over the next month, with the occasional nod to one of the most traditional, yet problematic holidays of the year: Thanksgiving.

He pondered this conundrum as he inspected the fish.

Xavier had made it clear to his mother that when Camille moved to Florida with her retired doctor, he and his family would not be making the trip for Thanksgiving. Xavier's own wife had pressured him to spend the holiday with her parents, and they'd compromised by having a second dinner with Lance on the Sunday following the feast.

That had suited him just fine. Thanksgiving was one of the busiest days at the restaurant.

But now that Xavier and his wife were separating, how would the holiday be managed? All the possible combinations made Lance's brain hurt.

He scribbled notes about how much of each variety of fish and shellfish he would get for the restaurant. The sea trout and small-mouth bass looked good. Shrimp were a requirement, as were catfish. Fortunately, both looked good this morning.

Did the artist he'd met the other morning like fish? He shouldn't give her a second thought. Chances are he'd never see her again unless she was fumbling around Jackson Square again.

He didn't try to stifle a smile. She had been so out of her element, but he had to give her points for effort. He had a hunch she wasn't going to give up, either.

He nodded at a fellow restauranteur and stopped to chat with the owner of a market not too far from his place. They both agreed the sea trout was looking good this morning, beautiful enough to stock.

After placing his order, he walked back to the apartment he kept not far from his restaurant. He'd sold the house in the Garden District where he and Camille had raised their children, needing no reminder of the happiness they'd once shared.

A second cup of coffee accompanied by a sweet beignet gave him the energy to tackle the endless paperwork running a business required.

But still his encounter with the artist ran through his mind.

She had a sense of what was probably regarded as flamboyance in Montana. He knew little of the state, beyond what movies and television had shown him. Images that she'd laughed at. What little he did know told him it was a beautiful place, with more than one well-known national park.

He could see her there—the single artist in a town full of practical people who were good at building log cabins and shoveling snow, both concepts that were alien to him.

No, it would be just as well if she never showed up at his restaurant. She intrigued him far too much. The end of his marriage still stung, but if he were to become involved with someone again, it should be with someone who understood the nuances of the Big Easy. Also, she should be willing to have a casual affair, nothing serious or complicated.

He knew in his heart the artist fit none of those criteria.

"IT HAS BEEN TOO LONG, cher," Lance said as he kissed the cheeks of Thérèse Cormier, his oldest friend.

"I've been busy," she said. "We're launching a new line of linens. You'll love them. They'll be great for your restaurant."

"I will certainly look at them."

"Look, but not buy," Thérèse said. "That is the problem with smart businessmen. They know when to keep their money in their wallet."

He laughed. He had loved this woman from the moment they met in grade school. It was too bad there had never been any sexual chemistry between them. She had been too ambitious to spend her time attracting boys. Now her lines of home housewares were known nationwide. She'd grown into a beautiful woman with a good fashion sense, often seen on the arm of some eligible bachelor at society events.

She'd never married any of them.

Lance escorted her to her preferred table, sending a waitress for his friend's favorite beverage on the way.

Once there, he sat with her a few moments as she told him about her latest line, an upcoming magazine article, and her appearance on a daytime talk show.

"It was so grand and exciting to be in New York. Those people know how to make things run," she said. "Even their political scandals move more quickly." She gratefully accepted her Sazerac cocktail. "But so exhausting. It's nice to be home." After sipping her drink, she asked, "So what is new? You look like something happened. Is it good or bad?"

"Nothing new," he said.

She shook her head. "You are lying. Probably to yourself. Who is she?"

"No one."

Thérèse laughed

He grimaced. He never could keep a secret from her.

"Impossible," he said.

She sipped more of her drink as a waiter slipped Lance's red wine in front of him.

"I don't even know her name," he said.

"Where did you meet her?" she asked.

He told her the story, including his comments about the woman's paintings.

"Oh, you didn't!"

"I did."

"You will never get another woman that way," she said.

"I don't want one. At least not long term. I'm fine with a few months of passion and then moving on. Most women these days are too."

"Lying to yourself again," she said. "You want what you had."

"I can't have it. That ship sailed to Florida."

"Time to find a new one, then. This woman from Montana sounds intriguing. You should go find her again. Invite her to the restaurant properly, not as a trade."

"Why would I do that?"

"To get to know her, of course."

"And then she goes back to the wilderness? A place full of guns, wild animals, and *snow*?" He gave a mock shudder.

"So go with her?"

"My restaurant cannot run itself."

"Hire someone to fill in."

Out of the corner of his eye, he could see one of the tourists becoming demanding.

"You are far too eager to spend my money," he said as he stood. "I'll send a waiter over to tell you the specials."

Leaving his wine glass where it was, he went over to handle the problem. The tourist was incensed there wasn't one offering of a good steak on the menu. It took all of Lance's patience not to point out that this was a fish restaurant. Instead he pointed out the pork and sausage dishes, even offering to create something not on the menu.

At that point the wife stepped in and told her husband to be satisfied with something off the menu, giving Lance and the waiter an apologetic smile.

She must be a saint to put up with him.

Although Camille had told Lance he was often overbearing and demanding in his own way. In her worst moments she called him a bully, which he definitely was not.

He simply had strong opinions.

He thanked the couple for being so understanding and whispered to the waiter to comp their desserts.

This was why it was necessary that he be the one in his restaurant every time it was open. He had to determine what to do in emergencies large and small. Every night brought people like this one.

A new group walked through the door. Whitney Goodwin was back with a few of her contemporaries. He greeted them and brought them to a table. She was young and new, but who knew what influence she might wield someday. Best to stay on her good side.

Once they were settled, he checked in with the kitchen staff. Everything was running smoothly, but he made a few corrections to remind them who was really in charge.

Xavier could never have this finesse. As a child, he'd seemed single-focused. He could play with the same toy far longer than his peers. Once he'd found the saxophone, he'd turned his attention there, playing daily. His phone, when he got one, had depths of jazz playlists that Lance envied. Xavier had brought together friends for trios and quartets. In college, he and some others had done well playing at small clubs. But when marriage was in the offing, his son had settled down and followed Lance's footsteps into the business world.

His son didn't have the background for a successful restauranteur. Not at all.

Giving another glance around the room, Lance made his way back to Thérèse who was finishing up her meal.

"Do you mind?" he asked, his hand on the back of a chair.

"Not at all," she replied. "Your company is always welcome."

He sat.

"Now where were we?" she asked, dabbing her mouth with the linen napkin. "Ah, yes. What you were going to do about the woman in Jackson Square."

"We settled that," he said. "Nothing."

"That would be a shame."

"Why?"

"Because she is the first woman you have mentioned since Camille left you for her doctor."

"Camille left because I opened a restaurant."

Thérèse laughed. "Men can be so blind. She left you long before the restaurant. She simply did not tell you."

"What do you mean?"

"She'd started looking a long time ago. No, she didn't act on it. But you didn't see it because you were so focused on business, you didn't see she no longer talked to you, or even noticed you much at all."

Lance's mind worked furiously trying to assemble a rebuttal to Thérèse's outlandish claim. When he couldn't come up with one, he slumped back in his chair.

He hadn't noticed his wife drifting away so he'd done nothing to stop it.

"Oh, don't look so sad. I've heard it said you are quite the catch."

"I don't want to be caught," he said.

"I think you already are ... just a little. You should ask her to coffee."

"I've already offered dinner for a painting," he pointed out.

"You are hopeless in the world of love," she said. "You offer. You do not demand, or trade, or whatever it was you were trying to do."

He forced a shrug.

"It's no matter. I'm not interested." He drained his wine and stood. "Enjoy the rest of your evening. I will see you again soon." He kissed her cheek and started to walk to the bar.

"Yes," he heard Thérèse say. "Very soon. You will need my help."

Chapter Five

Elaine stared at the ceiling of her winter rental, trying to find the enthusiasm to get up. The beautiful shower with its fluffy white towels awaited her. Her kitchen was stocked with her favorite breakfast foods with a few New Orleans delicacies thrown in. Now that she had purchased coffee, she'd programmed the pot the night before, and it was sending lovely aromas in her direction.

But still, she didn't move.

Her lovely dream of an artistic, sensual, and exciting winter was dying under the weight of loneliness. She'd finally made contact with the people in the next apartment. They were nice enough, but the connection wasn't there.

The problem was that loneliness was what had driven her from Promise Cove in the first place. Her best friend, Henrietta Paulson, had been gone for several years. That had left a hole in her life. She still thought of calling Henrietta to ask her what to do. Sometimes she spoke to her aloud, asking questions or explaining just how angry she was that Henrietta was gone.

Elaine had filled the void with busyness, but now Maggie was happily (finally!) married to Tom, and her granddaughter had started her own life as an adult. Even Elaine's home wasn't quite what it was. They'd sold the general store that had been her husband's dream to a younger couple in town. The new owners said she could live in her apartment above the store for as long as she wanted, but it wasn't the same.

When she went back, she was determined to find a new place to live.

Unfortunately, that would also be alone. She would no longer be able to connect with her daughter or grandchild across the hallway. That part of her life was over. And this time there didn't seem to be a compensating enjoyment.

Finally, she pushed back the covers and padded into the bathroom. The space was beautiful, even if she was going to have to get some cleaning supplies.

A maid service had been offered, but the thought of another woman in her space had made her shudder.

She'd cleaned her own bathroom all her life and that wasn't going to change now.

A half hour later she poured herself some steaming coffee and readied her bowl of fiber-laden cereal.

Her morose thoughts returned.

New Orleans was a sensual city, full of color and light, at least in the district she inhabited. Maybe that was part of the problem. This was a tourist area. One thing she'd learned from living in Paris was that art was sold in the tourist areas, but true art was created somewhere else.

She didn't know this city's soul. It was an alien place.

Maybe she should stick to known items, like flowers and mountains, no matter if strange men came along and declared them passionless. What did he know about art?

She had to give it time. She'd only been here little over a week. How long had it taken her to adjust to Paris? Or even to Montana?

Resolute, she finished her breakfast, gathered her things, and walked to the square.

DELILAH, THE ARTIST who always sat next to her, had thawed somewhat. They'd gotten in the practice of mutual coffee breaks and bathroom runs. Delilah had pointed out the public restrooms in the building behind them, so Elaine was no longer guilted into buying something just because she needed to use the restroom.

Surreptitiously, Elaine watched the artist. She was good at selling her art, acrylics of famous scenes around New Orleans. Delilah kept a stack of postcards to use as inspiration.

Clever.

Meanwhile, Elaine was trying to create an image of the Mission Mountains rising from beyond Flathead Lake from memory. She'd moved her set-up around so it was facing more toward the square, not wanting to take the rude man's suggestion, but also realizing the wisdom in it.

People stopped to watch, but then they moved on. They weren't in the south for mountains and snow, but for the heat, humidity, and exotic nature of a city teeming with jazz, superstition, and intrigue. It was a place where rules seemed to go out the window. Elaine suspected they weren't really gone, simply replaced with another set that she didn't understand at all.

Still she soldiered on, the vibrant blue sky of her home state giving way to the sharp peaks of granite that lined the edge of the Flathead Valley. While she waited for things to dry, which took longer in the humidity of the south, she played with color on a pad of bound watercolor paper. It had been a while since she worked in the medium, and she needed to relearn the color combinations to produce the effect she wanted.

"You might want to try something more local," Delilah said. "It's what they buy."

"I'm not sure I'm into selling. I'm trying to get back into the groove of painting."

"Then what are you doing here, taking up one of these spaces? We all wanna sell. It's a business for us ... how we feed ourselves. These spaces aren't for people who want to play ... or ... rediscover themselves." Delilah put her brush down. "'Sides, ain't you a little old for that?"

"You're never too old to learn something new about yourself," Elaine retorted. *Or too young* ... For all its finesse, the city could produce some rude people.

Her grip on her paintbrush tightened and tears filled her eyes. She couldn't paint. At least not here. Delilah was right. She was taking up space a more serious artist could use.

Footsteps approached behind her as she fought to regain control.

"Much better position," a familiar, if unwanted, voice said.

The man who'd been identified as Lance, the fish restaurant owner, walked in front of her and frowned.

"What's wrong? Who has made you so sad?"

"Nothing's wrong," she said, blinking rapidly.

"I can tell that isn't true."

"Then mind your own business." Elaine stood. "You are very free with your advice and nosiness. I didn't invite you into my life. So please leave."

Delilah stopped painting.

"But I wish to invite you to dinner. And I see you are painting mountains," he said.

"It's not for you. And it's terrible. It has no passion. Just like you said. I don't need your dinner ... or your sympathy. Just go away." She stood in front of him and attempted a glare.

"You are more beautiful when you are angry," he said. "Maybe dinner is too much. Thérèse told me so. Perhaps coffee?"

Elaine looked at the full cup on her small table.

"Then again, probably not," he said. "You drink the stuff all day."

She nodded, distressed to feel her anger melting away in front of his unrelenting charm.

"So dinner ... or lunch. There isn't as much pressure with lunch."

"Why are you bothering me?" Elaine asked. "There are dozens of people here. Some of them are even women around your age. Why don't you go bother them?"

His being younger shouldn't matter, they were never going to be in any kind of relationship. But for some reason, it bothered her.

He shrugged. "That is one of the mysteries of the universe. I feel compelled to invite you to dinner."

"Well, my answer is no. Go away. I have work to do."

"I could show you some of the beautiful places in the city," he said. "Maybe you could find inspiration and paint."

"And what would you do while I painted?"

"Um ... read a book?"

She shook her head. "Go away," she said again, but there wasn't as much energy in it this time. She picked up a brush and contemplated her next stroke on the painting.

"Go. Away," she repeated, avoiding looking in his direction.

"As you wish," he said.

"And don't come back."

"That's impossible," he said. "I pass by here almost every day."

"Find another route."

He shook his head. "Montana produces some hard women," he said. "But I will win you over. Have a good day."

"No point," she muttered at his back. "No coffee, no lunch, and definitely no dinner."

"He's not going to give up, you know," Delilah said.

"He may as well," Elaine said. She added dark green to represent the firs and pines that climbed the mountains to the tree line. It still looked lifeless to her. She forced herself to put her brush down before she destroyed the painting altogether.

"Why are you so hard on him?" Delilah asked. "He's a good-looking man. If he asked me, I'd go in an instant. The food at Fontenot's is divine."

"I'm not interested in a relationship," Elaine said. What did she have to do to make this painting work?

Delilah laughed. "Are all people from Montana this serious? It's dinner, not a relationship."

"Fine. I'm not interested in dinner, either."

"You're crazy. Either that or someone hurt you real bad."

Elaine shrugged. She was not getting into her personal life with this relative stranger.

"You could take pity on the man," Delilah continued as she added paint to her second canvas of the day. Several people had already commented favorably on the first.

"Why?" Elaine said, cleaning her brush and mixing a purple close to the color of lupines.

"His wife left him. They'd been married for decades. So happy ... at least that's what everyone thought. They had a beautiful home in the Garden District, newly remodeled after Katrina. Huge kitchen, everything." She leaned over toward Elaine. "They even had a spread in the local rich people's magazine. You know what I mean."

Elaine nodded. There were a few in Montana, displaying items for sale that would never be in her budget in this lifetime.

"Anyway, he retired, decided to start this restaurant, and she was gone so fast she didn't even leave a shadow."

"That's sad."

"See? You should go out with him. Cheer him up."

"I'm sure he has lots of friends. He's not my problem." Elaine would stay firm. No matter how many times this Lance person asked her out, she was not going.

Chapter Six

Elaine didn't know why she bothered opening her mailbox every day. No one was going to send her anything. Her daughter called or texted, her other—few—friends emailed, and she rarely heard from her closest friend, Betsy Wiznowski, now that her son Henry had taken over the general store. Betsy was too busy helping him add a small café to the store.

Elaine closed the mailbox and turned to go back up the elevator just as Nora Peterson, her next door neighbor, exited it.

"Hello," the warm Midwesterner said with a sincere smile. "How are you today? Are you going out to paint?"

"No, I don't have a permit for Fridays."

"That must be so exciting ... to be able to paint, that is. I mean, I have my crafts—knitting and scrapbooking—but that's not real art."

"Of course it is," Elaine said. "Anything creative is real art. Some people feel a need to make everything worth money. They stick a label on it to give it a mythical value, and then add a hefty price tag."

"Huh," Nora said. She checked her mailbox which was as empty as Elaine's had been. "What are you up to today then?"

"I was going to do some grocery shopping."

"Oh, that sounds like fun. Food is so exotic around here. I'm trying to adopt some of the local dishes, but Owen isn't too crazy about anything that isn't what he's used to eating."

"I see." She should just make her excuses and escape, but something about Nora's expression made Elaine realize the woman was lonely.

Two lonely people might not be a friendship, but at least it was company.

"But last year I convinced him to eat black-eyed peas and rice on New Year's Day. That's progress, right?" Nora beamed.

"Why did you make him eat that on New Year's?"

"It's southern tradition. Didn't you know that?"

"It's the first time I've been in the South."

"Well, then you must join us. I insist."

"I'm going to be in Montana over the holidays. My daughter, her husband, and my granddaughter are there."

"How nice for you. Owen doesn't like to travel in winter anymore. The kids don't even get together because the roads can be so bad. We have a family reunion in the summer instead. We all bring our RVs to a resort. Lots of siblings, cousins. It's great fun!"

Elaine tried to imagine it, but failed. Her Nebraska relatives had tried to entice her, her daughter, and grand-daughter for some similar kind of event, but she'd always found an excuse.

"I need to pick up some groceries too," Nora said. "Do you mind if I come along with you?"

"No problem."

Nora's smile broadened.

"In fact, why don't we visit some of the other shops in the area? I heard there's a store nearby that specializes in hot sauce. And we can stop somewhere and have lunch."

"Really?" The woman looked about ready to burst with happiness.

Elaine felt her own joy lift in response.

"Absolutely. Let's meet back here in a half hour."

"That would be wonderful."

They rode the elevator up together and waved as they went into their separate apartments.

It wasn't the same as going to lunch with the people in Promise Cove, but it would be fun.

NORA WAS A PLEASANT companion, someone with a glass-half-full attitude. As they walked, she told Elaine about her life in Minnesota, her children, her grandchildren, and her previous life as a public school teacher. The woman was Midwest traditional all the way. She'd married Owen right after college and, although she admitted life with him wasn't easy—what man was?—she still loved him. She was quite positive the reverse was also true.

The hot sauce place wasn't hard to find. Not only did it have aisles of the stuff, it had all types of other specialties, including kits that had everything needed for a savory rice and black-eyed peas dish to celebrate the new year. Elaine picked one up. It would make a great present for her friend, Ruth, who loved all types of stews and soups. A variety of hot sauces lined the walls and several shelf units. There were so many it was bewildering. Strange names dominated the labels: Slap Ya Mama, Trappey's Bull, Southern Art #1. There was even a clear hot sauce containing a single red pepper.

"I don't even know where to begin," Nora said. "Owen doesn't like spicy food, but these look so amazing."

"I imagine you'd have to be very careful in how you used them," Elaine said, grabbing a shopping basket. There were several men back home who would be more than delighted to have a few of these to experiment with. Especially Betsy's son, who was working on a lot of vegan recipes for his café. Ruth's boyfriend, Mike, who ran the local bar, would also love to play with some for his hamburgers, maybe slipping some into the burger of someone who'd had a little too much to drink.

Nora found the mildest sauce she could, and also picked up a package of rice and black-eyed peas. Once the women were checked out, they continued down the street with their purchases. They'd only gone a few blocks, stopping to admire the showy blossoms in a flower shop, when Elaine spotted a place for lunch. As she read the menu, she had to laugh.

"Do you mind vegan?" she asked Nora.

"I can't say I've had much of it. I'm willing to try it, though." She wrinkled her nose. "No kind of weird fish or anything, right?"

"No fish at all," Elaine said.

"But probably spicy," Nora said with a frown.

"Let's see if they can hold the spice."

"Okay," Nora said with a smile. "I'm willing to try."

"That's the spirit."

They sat and soon a waiter was with them to take their orders of vegan crab cakes, although Nora took some convincing that there was no actual crab in the cakes. "I don't do well with shellfish," she confessed. The waiter also said the chef could tone down the spice.

"And you, madam?" the waiter asked Elaine.

"Bring it as the chef prepares it," she said with a smile.

"Delighted," he said.

"How is your painting going?" Nora asked Elaine once they were served the iced tea they ordered.

"Terrible," Elaine confessed in a burst of honesty.

"Oh, it can't be that bad," Nora said. "I mean, you have painted before, haven't you?"

"All my life," Elaine acknowledged. "And it came easily in Montana." And even in Paris, but she didn't want to go into that with Nora.

"You're in a brand new place. It can be very strange here," Nora said. "Not at all like Minnesota. I like it, but sometimes ... sometimes I feel like I don't belong."

"Exactly."

"Maybe what you need to do is embrace it," Nora suggested tentatively.

"What do you mean?"

"Well, when I'm feeling at sea here—usually when Jack's totally sucked into some sports game on television—I find something unique to do. Last time I went to a voodoo museum."

"*You* went to a voodoo museum?"

"Of course. Why not?"

"I ... well ... I don't know. I'd never think of it, that's all." This woman had hidden depths.

"It was interesting, but a little bit creepy, if you know what I mean."

"I can imagine."

Their meals were delivered, and they dug in.

Elaine's crab cake was amazing. She'd need to pass along the idea. "Crab cakes" in a small Montana town would definitely be unique.

"Is it too spicy for you?" she asked Nora.

"No, it's perfect. Food in New Orleans is so absolutely wonderful. Have you had a chance to sample the restaurants yet?"

"Not really. Although ..." Elaine took another bite. "Never mind."

"Oh, tell me," Nora said. "I love hearing about other people's adventures."

Elaine sipped her drink. What had possessed her to bring it up in the first place?

"There's a man—he says he's the owner of Fontenot's Fish."

"That place is supposed to be wonderful ..." Nora said.

"He keeps saying he'll give me dinner if I give him a painting. No wait, that's not right. Now he just wants to give me dinner."

"So when are you going?"

"Never," Elaine said.

"Why not?"

"Well, for starters, I don't even know if he is the owner. What if I walk in there, and they have no idea who I'm talking about?"

"But what if it is him? A free dinner? What's to lose?" Nora asked.

"Then he'll expect something. Men always do."

Nora shrugged. "Just say no."

Elaine stared at her lunch companion. Apparently, the woman she'd assumed was a mousy little creature had more backbone than she'd imagined. Nora had gone to a voodoo museum, while she was afraid to go to a restaurant to find out if Lance was who he said he was.

"You should go," Nora said. "You might get some inspiration for your painting. I understand it's a beautiful place inside."

"That's not what I usually paint."

"Okay. It was just an idea." She forked another bite of the crab cake. "I'm sure glad I tried this. It's wonderful."

Elaine didn't miss the dig. This woman was not mousy at all. Not in the least.

In fact, the person who was shrinking from a challenge was the woman who looked back at her in the mirror every morning.

She should go. It would be fun and, as Nora had pointed out, a free meal. A very *good* free meal.

Except there were so many reasons why she wouldn't take Lance up on his offer.

Chapter Seven

After they parted on Friday, Elaine resolved to spend more time with Nora. Her first impression had been totally wrong. Instead of the stereotype of a conservative, church-going, doormat of a wife, she'd found Nora to be an intelligent, risk-taking woman with unexpected depths. Yes, she went to church and waited on her husband, but that wasn't the entirety of her identity.

Prejudice came in all forms.

It was time for Elaine to dig deep and banish her own gremlins or she'd never be able to get on with her life, no matter how long it was.

She put her groceries and the other small purchases she'd made away, then sat down with her phone to find a museum. Her college professor had assigned museum trips on a monthly basis. Their job was to draw what they saw, as accurately as possible, in order to learn previous painter's styles kinesthetically, through their hands.

Once he'd made arrangements with the local museum for them to bring paints, easels, and drop cloths with them so they could experiment with color.

Elaine hadn't been this stuck with her art in her life. Maybe it was time to go back to the beginning.

After scrolling through the art museums in the city, she made her choice. She'd go on Sunday. Tomorrow she'd set aside for the things that required doing in life: laundry, cleaning, and going over finances.

SHE SPENT SUNDAY MORNING with a pot of coffee, made from a local brew she'd picked up yesterday that promised a strong coffee reminiscent of New Orleans' best espresso bars. As she read through the local newspaper she'd picked up from a stand just outside the apartment lobby, she indulged in one of the sweet rolls she'd purchased.

New Orleans was certainly a vibrant, complex, and apparently scandalous place. Montana local papers reported the news, team scores, and opinion pieces. While the last often contained controversial topics, the paper she held in her hand let the controversy bleed over into other articles.

The art with which it was done amazed her. There were suggestions and hints, but never outright accusations unless charges had been brought. It was a bit like the gossip of Promise Cove written out in ink.

A grainy picture of a restaurant caught her eye. The mayor and some of his entourage celebrating His Honor's birthday at his favorite restaurant, Fontenot's Fish House.

Elaine studied the picture. She found him over the mayor's left shoulder. The man who had been asking her to dinner really was, it appeared, the owner of the restaurant.

If so, Delilah had been right. He was one of the more sought-after bachelors in town. Had the story she'd told about his failed marriage been accurate? Or was there more to the story, like the woman's point of view?

There almost always was.

It would be best not to get entangled. From what she was reading, once a person was captured in the net of New Orleans gossip, struggling against the webbing only ensnared them more in scandal.

She turned the page, just as her phone rang.

"Hello, sweetheart," she said to her daughter. "How are things going?"

"It's a disaster, Mom," Maggie replied. "Why did I ever think this was a good idea? George told us he'd get the outside framing up by first snowfall so we could work on the interior, but it's been snowing for a week already."

"You know those early snows melt," Elaine said.

"Only if it stops snowing. We've got six inches. Everything's wet!"

"I'm sure you'll get through this. You can handle anything, remember? You're the mayor of Promise Cove."

"Only because I can't find anyone else to take over," Maggie said.

"The town knows a good thing when they see it. Trust George. He's a good contractor and he's been doing this a long time."

"Now you sound just like Tom."

"Then listen to your husband. Other than the house, how are things going?"

"I've finally talked him into letting me add a greenhouse to one side of the house. I want to be able to start some plants that I can use to show people the kinds of flowers I'm talking about. I'll still source from nurseries, but ..."

Elaine tried to pay attention as her daughter told her all her plans for the relaunch of her garden design business now that the store was sold. But by the time Maggie got done, she was exhausted simply from listening.

"Those sound like great ideas. How is Henry doing with the store?"

"There have been a few rough patches, but the manager we hired before we sold is helping him through it. It's not going to be the store Dad built, though." There was a tinge of sadness in Maggie's voice. Selling the store had been the right thing, but it had been a loss as well, as all change was.

Her daughter caught her up on the town gossip, and they talked about the possibility of Maggie and Teagan coming to visit Elaine in New Orleans. It would be good to have them here.

After they ended the call, Elaine picked up her cup of coffee and drifted back to a time when her husband had first presented her with the idea of opening a general store in Montana. They'd been on vacation visiting Glacier National Park and had fallen in love with the ruggedness of the terrain and the people. She'd naively imagined that his big ambitious dream still had space for her own ambition to become a serious artist, respected and financially rewarded.

But bit by bit her time was chipped away. First, by the necessity of working while her husband renovated the old general store they'd purchased in the small town of Promise Cove. Then by continuing to work both outside their business plus take care of the books, all while they convinced people to buy locally instead of traveling to the nearest big town for all their shopping. It took them a while to figure out what to stock for the locals, as well as enticing the tourist trade out for scenic drives or to take over their vacation cabins on the lake.

When Maggie came along, Elaine had packed away her art supplies in a cupboard.

THE OGDEN MUSEUM OF Art turned out to be a several-storied building in the Warehouse District of New Orleans. Its outside was pedestrian, especially in contrast to the more traditional art museums of her college years. But once inside, the familiar trappings of art museums everywhere made Elaine feel at home.

She wandered through the exhibits from the temporary curated shows to the permanent galleries. As she did, her sense of alienation grew. It was so very different from either her Nebraska roots or her Montana life. Southern paintings were lush with color and vibrancy. From people in colorful and flamboyant costumes, to the sensual undulation of waves encroaching on a beach, the art evoked ... what?

It was hard for her to pin down. It wasn't the awe she'd felt when she first saw paintings of the Rocky Mountains, a glacial lake, or the mighty Missouri. No, this was almost arousal.

No wonder Lance thought her work was passionless. It never occurred to her to put ... well ... sex into a painting of a flower. It was something Georgia O'Keefe might get away with, but not a grandmother from Montana, no matter how much Elaine had played the artist with her colorful clothes, bright hair, and flashing jewelry.

The closest she'd come to this feeling had been with her lover in Paris. It had been the first time she'd risked her heart since her husband had died. In the beginning, it had just been a small fling, a way to slow down the passage of time. Soon she was included in outings with all his friends and had moved her things to her own room in his flat.

But then he'd wanted more, something full time. It had sounded so romantic, and she'd actually considered it, until she went home for the summer. She'd proposed a split living arrangement, but by the time she was ready to go back to Paris to convince him to try, he'd already moved on.

It was silly really. It had only been a fling that had gotten out of hand.

She shouldn't have felt as devastated as she'd been.

After nights of crying herself to sleep, she'd resolved to never get involved with anyone at that level again. Even a brief affair was out of the question.

She was going to concentrate on her art. Lance had been right about one thing. She could channel the passion she felt for life into her art.

Sitting down on the provided bench, she took out her sketch pad. A painting of a woman in her garden was on the wall in front of her, the flowerbed full of lush primary colors. Designing an outdoor living space here would be much more of a challenge than in Montana with its limited options due to the climate.

Elaine studied the painting and then began, her fingers manipulating the pencil in imitation of a vibrant orange-yellow candelabra plant. At first her efforts were stiff and unrewarding, but eventually the image she was seeking to reproduce came alive under her pencil.

Chapter Eight

Whitney Goodwin pressed her hands against the city council desk to keep them from trembling as she read the financial report to the other members. She'd taken care with her nails today, a conservative blush polish with a hint of brown picking up the tint of her skin. Likewise, her outfit had been chosen with care, a suit she'd picked up in a consignment place, its original label carefully snipped out.

But she had been able to tell it was quality. Her mother, a seamstress who worked for the clothing line of Thérèse Cormier, had taught her to look at the details of the garment: the width of the seams, the stitching on the hem, the number of buttons on a suit jacket cuff, and the length of its lining. Did it cover the full jacket? Or had the manufacturer tried to skimp with something that came halfway down the back or didn't extend to the sleeves?

Attention to detail was what she'd inherited from her mother and what had made her so good in her current job on the city council. She was one of the youngest financial managers they'd ever had. She'd achieved the position by demonstrating her ability with figures, a solid plan for managing the complex financial system, and that most important of all items for a prospective member on the city council: her reputation.

Once she was finished, she answered the inevitable questions, some genuine, some meant to cast doubt on her ability. Finally, the budget was referred to committee, and the meeting droned on.

Hours later, it concluded with a report from Vince Landry, a deputy superintendent in the police department. They were seeking an increase in their budget, something they did on a regular basis. The request, inevitably, was assigned to her.

As she packed away her things, the deputy superintendent made his way to her. He was a good-looking man, if somewhat older than she was. He had kept himself fit, something that couldn't be said of every police administrator, and his hair was a thick and wavy brown.

"Hello," he said, holding out his hand. "I'm Vince Landry."

"I know," she said with a polite smile. "I was here when they introduced you."

"Ah, yes, of course." He took a few steps away from the others gathering their things, and she was forced to follow.

"I was wondering if you were available for a drink?" he asked. "I know you're new on the council. Getting a leadership role, especially in finance, that's very impressive."

"Um … I don't know if that's appropriate," she told him.

"It's fine," he said. "People do it all the time. It's how business gets done in New Orleans, whether it's corporate or government. Your predecessor and I met all the time."

She'd heard rumors about Vince Landry. The image he portrayed was on the up and up, with one of the most respected districts in the city in terms of safety and policing. So far the only scum that had floated in his direction was in regard to his tumultuous relationship with his wife.

"We'll just discuss the police force," he said. "There are things … nuances … that you may not grasp, being new and all. I promise … no prying on my part. And no pressure. Just a friendly discussion."

His dark eyes seemed honest, and his smile was genial. There was no harm in listening. Going out for a drink with a reasonably attractive man, even if it was only business, sounded wonderful. She'd been working herself hard, trying to be worthy of the honor they'd given her by naming her to the post.

Once again that worry flitted through her brain. *Why had they done that?* There were a few others on the board who had more experience than she did.

"Sure," she told him. "Tell me where you'd like to go, and I'll meet you there." Self-preservation hadn't entirely left her mind. Her own vehicle meant she could leave if things got dicey, and she wasn't trapped in a car with someone.

Not that she believed Vince was really a threat. He was a sharp negotiator—all the people dependent on the city's budget were—but there was nothing inherently evil about him.

He told her where to meet him, then left, shaking hands with several people on the way out.

What did he want from her? Was he telling the truth?

Too bad he wasn't single. There was something about an older man with power that had always turned her on. She didn't like to think she was that shallow, but it had been one of the reasons she'd gone into politics in the first place.

Plenty of good-looking men eager for an edge over the rest of the populace.

THE BAR WAS, LIKE MOST local places in New Orleans, full of dark wood and dim light. And, like many of them, a musician was playing for background music. The atmosphere in this city almost compelled everyone to try their hand at an instrument at some point in their lives.

Whitney's affair with the piano had been short-lived.

Vince had beaten her to the bar and was waiting at a table near one of the walls. He rose when he saw her and pulled out a chair. With as much grace as she could muster, she sat down and let him help push the chair in.

"What can I get you?" he asked.

"White wine will be fine," she said. She wasn't picky about the kind of wine as long as it wasn't red. Red wine gave her a nasty headache.

She looked around while she waited. There was nothing extraordinary about it. It was a neighborhood bar, one of hundreds in the city. Like many, the atmosphere was comfortable, and no one was drinking too much or trying to impress, which happened a lot in many of the tourist places.

It said something about Vince that he picked a place like this. No hype and no gossips.

He returned with her wine and sat down with his drink, a scotch or whiskey of some sort on the rocks.

"Here's to a successful term on the city council," he said, raising his glass.

They clinked and sipped. While they did, his gaze was steady on her, measuring her.

She had to look away.

"How long have you lived in New Orleans?" he asked.

"All my life. I went to school at Tulane."

"Always interested in politics?"

"Always," she said. "It's my passion. I love it here, but we can do more for the people. There's millions of dollars coming in every day from tourists, but it's not getting into the budget for improvements in everyone's lives. You know, it's not only the tourist areas that need good infrastructure, but the restaurant and store employees need habitable living conditions, too. And don't even let me get started on teachers' salaries."

"I won't," he said with a smile. "You're really passionate about this. Is it city council for life?"

"Well ..." She didn't like talking about her dreams. Some superstition, probably instilled by her overly suspicious mother, made her believe if she spoke them aloud, they'd fracture into a million tiny pieces and disappear.

"It's okay," he said. "Your secret's safe with me."

She twirled her wineglass around.

"Is deputy superintendent as far as you want to go?" she asked.

He laughed. "I knew you were a smart one," he said. "Always ask another question when you don't want to give an answer to the one you've been asked. Clever."

She blessed her darker skin and the dim light as heat flamed her cheeks, and gave a slow, deliberate shrug. If nothing else, talking with Vince was going to hone her political skills.

"I hate to be that guy," he said, his expression becoming more serious. "But you're very pretty. You probably know that already."

She stilled. This wasn't how the conversation was supposed to go.

"Sorry. I didn't mean anything." His expression shifted to one of genial "aw shucks."

"No problem," she told him. Like he said, he was a guy. More than one of them had told her she was attractive.

"My wife and I separated. Again," he said, wrapping his hand around his drink like he was protecting it.

"I'm sorry to hear that," she said.

"Like I said, it's happened before. She'll calm down and take me back. Like always. But it's getting tiresome. I may not go back this time." He picked up his drink and looked over its top before taking a sip.

Whitney had made it a point never to get involved with a married man.

"What did you want to discuss?" she asked, uncrossing her legs and squaring her shoulders.

He put down his glass and folded his hands.

"It's important you understand what role the police actually play in keeping this city safe. Not only for the locals, but for the tourists. As you rightly said, the tourists bring a lot of money here. We want to make sure they aren't harassed by pickpockets, beggars, or window washers."

She nodded.

"I know there's a lot of distrust of police departments these days, but we're the good guys, Whitney. You have to remember that. We put our lives on the line so you can walk into your apartment safely every night. A good budget for the department means we can hire the best people and supply them with the right safety gear."

She nodded. Everything he said made sense to her.

"There's a lot of demand for the money. I know that. And you're right, more of the money tourists spend should come into our coffers. At the same time, we need to make sure the money goes to where it's needed most. If you don't have a safe city, you have nothing."

"I understand," she said.

"I hope so," he said. "What I want to do is to help you understand how our budget is used so you can fight back when some of those do-gooders want to implement programs that supposedly 'keep people out of jail.' It's never worked. What we need is a strong police force."

She nodded. She could listen, couldn't she? Then she'd make up her own mind.

"Another?" he asked.

She looked down, surprised to see her glass empty.

"Sure."

Chapter Nine

"What are you doing here?" Lance asked his son when he walked into the restaurant kitchen.

Xavier was adding garnish to a plate of what looked like an open-faced po'boy.

"What's that?" Lance asked, his irritation growing. "We don't have po'boys on the menu."

"You should."

"Why? They're messy. Street food. They don't work with the atmosphere I'm trying to create. No one wants to pick up a sandwich in a fancy restaurant."

"You don't pick this up. Knife and fork all the way. Taste it." Xavier pushed the plate his way, along with a fork and a steak knife.

Lance poked at it with the knife. Under the traditional dressing of shredded lettuce, tomato, pickle, and mayonnaise, there appeared to be a piece of fish.

"It's boned," Xavier said.

Lance cut out a piece in the middle, stabbed it, and put it in his mouth.

Immediately, his tastebuds woke up, taking in the explosion of flavors in his mouth, the associated nerves dancing with joy. Even the texture was perfect, a mixture of hard crust, soft fish, and crunchy lettuce.

It was amazing, but he wouldn't serve it in his restaurant. He loved his restaurant, but it had cost him the love of his life as well as most of his savings, and he wouldn't make his son deal with the same fate. Xavier had enough problems, mainly from choosing the wrong woman to marry. He didn't need any more.

"It's very good," Lance said. "Why don't you serve it to me some night for dinner? Now, you need to get out of here so we can prep for dinner."

As tempted as he was to dump the rest in the trash for dramatic effect, he couldn't waste such beautifully prepared food. He stuck the plate on a high shelf.

"Dad, I want to work in the restaurant. I made that dish to show you I know how to cook."

"One dish doesn't make you a chef. Have you been taking culinary classes at the community college? Online?"

"At NOCHI," Xavier said quietly

"NOCHI?" The New Orleans Culinary and Hospitality Institute was one of best schools in the country.

"Yes." Xavier took off his apron and hung it up. "I'm serious about this, Dad. If you won't let me in, perhaps someone else would be happy for an unpaid intern."

His son working for someone else?

"At least bring me in for Thanksgiving," Xavier said. "It's one of your busiest times. Harper has Avery for the holiday. Let me help."

"You have a job," Lance pointed out.

"A job I dislike intensely."

The kitchen staff was giving them side looks. They were becoming too aware of the altercation. Lance nodded to the door. They walked to the bar where Prosper set out two club sodas with lime.

"You have a family to think about," Lance continued. "Girls are expensive. They need things. You have to make sure she goes to the right schools, meets the right people."

Xavier laughed. "Sometimes I forget how helplessly old-fashioned you are, Dad."

"But of course he is," Thérèse said as she walked to the bar.

She must have gotten one of the waitstaff to let her in.

She placed her hand on Lance's arm. "It's one of the reasons he's such a catch. Women may say they want independence, but they also love the old-fashioned courtesies."

"You own an empire," Xavier pointed out.

Thérèse shrugged. "A woman can have both. There is no law against it, cher."

"Anything?" Prosper asked.

"Seltzer water," she said. "With a lemon, thank you, Prosper."

"No problem."

"Has your father told you about this woman he's chasing?" Thérèse asked Xavier.

"I'm not chasing any woman," Lance said. "And Xavier doesn't need to know my business."

"Half of the district knows your business," she said. "You think the artists don't gossip?"

"Xavier thinks he wants to be in the restaurant business," Lance said. Time to move the topic off him.

"But of course," she said.

"Why 'of course'?"

"Because he is a smart young man."

"It is not smart to go into the restaurant business!"

"You did, Dad," Xavier pointed out.

"That's different. My responsibilities are done. While you were young and your mother ... well ... you know ... I took care of both of you. I did what I had to do. What a man is *supposed* to do." The depth of his anger surprised him. He wanted to put Xavier over his knee and spank some sense into him, something he'd *never* done in his life.

"Interesting," Thérèse said.

"What!" he barked.

"That," she said. "You're making a very large mountain out of a very small molehill. Just because you did something you thought was right, doesn't mean it's right for Xavier."

"But he has a child he has to take care of. And if he wants his wife to come back to him, he's got to toe the line. Give her what she wants so his child doesn't need to make choices between parents."

"And you think that only happens between parents who are split up? No. My parents had a war between them all the time. And they demanded we support one or the other in their fights. It was a relief when they split up."

"We never made Xavier choose. In fact, we never fought in front of him."

"But I knew, Dad," Xavier said softly.

Lance looked around. The restaurant was still closed, and Prosper was cleaning glasses at the other end of the bar.

"This is not the place for this discussion," he said.

"True," Thérèse said.

"What we were discussing was whether or not Dad will let me work on Thanksgiving. Help him out. My wife has Avery with her family, so I'm free."

"What a splendid idea!" Thérèse exclaimed.

"It is not a good idea at all," Lance said. Letting his son work the holiday was giving him a foot in the door to a career he had no right to contemplate.

"You don't have to pay me," Xavier said.

"What is the poor boy supposed to do?" Thérèse asked. "You want him to sit in his lonely apartment and stare at football while he eats take-out turkey?"

"Of course not," Lance bristled. "He can come here and sit at a table and eat like all my friends do."

"Dad, please," Xavier said. "Maybe I'll hate it. Then your wish will come true."

Lance contemplated the idea. Working a large crowd, especially during a holiday when expectations ran high, was hard, stressful work. It was the best and worst the business had to offer.

"Let him work," Prosper said, refilling the glasses with the appropriate fizzy water.

Lance glared at him.

"Just sayin', boss," Prosper continued. "We could always use the help. You know these young people ... some of 'em always cancel las' minute."

Prosper had a point. At least Xavier would show up.

But ...

"He was in my kitchen," he complained to Thérèse. "Thinks we should serve some kind of po'boy here."

"Did you taste it?" she asked.

"Well ... yes."

"And?"

"It was good," he had to admit.

"Your son is a good cook."

"How do you know?"

"He made me a sandwich one day when he stopped by to see me at my office. You know I have a full kitchen there so I can cater events and do videos and such."

The workings of his friend's business were full of projects and details that escaped him. It was hard to recognize this wealthy, sharp businesswoman who'd started in one of the poorer sections of the city. A scholarship student, she'd attended his private Catholic school. He'd first seen her crouching in the dirt with a fistful of rocks, ready to fling them at anyone who dared bully her.

He'd talked her into putting her handmade weapons down. They'd been friends ever since.

Seeing her expression, he realized he'd already lost this discussion.

She must have seen it on his face because her face relaxed into a smile.

"Okay. You can bus tables on Thanksgiving," he told Xavier.

"Thanks, Dad." Xavier grinned.

"We'll see how you feel at the end of the day," Lance warned.

"Got it ... now what about this woman Thérèse was talking about?"

"Just because you won doesn't give you the right to pry into my private life."

"So you admit there is a woman," Xavier said.

"He wants there to be a woman," Thérèse said. "So far she has the good sense to resist."

"I thought I was a good catch," Lance said, putting on a mocking tone.

"You are. But that doesn't mean there aren't issues."

"Of course," Lance said. He ticked them off on his fingers. "She doesn't live here. She's from Montana, a place truly in the middle of nowhere. She doesn't understand the nuance of New Orleans. She thinks she's a painter, but her work is terrible."

"Yet you offered to buy one," Thérèse said.

"How do you know that?"

She shrugged.

"Besides all of that," he said. "I think she's older than I am."

"How terrible," Thérèse said, deadpan.

"I know," Lance said. "It shouldn't matter. Men date younger woman all the time."

"How mature of you to understand," Thérèse taunted him.

"Enough of this," Lance said. "The restaurant needs to open." He pointed to Xavier. "You, stay out of my kitchen."

"Yes, sir." Xavier gave him a mock salute.

"And you." He pointed to Thérèse. "Stay out of my business."

"Of course, cher," she said.

"Prosper, get ready. I'm opening the doors."

"Yes, boss."

Lance went to the front door to unlock it, Thérèse trailing behind him.

The mayor was standing at the front with several of his donors.

"Ah, Thérèse," he said as he came in and bestowed kisses on her cheeks. "Thank you for meeting me here."

"Your table is ready," Lance said, walking toward the regularly reserved circular table.

Thérèse and the mayor. Interesting. She had money enough to donate to his campaign, but what did she want in return? Because Thérèse always wanted something.

It was the way of the city. Always undercurrents, deals being made, people skirting the edge of the law and sometimes crossing over.

A plainspoken woman from Montana sounded very appealing.

Chapter Ten

Before she left for Jackson Square, Elaine spent several minutes perusing the website for Fontenot's Fish House. It would be a shame not to take the owner up on his invitation.

It would also be foolish to go.

This trip was for her to rediscover herself alone, not who she was with a man. She already knew how that story went.

Ever since her trip to the museum, she felt like something had broken loose. Reminiscing about how life had been with her husband and with Henri had hopefully settled those two parts of her life firmly where they belonged: in the past.

Following Delilah's cue, she'd collected several postcards of iconic New Orleans scenes. She'd paint something totally unfamiliar. No matter how bad it was—and Delilah would surely let her know—it would open her up to more ideas.

She definitely needed to get away from mountains and flowers, and she wasn't ready to open herself up to the style she had been doing in Paris.

She wasn't sure she ever would be. Was that style something she'd been developing on her own, or had it been an imitation of her lover's art in hopes of winning his approval?

How shallow could she get?

She packed up her gear and went out the door. There she ran into Nora, returning from her morning walk.

"Off to paint," Nora noted. "I admire your dedication. I'll have to walk down there someday and watch you in action."

"Oh, please don't," Elaine replied.

"It can't be that bad," Nora replied. "I'm one step beyond the square-bodied people we used to draw in grade school. I have a very low bar of what's good and bad. Besides," she said with a smile. "You're my friend. I promise I'll tell you it's wonderful no matter what I really think."

"Thanks," Elaine said. "Coffee and beignets Friday morning?"

"Sounds wonderful," Nora said. "We can catch up on our adventures." She leaned closer. "Maybe your friend from the restaurant will be back to see you."

"I hope not," Elaine said firmly. She hadn't seen Lance for over a week, and that suited her just fine. She waved at Nora as she walked toward the elevator. "See you Friday."

As she walked out the front door of the building, she took in a big breath of air. She was almost getting used to the heavy humidity of the South. Her skin felt dewy, like it had dropped several years of age. It was pleasant to avoid using tons of moisturizer like she'd had to do every day for the last few decades.

She smiled at several people she saw every morning on her walk, and exchanged pleasantries with the woman who ran one of the many antique stores in the quarter. She set up her easel, chair, and the travel mug she'd purchased last week. After placing the blank sheet of watercolor paper she'd prepped last night on the easel, she pulled out her stack of postcards and chose the one of Louis Cathedral.

May as well paint what was directly in front of her.

"I see you've stolen my trick," Delilah commented.

"It's always good to borrow ideas from the smart people," Elaine said, sorting through her tubes of paint to pull out the one she wanted to start with.

"Oh, so you think I'm smart now," Delilah said.

"You've been doing this a lot longer than I have," Elaine pointed out.

"Good point."

Nabbing the tube she wanted, Elaine began to work, laying down a wash of blue, not as vibrant as the hue she'd use for Montana's sky, but a paler, almost grayer color. When she painted the cathedral, its color would pick up what she'd already laid down in the sky.

She'd been working for about an hour when she felt someone behind her. Without looking, she knew it was going to be Lance Fontenot.

Perhaps if she ignored him, he'd go away.

"I brought you espresso," he said.

She waved her brush toward her travel mug.

"But this is superior espresso," he said. "Whatever you have in that mug cannot compare to this beverage."

"I'm busy," she said, not turning around.

"I'll take it," Delilah said. "If Elaine doesn't want it," she added quickly.

The aroma drifted to her nose. It *did* smell divine.

She held out her hand, still not looking at him.

He laughed and placed the cup in her hand.

Cautiously, she put the cup to her lips. Not too hot. She sipped.

"Ahh," she said.

"Exactly." Lance walked around to where she could see him.

"Thank you," she said.

"No problem."

What was she supposed to do now? She took another sip, then placed the cup on her table and dabbed it in some paint.

"What are you painting?" he asked.

"I'm attempting to paint the cathedral."

"I'm sure it will be wonderful."

"It's a work in progress," Delilah commented.

Elaine shot her a look, and the younger woman smirked.

"I'm experimenting," Elaine said. "It doesn't have to be perfect. Not yet." She looked up at him. "What do you want?"

"To again invite you to my restaurant. Tonight, if you will come."

"I'm busy."

Delilah snorted.

"I *am*," Elaine repeated.

"That is a shame, cher," a woman's voice stated. "The food at Fontenot's is very, very good."

Elaine looked over her shoulder. The woman in her view was slim, with skin the color of a good espresso, dark black eyes with thick lashes, and thick black hair styled to stay off her face while retaining its curls. Her clothes were studied casual and must have cost more than Elaine paid for three pairs of good jeans at Murdoch's.

"And you are?" Elaine asked.

"Thérèse Cormier. I own Thérèse Cormier Designs."

"Okay, but why should I listen to you?"

Thérèse laughed and turned to Lance. "Oh, cher, you are so right. She is unique."

Delilah leaned close to Elaine. "Um, she's like famous. Martha Stewart famous."

Elaine shrugged. Fame had never meant much to her. At the end of the day, stars, athletes, and politicians were just like every other human being; they put their pants on one leg at a time.

"She knows *everyone*," Delilah continued. "If you want to do business in this town, it's good to have her on your side."

"I'm only here for the winter. Then I'm going back home where my daughter is mayor." She shot Thérèse a triumphant look.

No need to tell her Promise Cove was a tiny town with no stop lights, or that Maggie was mayor by default.

"You *must* come," Thérèse said. "The patrons will be so delighted to see you. You will be the talk of the town, a single woman coming to the restaurant of one of the most eligible bachelors in the city. I will introduce you to all kinds of people who will love to hear about the Wild West." She peered at the painting Elaine had on the easel. "Maybe we will wait a little while to tell them about your art, though."

Elaine huffed. No need to dis her art.

Then she looked at the painting again.

It did need some work.

She looked up at Thérèse who was smiling at her in a kind way.

"I tell you what," she added. "You will come to my salon for breakfast some morning. I will tell you all about New Orleans, and you will grow to love it. You will want to stay forever."

"Doubtful," Elaine said. "But thanks for the invitation. I appreciate it, but, as you pointed out, I need the time to work on my painting." She picked up her brush and mixed a new shade of gray, suppressing the urge to tear the paper off the easel, rip it up, and start again.

Maybe tomorrow.

Maybe somewhere else where the pesky restauranteur couldn't find her.

"What's your favorite dish?" Lance asked.

"Fresh-caught trout grilled on an open fire," she said as she added shadow to the edge of the cathedral. "Emphasis on fresh caught."

"Someday I will catch you a fish and serve it to you."

She barely kept herself from snorting.

"Tonight, I will find you the freshest sea trout we can prepare, flavor it the New Orleans way, then grill it for you so you can have a mix of old and new."

He was pulling out all the stops.

"I don't know what's with you," Delilah said. "If a man offered to do anything so nice for me, I'd be eating out of his hand. And to have a good-looking man do that?" She shook her head. "You're crazy not to accept that."

She was, Elaine acknowledged to herself, being so stubborn she was cutting her nose off to spite her face. It was something that her dear friend, Henrietta, had pointed out to her innumerable times before she'd had the bad taste to die one winter's day.

Lance crouched beside her. "Please say you'll come."

"You must," Thérèse said. "The poor man has been pining over you for weeks now. I've never seen him so crazy over a woman, and I've known him all my life."

Elaine made the mistake of looking over at the man beside her. Lance had the open expression of a puppy dog begging for attention.

She threw down her brush, and threw her hands in the air. "Okay. Okay! I'll be there."

"Thank you," Lance said, rising. "You will not regret it."

"I'm only there to eat," she stated. "I don't need to be introduced to anyone else, thank you very much," she told Thérèse. "And only eating," she pointed out to Lance. "No more than that."

"Agreed," he said.

"What time shall I be there?" she asked.

"Around seven would be good if you can wait that long," he said. "By that time, the tourist rush will be over. My staff can handle the locals while I tend to you."

"Fine. Now go away so I can work."

"Later," Lance said as he and Thérèse threaded their way through the artists back onto the street.

When they were out of sight, Elaine tore the paper from the tape holding it to the easel, put up a fresh sheet, and began again.

Chapter Eleven

Elaine hesitated outside the door to the restaurant. Mid-November evening had already arrived, but the old-fashioned street lamps of the French Quarter, as well as lights spilling from the still-open establishments, made it feel like twilight. The heat of day had relented, and it had been cool enough for her to wear one of the shawls an artist in Promise Cove had made for her over the pink satin shirt and dark black skirt she'd brought with her just in case an occasion arose.

Why did crossing this threshold feel like she was about to change her life? It was ridiculous. Her life—at least the signatory events—was over. She wasn't going to get married again, and her child-bearing years were well behind her. Instead of getting her driver's license, someone was going to forbid her to drive at some point. The next official church rite in her life would be the last sacrament.

She was being way too morbid for a fun night at a well-known restaurant. She'd taken some time in the afternoon to search the internet. Not only was Fontenot's listed on the tourist recommendation sites, but the restaurant and its owner were often noted for its charity events, and the celebrations of notable people in the New Orleans scene, including the mayor.

Squaring her shoulders, she pulled open the door.

As she stepped into the entryway, her jaw dropped. It was a fantasy, a scene of the Belle Époque of Paris, Gigi learning to be a courtesan in the movie of the same name.

White pillars rose to a lofty ceiling of arched ivory, triangular panels separated by molded vines and flowers. Windows were plentiful, all reflecting a deep blue tint that might be the real evening sky, but was more likely artificial. There were plenty of good-sized round tables, glistening with polished wineglasses, gleaming flatware, and crisp linen tablecloths and linens. In addition, small tables took over the edges of the restaurant, lit with small crystal candleholders flickering with light. Soft music played in the background.

"It's beautiful, isn't it?" Lance said, standing next to her.

"Amazing. Did you do this?" she asked.

"The bones were here. I worked with an interior designer to bring it to life."

"I feel like I've been transported back in time. I half expect to see women in elegant gowns and men in formal dress."

"Exactly," Lance said. He hesitated a second then held out his arm.

She took the same half-second moment, then took it.

He guided her to a small bar tucked in the corner. There was a waitress station at one end and a couple of stools at the other. An older black man with a thin dark mustache polished glasses behind the bar.

"This is Prosper," Lance said. "He makes the best cocktails in the city. I snagged him away from a very prestigious restaurant."

"More prestigious than this?"

"Their dinner prices begin where ours end, and that only covers a small bowl of gumbo."

"And you got him to leave there and come work for you?"

"He joshin' you," Prosper said. "I didn't even know how to make a cocktail before I got here. My dad taught me to fetch a beer from the fridge, and my buddies could count on me for good whiskey. Nothin' more."

She grinned. Prosper reminded her of some of the older men who'd been living in the mountains all their lives. Their lives were simple, their tales were tall.

"Have you lived here all your life?" she asked.

"Pretty much. There were a few years I spent in the war ... best forgotten. And I went away for a bit."

She opened her mouth to ask what Prosper meant by "away," but Lance gave a slight shake of his head.

Then the answer leapt into her mind. Prosper had served time.

But in spite of whatever he'd done, Lance had given him a second chance.

"There's a number of people where I live that served as well," she said instead. "I know how difficult it can be, and how many scars it can leave. Thank you for serving."

Prosper nodded his head but didn't look up from the wineglass he was rubbing with a bar towel.

"Can we have a couple of aperitifs?" Lance asked.

"What are you making for the lady?"

"Sea trout. Not as fresh as she requested, but I'm sure she will be happy."

"You can stop talking about me like I'm not here," Elaine pointed out.

Prosper chuckled. "I like this one, boss."

"Does he bring many women by for your approval?" she asked.

The bartender laughed even harder. Then he leaned across the bar. "Trade secret. Boss swore me to silence. But not too many."

"Got it," she said with a grin.

A waitress came by with a drink order, and Prosper took care of it, leaving her to scramble for something to say to Lance. The bartender had been easy. She was used to talking to people who were going to be casual acquaintances. She'd done it at the store for years.

Lance was never going to be a mere acquaintance.

"How does this stack up against the fine establishments of Promise Cove?" Lance asked.

"You mean Moose's Saloon?"

He looked at her as if she were joking.

"Mike serves a mean burger and a cold glass of beer, but if you want anything else to eat, you're out of luck. You can also get a glass of wine, but nothing stronger. There's too many people who get nasty on the hard stuff living in the woods."

"I heard there was a bunch of survivalists up that way."

"Not survivalists necessarily. Just people who'd prefer not to be bothered."

Prosper slid their drinks in front of them. He pointed to her glass. "This here is a spritzer made with a fruit wine from Pontchartrain Vineyards, some seltzer water, and a few other ingredients I'm not going to tell you about."

She left the drink on the bar until Lance picked his up and gestured to her as if to clink.

"I don't usually drink a lot," she said, lifting the glass.

"It's mild," he said. "Designed to whet your appetite for the best fish you'll ever have ... at least this side of Montana."

"Okay." They clinked, and she took a sip. It was exactly as he'd told her, fruity and light, not cloyingly sweet which would have put her off.

"Very nice," she told Prosper. "Thank you."

"Yes, ma'am," he said, as he continued to make drinks for the orders that were steadily coming in.

It was all very elegant: the place, the drinks, the low murmur of conversation she could hear behind them. This was Lance's world. He fit right in.

But this wasn't where she belonged. Her world was sitting by a beautiful mountain lake, watching the sun slowly dip below the jagged peaks of the Rockies.

He was an urbane man about town, a good number of years her junior.

She was a woman adrift, trying to figure out where life had gone. It seemed like just yesterday that she was walking down the aisle to get married. She'd spent her life taking care of others and sublimating her own needs to theirs, and she didn't regret it at all.

If she didn't learn her own value, besides being a caretaker, she'd have failed one key aspect of living for herself. It wasn't important for everyone, but she was discovering it was vital to her.

"Where did you go?" Lance asked.

"What? Oh, just thinking."

"I could see that," he said with a smile. It was a kind smile.

"I'm not looking for anything," she said.

"I know that. Neither am I. For tonight, I am making you a wonderful dinner because I very much want to do that for such a beautiful woman."

"I'm no longer beautiful," she said. "People barely see me." She couldn't remember when a man had last given her a second glance.

Until Lance.

"Oh, cher, you are still beautiful." He ran the tip of his finger down her no-longer-firm jawline. His touch was light. "Age doesn't preclude beauty. It's a different kind of attractiveness, far better, I think, than the sharp angles and greedy seductiveness of young people. I can see the caring in your eyes. I suspect your friends and family think you are very beautiful indeed."

The air had escaped her lungs and failed to return.

"And after dinner?" she asked.

"We'll see," he said. "Nothing has to be serious. It might simply be dinner. Or we may decide to *laissez les bons temps rouler*, let the good times roll." He shrugged. "There are no rules for what we do."

"There are always rules," she said. "We may not always know what they are, but they're there."

A waiter came over and said something to Lance.

"Excuse me for a moment," he said. "There is something I need to take care of."

She watched as he walked back to the main room. He'd kept himself in shape, but hadn't overdone it.

Her cheeks flushed, and she turned back to the bar.

"Do you want another?" Prosper asked.

"No. No thank you."

Prosper nodded.

"What kind of a boss is he?" she asked the bartender.

"Fair." Prosper leaned his hands on the bar. "He's a good man. Gave me a chance when nobody else did. Only thing." He grinned.

"What?" she asked.

"He not always smart about women."

"That's fine," she said. "This isn't serious."

"That what he think too, but he be wrong." Prosper shook his head. "You've been like an obsession for that man. After his wife ran off, I think he never look at a woman that way again. But here you are."

"It's just dinner," she protested.

"So you both say."

A waitress approached the bar, and Prosper moved away to tend to her.

"The problem with running a popular restaurant," Lance said. "People always want to talk to the owner so they can show their proper place in the pecking order. When I come over at their bidding, they think they are demonstrating that power." He shrugged. "I let them keep that illusion. It's good for business."

"I'll never understand this business," she said. "At least not in this city. At home, Mike's a good listener to those who need it, tells people to get their act together when they're a mess, and opens the space for all kinds of community events."

"Sounds like a nice place. Less complicated."

"Maybe ..." There were times when Promise Cove had its own craziness.

"Your table is set," he said. "Are you ready?"

"Yes. Quite hungry, actually."

"Good. I like a woman with an appetite." He guided her through the maze to an intimate table in the back, not too far from the kitchen.

As they walked through the restaurant, there were multiple glances in her direction, and the conversation increased slightly in volume.

In Promise Cove she drew attention because of her colorful apparel and friendliness. Here it seemed to be more important who she was with.

Decidedly uncomfortable.

He got her settled then went off to the kitchen and returned with a small steaming bowl of soup. "This is crawfish bisque. A little spicy, but very, very good."

A young man dressed in black placed a bread basket on the table and filled her water glass.

"The baguette is freshly made in the New Orleans style, so it may taste a little different from any you've had other places." Lance grinned. "And the busboy will keep your water filled in case it is too hot for your tongue."

"I'm used to a little spice," she said. How hot was the food going to be?

"Good. I'm going to let you attend to your soup while I see what my troublesome customer of the night is complaining about."

"I can't wait to taste it."

"Bon appetite," Lance said and walked rapidly to a table of four people. One of the men at the table stared at her for a few moments before turning back to the other men.

Prickles rose on the back of her neck, but she sloughed them off and concentrated on the soup.

It was delicious.

"IS THERE A PROBLEM?" Lance asked the four policemen as he reached their table.

"Not at all," Vince Landry replied. "We're simply disagreeing about the best way to do something. You know how that goes." He tried on a smile, but it didn't make it anywhere near his eyes.

Lance didn't trust him, even if he was a high muckety-muck in the police world. New Orleans was known for the continual corruption in the department, no matter how hard the city tried to root out the problem. There was always someone on the take.

Bribery and wheeling-dealing were baked into the New Orleans culture.

"Yes, I can appreciate that," Lance said. "However, our other customers are here for a relaxing evening. If you could save your argument for later …"

Vince eyed him, vying a bit for control, then said, "Sure. We didn't mean to cause any trouble."

"No problem," one of the others said.

"Good to know," Lance said. As he turned away from the table, the mayor's entourage entered the restaurant.

Was it a coincidence the cops were in his restaurant on the night the mayor usually showed up?

With a smile, he went to greet the mayor, a man he genuinely liked, although there were corruption rumors swirling about him as well.

"How was your week?" he asked, enduring the man's excessive handshake.

"Excellent!" the mayor boomed. Then he leaned closer and added, "Finally brought the plumber's unions to heel."

"What he really means," the mayor's wife said, "is they finally came to a settlement that pleased no one."

Lance laughed. The woman was a clear-eyed counterpart to the mayor's bombast.

"She never lets me enjoy my little victories," the mayor said in mock sadness. "Shall we go to our table? I'm famished. What's fresh today?"

After he walked with the group of six to the mayor's reserved table, Lance laid out the specials. He glanced over to Elaine who had finished her soup and was watching the performance. He grinned at her, and she smiled back.

The mayor missed nothing.

"There've been rumors you've been harassing some artist down at the square. Is that her?"

"I'm not harassing anyone," Lance protested, gesturing to the chairs. "Enjoy your dinner."

The mayor laughed, but didn't press it ... for now.

Lance walked over to the bar to get a glass of wine for his guest.

"What do you think?" he asked Prosper.

"Uh-uh. You don't pay me to think," he said. "You pay me to make drinks. You want your glass or something for the lady?"

"I know you have opinions."

"Which I am smart enough to keep to myself," Prosper said. "What do you want? We busy here." He gestured to the waiter approaching with a cocktail tray.

"I think a Riesling will do," Lance said. When the bartender decided to get tight-lipped, there was no hope of prying them open.

"Good choice." Prosper nodded and poured a full glass of the good stuff instead of the house wine.

He must approve of Elaine.

"What did you think?" Lance asked her when he arrived at her table. The busboy had already cleared her bowl.

"Delicious. And hot."

"This should help," he said, placing the wineglass in front her. "Riesling. A little bit sweet to counteract the heat."

"Thank you. I hadn't expected the soup. You're very generous."

"Only the best for a welcome guest."

Her cheeks pinked. After a sip of the wine, she said, "Interesting crowd you have here. I have a sense there are a lot of 'important' people here."

"It's something I've tried to cultivate. We're known for our discretion, but also as a place where people can be seen."

"Odd combination."

"It's New Orleans. We do things a little differently. Instead of hiding away our indiscretions, we flaunt them a little ... but not too much. The city is an aging courtesan."

She laughed. "Not at all like Promise Cove. The forests keep a lot of things hidden. There's gossip, but it's done in whispers, not restaurants."

"You're missing out on so much," he said. He touched her hand, feeling compelled to connect with her. Too late he realized the gesture gave his words a double meaning.

She withdrew her hand. "It works for me."

"Do you like anchovies?"

She wrinkled her nose. "I had them once on pizza. Never after that."

"Then I will bring you a plate with your salad so you can pick them off, but try them again first. For me?" He wanted her to like the food as he prepared it, to fall in love with the flavors of his city.

And after that?

"I'll be right back."

He retrieved the salad from the kitchen and placed it in front of her. "Pepper?"

"A little."

He ground the mill twice, then said, "Enjoy."

"Wait!" she said.

"Yes?"

"Aren't you going to sit with me at all? The food may be wonderful, but it is better with company, isn't it?"

"Of course," he said, sitting down.

"Why a restaurant?" she asked, pushing the anchovies to one side as she stabbed a bit of lettuce and cucumber.

"It was one of the few things I did with my dad," he said. His dad had always been in and out of the door, briefcase in hand. When he *was* home, he was holed up in the den with orders to be left alone. Lance had learned his work ethic from him.

"On Saturday mornings, he'd take me to the markets," Lance recalled. "Other boys went fishing, I went to the fish market. Then the farmer's market. Often a trip to a store specializing in spices and hot sauce." Both his parents had distant branches of their families with Cajun roots, frail enough to leave most of the culture behind, strong enough to maintain its food traditions.

Lance leaned back in his chair. "Later in the day, after Dad had done more of his endless paperwork, we'd cook. None of my siblings were interested. Mom was always taking them to one sporting event or another. But Saturday afternoons were my time."

It was a tradition he'd passed on to his own son.

Probably why Xavier wanted into the restaurant business. It was his own fault.

"Sounds wonderful," Elaine said.

He glanced at her salad. She finished most of it, including the tiny fish, before laying her salad fork across the dish to signal she was done.

"And the anchovies aren't bad," she added.

"Then I must go to prepare your entree," he said.

"May I see your kitchen?" she asked. "I promise I won't bother anyone. I'm curious. In Montana, at the general store, we did a little breakfast and lunch service. I used to cook."

"Really?"

"Really. I make a mean panini."

He laughed.

"Of course. This way."

Her eyes grew wide as she witnessed the fast operation that kept everyone fed. Flames flared from the six-burner gas stove, orders were shouted, and sharp knives kept up an ever-present clatter.

"And I thought the general store could be a little nuts," she said as he brought her back to her table.

"Ah, there you are, cher." Thérèse leaned in to air kiss Elaine's cheeks. "Are you keeping her all to yourself?" she asked Lance. "The room is buzzing."

"I've been busy," he said. "And now I'm going to go cook her fish."

"*Ça c'est bon*," she said. "I'll introduce her while you cook."

"Be gentle," he told her, trying not to think of the consequences of letting Thérèse loose with Elaine.

It couldn't be helped. His friend was going to do what she did best: determine Elaine's character by introducing her to the vast range of the New Orleans populace who dined in his restaurant.

Heaven help her.

Chapter Twelve

The meal had been wonderful. She'd thanked him profusely after dessert and left before he could suggest anything else.

But his food must have seriously bewitched her. That was the only reason Elaine was sitting in a café with Lance Fontenot, sipping bitter espresso and delighting in small bits of sugary beignets at nine o'clock on a pleasant November morning not long before Thanksgiving.

They were quiet; their small talk giving way to a comfortable silence. Birds twittered in the city trees. The people who wandered the streets no longer contained the determined group on their way to work, but hadn't yielded to the crush of tourists looking for the same unique experience to tell the folks back home.

In that way, it wasn't much different from the short-term tourists who came to Big Sky country to check things off their bucket lists: Glacier National Park, fly-fishing a world-class trout steam, seeing a rodeo, walking in the footsteps of Lewis and Clark, and finally ending up in Yellowstone National Park. They checked off experiences, but never understood them. It took a lifetime to know a place ... or at least more than a few days.

She would never know New Orleans the way Lance did. Its music pumped his heart, and its food and culture drove his neurons to fire across the synapses.

"Tell me about yourself," she said. "You told me about your time with your dad, but where did you grow up? Do you have any kids of your own?"

"I have a son, Xavier, who is married with a daughter. Avery is the delight of my life." He smiled. "As for growing up, we had a house in the Lakeview District. In fact, my father stills lives there. We had to renovate after Katrina, but there were long overdue improvements that needed to be made so Dad could age there gracefully."

"How old is your dad?"

"He's in his mid-eighties. Since he retired he's been learning how to enjoy life totally. He goes dancing every Saturday night, plays poker with his friends, and is learning to play pickleball. He even has a girlfriend in her mid-seventies."

Elaine tore another bit off her beignet. Mid-seventies wasn't that far away.

"My younger brothers went into law enforcement. One's a cop in Cincinnati, the other a DA in Baton Rouge. My dad had been a DA here in New Orleans, so that made sense."

"You didn't follow in your father's footsteps?" she asked.

"I didn't really want to know the underbelly of the beast. People do some horrific things to each other. I can live without it."

"Yet you enjoy the mystery and intrigue your guests bring to the restaurant."

"I'm detached from it." He traced the rim of his espresso cup with a long finger. "It's like reading a suspense novel full of blood and gore. Those aren't real people to me. My brothers have to look at photographs." He shuddered. "Not for me."

"Not me, either."

They smiled at each other, then she looked away, suddenly shy with the openness of it.

"Did you grow up in Montana?" he asked.

"No, Nebraska." She told him about her early life growing up with four siblings during the contentious sixties, and how the turmoil of the times had strained relationships between them so much that they never really connected.

"My brothers have died; so have my parents," she said. "My sisters are in Nebraska with their families. We get together occasionally."

"I'm sorry. It must be difficult."

"Not really," she said. "I got caught up in my own life. Promise Cove became my family."

"And the art?" he asked.

"Ah, yes, the art." She didn't have a good answer for that. When she was younger, she enjoyed painting and drawing. It was a way to drift away from the reality of all the noise in the world. One of her sisters drifted into books, the boys, like Lance's brothers, had devoted themselves to sports. Her other sister played with Barbie.

Unlike her husband, Lance didn't press her. Jack had been a pragmatic Midwesterner, little given to dreaming. He'd left that to her. She'd hoped to be an art teacher and completed two years of college before Jack swept her off her feet. Once they got married, she'd never gotten back on track with her own life.

All those years ...

Lance placed his hand on hers. "You seem sad," he said.

"When you're young, it seems like there's so much time in life. But there are so many things a person has to do, especially if they have a family.

He nodded.

"Once Maggie took over most of the store duties, I had more time. I painted everything. I went through my wild painting period, simply splashing color about until it looked pretty. I spent hours outdoors doing plein air paintings. When I went to Paris, I tried to imitate the Impressionists. After I met ... well ... later I imitated someone else's style."

"You've been to Paris," he said quietly.

"Yes. I spent two winters there."

"It is the most beautiful city I've ever seen," he said. "Next to New Orleans, that is."

"It is."

On a whim, she'd traded the comfortable shoes of Promise Cove for the exquisitely crafted high heels of Paris, with disastrous results. Now she was trading shoes again, except the fashionable footwear of New Orleans were scuffed with wear.

Would the results be equally disastrous? She needed to be careful about getting too close to Lance. Noticing he was still holding her hand, she pulled it away.

"What do you want to do with your art now?" he asked. "Forgive me for saying so, but sitting in Jackson Square doesn't seem comfortable for you."

"It isn't," she admitted. "I got the permit on a whim. It sounded so romantic, you know."

"And you are very much a romantic, aren't you."

Something in his voice caused her to look at him where she was once again snagged by his gaze.

"Yes," she whispered.

For a few moments, they sat like that. His essence seemed to grow bigger, more important. On its own, her hand drifted closer to his. She longed to touch him, but more than that, to get to know him. How did his laugh sound when he totally let go? What was his expression when he gazed at his granddaughter asleep? How did he express sorrow? Anger? Joy?

Would he accept all her ways of expressing herself?

"What are you thinking so hard about?" he asked.

"It's hard to express. I guess it boils down to ... well, I'd like to get to know you better. At the same time, it's ridiculous. Look at us: city mouse and country mouse." She gestured to him. "May." Then she touched her chest. "September."

"You are a very young September," he said, but he wasn't mocking her. "I want to get to know you, as well. You fascinate me. An upbringing so different from mine. You were raised to be practical and conservative, but they didn't box all of you in. There is a fairy soul that flits through your body."

"Henrietta used to say something like that."

"Henrietta?"

"She was one of my closest friends, an amazing woman. She was a poet laureate of Montana, and ran retreats for people who were stuck in their artistic careers. Famous artists, dancers, and entertainers have come to our little village. She passed away some time ago."

"Sounds so fascinating. I'm sorry I won't get to meet her."

"Yes." That was all she could manage to get out. Even though it had been many years, her heart ached every time she thought about Henrietta being gone.

"Come walk with me," he said. "I'll tell you all about the quarter, and we'll go down to the river."

"Don't you have to work?" she asked.

"Later," he said. "My head chef knows how to get started. And it is the first day Xavier is learning the ropes so he can help out on Thanksgiving. He took the day off from his good job to do this. Hopefully, when he learns how hard and dirty it is, he will come to his senses and give up the fantasy of working in a restaurant."

"Xavier is your son, right?"

Lance nodded as he stood up.

"What's wrong with him working at your restaurant? I loved it when Maggie started helping out at the store."

"Because he has a family. It's his job to have a secure income to make sure they're taken care of. Working in a restaurant is risky. I worked hard all my life to earn the right to take a little risk. Xavier and my wife always came first. They never had to worry."

"Now who's being conservative and old-fashioned?" she asked.

He looked at her for a moment, then laughed. "You're good for me, cher."

"I'm glad."

As they walked, he told her about the different sights they were seeing. There seemed to be someone on every street corner who he knew. It was as if Promise Cove had a main street, and she took a stroll. She'd know almost everyone.

Except this was on steroids.

"I'm trying to get Maggie and my granddaughter to come down in January. Teagan, my granddaughter, has the month off, and no one's designing gardens in January. At least they shouldn't be."

"Your daughter designs gardens? I thought she worked in the store." Lance frowned.

"We sold the store. Now she's following her dream of designing gardens. She's really good at it. She'd love all the different flowers down here, even though they wouldn't stand a chance in Montana."

"If you no longer own the store, you have nothing tying you to Promise Cove."

"I have my friends," she said. Her voice was firm. Ultimately, she belonged in Promise Cove. He needed to understand that.

He nodded.

They crossed the broad levee that attempted to hold the Mississippi River captured. The open space was full of flowers, benches, small neat kiosks, and people strolling. A massive old riverboat was moored at one end.

When they reached the edge of the mighty river, she stood in awe. "I never knew it was so massive. I thought the Missouri was big, but this is amazing."

"It is beautiful, full of depth, and can be very treacherous. Like a woman," he said. He took her hand and turned them to walk beside the rolling waters.

She let him.

Chapter Thirteen

"This is a great idea," Nora said as they climbed to the top of the red bus. "I've always wanted to do this, but it was too hokey for Owen. And it didn't seem like much fun by myself."

"I get it. Hokey is much more fun if there are two of us," Elaine said with a grin. After her walk with Lance, she decided it was time to get to know the city better. It was easy to get Nora to come along with her.

Owen was a real stick-in-the-mud.

"You hear about the Garden District all the time," Nora said. "I can't wait to see it."

"I'm sure it's quite beautiful," Elaine said, not revealing her real reason for wanting to see the famous district. She'd spent over an hour searching until she finally found an old listing of the sale of Lance's home. She'd memorized the address and the photo of its exterior.

It wasn't really stalking. She was simply gathering information about a man she was seeing.

Was that what she was doing? Seeing him?

Although she hadn't been back to the restaurant, they'd made some vague plans to see each other again. He wanted to expose her to a jazz club and nightlife, but running a restaurant made nighttime plans difficult.

She'd already given up parts of her life for a man; it wasn't something she wanted to do again.

"How was it?" Nora asked as they settled into their seats.

"How was what?"

"Dinner! I haven't seen you much since you had your meal at Fontenot's. How was it? Was he as charming as everyone thinks he is?"

"Extremely charming," she said. "He seems to know everyone."

The bus pulled away from Jackson Square and began its tour around the French Quarter. She and Nora ignored the tour guide and continued their conversation.

They knew this section of town.

"And the food?" Nora asked. "Tell me everything."

Elaine told her about the restaurant décor, the appearance of the mayor, and the sense of intrigue she'd felt.

"They say New Orleans is a place where a deal is always being made," Nora said.

"That could very well be true."

The question in Elaine's mind was how much Lance was involved in the intrigue. Did he merely provide a place for it to occur and bask in the undercurrents like he said? Or was he a player himself?

She'd never been someone who tried to play one person against another or leverage a secret to gain power over someone. In grade school, particularly in the later years, some of the girls would get together to form cliques. There was always a lot of whispering going on with those girls.

Sometimes a girl who was in the group was suddenly out. She either became angry and plotted her revenge—some of it very nasty—or hid in the girls' bathroom and cried her eyes out.

Elaine stayed far away from those circles. She was polite, but distant. Even so, more than once a girl had slung rumors about her. Once it was so bad, she'd been hauled in front of the teacher and punished for something she'd never done.

The smirk on one of the girls' faces had devastated her. She'd done nothing to deserve that treatment.

Nothing.

Since then she'd stayed far away from people who traded in lies, innuendos, and secrets.

"Are you seeing each other again?" Nora asked.

"Perhaps." Elaine turned quickly to Nora. "But he's being kind to a temporary visitor. That's all this is. I have no desire to get caught up in his life."

Which begged the question: why was she searching out his former home in the Garden District?

"Except you're blushing," Nora said.

"I am not." She could feel the heat in her cheeks. "Women my age do not blush."

"That's a lot like saying a woman has a dewy mist instead of sweat," Nora countered.

Elaine laughed. Just when she thought she had Nora pegged, the woman came up with something unexpected.

The tour guide announced their arrival at the Garden District.

"For those of you who wish to take the walking tour," he said. "Please get off at the next stop. You can hop back on whenever you want. Check the times of departure listed on your itinerary or on our app."

Why did everything have to be an app?

She and Nora made their way down the stairs to the exit. In front of them, a large, enticing shopping center that included a bookstore anchored the corner. Definitely a stop before leaving.

When the tour guide, holding a red baton high in the air, gestured for the people getting off the bus to join her, they hurried over. The guide checked their tickets, then began an overview of the district.

"This area once had a lot of plantations, but land was sold off over time. Most of the people who bought were wealthy Americans who didn't want to live in the French Quarter because that area was populated by the Creole people. Remember Louisiana didn't become part of the United States until after the Louisiana Purchase in 1803. The British tried to take possession of this important port in 1815, only three years after Louisiana became a state, but were defeated. It was one of the most decisive battles of the War of 1812."

The woman began to walk, and the group followed in a herd.

Soon they were in front of Lafayette Cemetery, where the woman began to talk again.

"I came here once for a nighttime ghost tour," Nora confessed. "I swear there were real ghosts."

"You continue to amaze me," Elaine said.

Nora grinned.

After the brief walk in the cemetery, they were led back past the shopping center where they viewed a well-kept Victorian the tour guide announced as Colonel Short's Villa, built in 1832 after some of the Livaudais Plantation was sold off. The tour guide went on to inform them that some of the original parcels were subdivided in the late 1800s. "This is why there is such a mix of architectural styles in the district."

The walk was fascinating. It was clear why the district was still sought-after by the social climbers and those with disposable wealth. What would it be like to have that kind of money? People in Promise Cove had often thought Elaine and Jack had money because they owned the general store.

That illusion was only because they hadn't seen the debts and bills that needed to be paid off every month.

The relief she'd felt when Maggie approached her about selling the store had surprised her.

After about a half hour of lecture and walking, Elaine saw the house on Prytania Street. It was easy to distinguish with its round tower and arched entryway. It was definitely one of the parcels that had been created at the end of the nineteenth century. The listing had been for over two and a half million dollars.

Elaine couldn't fathom spending that kind of money on a house.

"What's so interesting about that house?" Nora asked.

"Uh ... it's so different from everything else."

"Yes, looks like something we'd find in the nouveau riche section of Minneapolis."

"Why, Nora! You're a snob."

"A girl has to have some defects," Nora said with a grin. She gestured to the tour guide who was on the move again. "We'd better catch up."

AN HOUR LATER, THEY were deposited back at the original spot.

"I don't know about you," Nora said, "but I'm starving, and my feet are shredded ... at least they feel that way."

"My head is crammed with history and architecture," Elaine confessed. "Where do you want to go for lunch? Every time we passed a restaurant with yummy aromas, I wanted to skip the rest of the tour and go right in."

"I know what you mean," Nora said. "But the tour was fascinating." She pulled up her phone. "Fortunately, I foresaw this possibility and scouted out a place. How does Gracious Bakery and Café sound?"

"Well, I hate to say it, but it sounds ... *gracious*." Elaine grinned.

"Bad," Nora said. "It's this way."

The entrance to the bakery and café was a corner door, slicing across the sidewalk at an angle. As soon as they walked in, Elaine was delighted with it. They placed their orders for sandwiches, got their drinks, and found a table.

"Now," Nora said. "Tell me what was really up with that house. I'm not buying your architecture excuse."

Elaine's new friend was getting to know her far too well.

"It was interesting, that's all," she tried.

Nora tilted her head and frowned.

"Oh, all right. Lance used to own that house. It's where he and his wife raised their son."

"That big house just for the three of them?" Nora said. "Although, I shouldn't be surprised. Clusters of large homes are sprouting from former cornfields all over our state."

"Around our bigger cities as well," Elaine said.

"It sounds like there's a little more to your relationship with Lance than a nice guy showing a tourist around," Nora pointed out.

"That's all it can be," Elaine said. "He's fascinating, but we're opposites." Should she tell Nora the other problem? She'd finally looked for Lance's age last night and found it. Maybe saying it out loud would convince her that any relationship with him was ridiculous.

"What else?" Nora asked.

"Well, he's eight years younger than I am." There. She'd said it. And it didn't make her feel any more resolved to keep things light. In fact, it made her miserable.

"So?" Nora asked.

"So? What do you mean ... so?"

"Men are with women younger than they are all the time."

"But not the other way around," Elaine maintained.

"It's changing," Nora said. "You can be a pioneer. Don't let age stop you. Not if there's something really there worth pursuing."

That was the question, wasn't it? Was any relationship, even the possibility of one, with Lance Fontenot worth the effort?

Chapter Fourteen

Avery giggled as the penguin waddled to the edge of the platform and dove into the water. The bird was much more graceful as it swerved and circled, almost disappeared into the depths of the water they couldn't see, and then zoomed close to the glass.

Lance's granddaughter jumped back and laughed some more. "Pengin," she said with a delighted smile.

Glancing at his son, Lance said, "She's going to be a heartbreaker."

"I know," Xavier said. "She's got her mother's ability to wrap men around her little finger. And she's only five." He groaned.

"Let's hope she inherited my sense of responsibility," Lance said.

"Why not mine?"

"Because you want to go into the restaurant business."

Xavier shook his head, but the argument was delayed because Avery tugged at his hand. "I want to see the lion."

"They don't have lions here," he said. "This is an aquarium. They have fish."

"And birds."

"And a few birds," Xavier agreed.

Lance had never been sure why the birds of prey had landed in the aquarium, but it probably had to do with some ecological or anthropological theory that fish had evolved from birds or vice versa.

Cooking was far easier to understand.

"And lions," Avery said.

"No lions."

Her sigh indicated that she didn't understand how her father could be so ignorant.

"Fish with stripes. And squiggly things around their heads." She waved her fingers around to demonstrate.

"Oh, a lionfish," Xavier said with great exaggeration. "They're over here."

Lance trailed behind them as they walked to the tank that held the vibrant creatures. His son was turning into a great dad. It was too bad he wouldn't take his financial responsibilities seriously.

Now wasn't the time to discuss it.

"What shall we do after the lionfish?" he asked when they got to the exhibit.

Avery ignored him and focused on the fish. Every ounce of her being was concentrated on the wavy spines of the species. She turned around and beckoned him over.

Lance crouched down beside her.

"Aren't they beautiful, Gran-papa?"

"Yes." He watched the fish. Children had a way of reminding him that it was important to be present in the moment, not always thinking about the next thing that needed to be done.

The striped fish swam back and forth, their deadly spikes waving like the mane of the animal that had inspired their name. Their unblinking round eyes never moved as they traveled, but some instinct led them to open their mouths to snap at a speck of food.

They were the only ones in the tank, swimming back and forth endlessly, going about the basic business of life without thought of art, education, or the existence of a higher being.

"But not good to touch."

Avery brought him back to reality.

She shook her head, brown ringlets waving about as the spikes waved around the fish. "They have poison. They hurt people."

"That's right," he said.

"But they don't bite."

"No, they don't."

"Sharks bite. And alligators. Not lionfish." She seemed to consider this for a moment. "Let's go to the shark tank," she said and grabbed for her father's hand.

Marine life fascinated his granddaughter. As often as he could, Xavier indulged the fancy. And when possible, Lance went along with them.

What would happen to these Sunday outings if Xavier went into the restaurant business? His son needed to think about these things. Food service played the devil with one's personal life. People liked to eat out at the most inconvenient times.

It was why Lance had waited until his son was grown before he'd even started talking about opening his own place. Camille had indulged him as long as she thought it was a fantasy. She liked his paycheck and the fact that he could be counted on to show up at her parents' Sunday dinners. He'd set her expectations early on for fine pieces of jewelry on her birthday.

When he'd started viewing real estate listings and making appointments to see businesses for sale, she'd gotten concerned and had started dropping hints about her desire to travel after they retired.

He'd known better. New Orleans had bound Camille to her as surely as a spider wrapped a trapped fly. His wife hated sleeping anywhere but her own bed.

At least until *he* had come along.

Lance pushed away the images. This was time for his son and granddaughter, not for bad memories.

Avery seemed to understand her role of rescuer.

"Gran-papa, look at that one! He's coming right at us! I think he wants to eat us."

"He's a little small to eat a big girl like you," Lance said, watching the spotted shark come toward them. About twenty-eight inches long, it had a slender body with two fins at the back.

The shark continued to come toward them, inches off the sand at the bottom of the tank. At the last moment it turned, the almost human-shaped eye about the same height as Avery's.

She gripped his hand tighter.

"He looks mean."

"He probably is if you're a small fish or something. I don't think we're in danger."

"What if we go swimming?" she asked.

"You don't need to worry about him," Xavier told her. "He's not interested in you."

"But what about the big sharks? They could eat us." She let go of Lance. "They have really big mouths." She used her hands to demonstrate the size of a shark's mouth.

"Oh, I think bigger," Xavier said. He pulled his daughter's arms wider.

"Wow." She stood quietly for a few moments, then dropped her hands. "Do they have those sharks here, Daddy?"

"No, honey, they don't."

"Then you have to take me to see them."

Xavier scooped up his daughter. "I'll see what I can do," he said. "But not today."

"Not today," she said. "I'm hungry."

Lance shook his head. The women in this family were not for faint-hearted men. Avery was going to be the type that made Scarlett O'Hara look like an amateur.

They made their way to Bite, the aquarium's restaurant. Once they'd ordered their food, Lance handed Avery the kid-proof tablet he'd brought with him. He showed her how to get to the pictures and videos of sea life and soon she was engrossed.

"I'm looking forward to working Thanksgiving," Xavier said.

"How was your first stint as a bus boy?"

"Fine. I know I have to start at the bottom. The waitresses are nice. They share their tips. I know not every place does that."

"I encourage it. Everyone is working hard. They deserve to be compensated for their efforts."

"Starting on the bottom, I'll learn the business well. But I also want you to teach me. You didn't start that long ago, and already you have one of the most successful restaurants in the city."

"I thought about it a long time before I did it. I took care of my responsibilities first." Lance nodded at Avery. "You think she's demanding now? Wait until she becomes a teenager. And needs dresses for all those fancy balls women seem to require for their daughters."

"That's old fashioned. Avery's not going to want that."

"Maybe not, but her mother will. And all those traditions are still going strong. Avery will get swept up in it, you'll see."

"How do you know?" Xavier challenged him. "You only had brothers."

"Who do you think those women danced with?" Lance asked. "My mother, bless her soul, always made sure we went to the right parties and dances.

Fortunately, she also turned a blind eye to the not-so-sanctioned parties we went to."

"The ones you were always forbidding me to attend?"

"Yep. I knew what went on at those parties."

"I bet all the girls wanted to go out with you," Xavier said.

"I didn't lack for dates, let's put it that way."

"So what about the woman Thérèse mentioned? Are you dating her?"

Lance hadn't seen that coming.

Fortunately, that was the moment their food was delivered. By the time they got Avery settled again, he could redirect the conversation. He did not want to discuss Elaine, mainly because he wasn't sure what they were doing.

Besides having fun. In fact, he couldn't remember the last time, if ever, he'd had this much fun with a woman who wasn't his granddaughter. Even Thérèse was more work than Elaine.

"Tell me about her, Dad."

"Who?"

Xavier rolled his eyes, a skill he'd adapted as a teen when his parents were just too awful for words.

"There's nothing to say," Lance tried.

"Mom says you've been seen with her."

"How does your mother know anything? She's in Florida."

"The same way she's always known everything," Xavier said. "She's very tapped in. So is my wife, Harper. She's heard things too. You're considered a very eligible bachelor for a certain set, you know."

"The same group of woman who can't understand I'm not interested."

"That's why they're all unhappy you're dating this woman who's not from here. They're sharpening their claws."

"They'd best leave her alone," Lance muttered. "We're not dating. I treated her to dinner. And to beignets at Katie's. And, of course, I'll ask her to come to the restaurant on Thanksgiving."

"Of course," Xavier said. "I hate to break it to you, Dad, but that's dating."

Lance waved his hand in dismissal. "How can that be dating when she's only here for the winter? In my day, dating had a purpose. It was to check out a person to see if they would be a good life companion. See if you were in love with them, a strong enough love that would carry you through the times of life that were difficult."

"It didn't last with Mom," Xavier pointed out.

"We made it through the rough spots for most of our lives. We really did love each other. Believe that." He focused on Xavier to make him understand that his parents had had a good life together and with him. "But somewhere along the way our dreams diverged. We separated." He shrugged. "It's okay. We've moved on."

"And that's not what you want with this new woman."

"No. We're having some good times. That's all."

"That's enough?" Xavier asked.

"Absolutely."

Chapter Fifteen

Whitney's insides were a mess. She shouldn't be doing what she was doing, but this was the world of politics, the world she desperately wanted to be part of. There was so much good she wanted to do for her city and her people. If dancing close to the line was the price she had to pay to get the job she wanted, then she'd just have to do it.

She'd opted for the bus. That way her car wouldn't be spotted anywhere near this city-owned apartment. It was supposed to be for guests of the city. The mayor and the head of the city council had discretionary use as well.

How did Vince have access? When she'd asked, he'd told her not to worry; it was all on the up and up.

She decided to believe that answer.

As she walked from the bus stop to the apartment building, she glanced around her. What would she do if she saw someone she knew? How could she explain her presence in the business district on a Sunday?

The rat-a-tat of her heels clicking on the sidewalk increased in tempo.

Soon she was at the building. She pressed the call button for the apartment. "It's Whitney."

The door buzzed, and she pushed through it. A slow-moving elevator took her to the fifth floor. Once disembarked, she checked the sign for numbers and headed in the correct direction of the apartment number Vince had given her.

She tried to sound self-assured as she rapped on the door.

Vince opened the door and gave her a beaming smile. "It's good to see you again."

To her surprise, he gave her a kiss on the cheek. He was freshly shaven and had used a cologne with an aroma of cloves. He wasn't in uniform, but his shirt was pressed and his jeans clean.

"Come in. I stopped to pick up some brunch items. Can't talk about business on an empty stomach. Coffee?"

"Please." Coffee wouldn't help her jittery stomach, but she needed something to do with her hands.

As he went to the kitchen, she walked to the windows. By and large, New Orleans was a low-rise city. From this angle, she could see all the way to the river, even at this relatively low height.

"Nice view," she said as he came back into the room and handed her a mug of coffee.

"Yes. Too bad your constituents can't enjoy it." He shrugged. "But those are the kinds of perks that come with this job."

His breath brushed against her neck.

"Of course," he added. "You'll have even better perks as you climb the ladder."

That wasn't why she was ambitious, but he wouldn't understand that. Men like him were ambitious for the power, not for the good they could do for others.

Why was she here? With him?

Politics. It was the way things worked. They shouldn't have to, but they apparently did.

"Let's eat," he said.

It was the last thing she wanted to do, but he was calling the shots. At least until she figured out what he wanted and what he was offering in return.

The brunch spread he'd laid out on the dining room table was bountiful. Eggs, ham, a po'boy sandwich sliced in two, and a couple of salads, along with the inevitable beignets, lay in front of her. In addition to coffee, there was a clear glass pitcher of orange juice.

"I've got some champagne we can add to that later," he said. "Once we finish talking about business."

She murmured acceptance as the acid from the coffee added to her stomach's turmoil.

After ladling some eggs on her plate, along with a piece of ham, some green salad, and a croissant, she took her time adding butter to the light French roll.

Vince piled his plate like he hadn't eaten in a week. He must have a good workout routine to eat like that and maintain his weight.

"How well do you know Lance Fontenot?" Vince asked after they'd exchanged a few more pleasantries and started their meals.

"Not well at all," she said. "I've met him when I've gone to the restaurant with the mayor, but I've never been there on my own."

"The mayor is important. Lance likes to hang out with the bigwigs. Makes him feel like he's got power." Vince barked a laugh. "Some people don't understand what real power is." His gaze zeroed in on Whitney. "That's what I've got. Real power. And you'll have it too. All you have to do is pay your dues, and you'll be on your way."

She waited. Where was he going with this?

"I need you to go to the restaurant by yourself. Get to know him."

"Why?" she asked.

"Because he's pals with the mayor. I'm looking for gossip. You're young. He won't suspect you of doing anything underhanded. And you're pretty. What man doesn't like a pretty woman?" Vince reached across the table and stroked a finger down her hand. "I know I do."

His touch should have given her the creeps. Instead, her body buzzed in reaction.

"Lance is in his sixties," she said, moving her hand.

"I don't care how old a man is. A pretty face is a pretty face." He grabbed one of the po'boy halves. "Will you do that for me? I'll even throw in some cash to pay for those fish."

"Not necessary," she said. "This is my future too, remember?" He still hadn't told her what she was getting from this deal, and she wanted to remind him.

"Of course," he said.

"I really don't see how this helps."

"That's the beauty of gossip. You never know where it will lead." He pointed his fork at her. "And keep up whatever you're doing with the mayor. He likes you. Or he's trying to score diversity points. Whatever. Just keep working him."

This whole dialogue was beginning to sound like something out of a bad thriller. Maybe books were written that way because the conversations were based on reality.

It didn't matter. What mattered was getting to the kind of position where she could really make a difference.

"Okay." She put another forkful of lukewarm eggs into her mouth.

"You're not seeing anyone, are you?" he asked.

"Not at the moment."

"Like I told you, I'm separated from my wife. Looks permanent this time. How about we go for dinner sometime? Or to a jazz club? I know some great ones."

"I don't date married men."

"I'm separated."

"Not much of a distinction."

"It could be mutually beneficial."

There was a coolness to his tone that made her uncomfortable.

"Say you'll think about it," he added.

"Sure," she said. She could think about something all day long and never feel the need act on it.

What if he made it a prerequisite to helping her? It was a trade as old as humans.

She forced herself not to shudder. Instead, she tried to change the topic.

"What do you think about the move of the city's investments to a green bank?" she asked.

"What a revolting name," he said. "Green bank. It's another marketing ploy."

"Actually, no," she said. "They're working to fund clean energy technologies. Instead of investing in oil companies, the city is using the bank to invest in tech that will help it survive."

"All New Orleans needs to do to survive is build a higher wall. We don't need smart cars that a man can't fix on a weekend. It's already a pain with all that computer stuff gunking up the works."

"From a financial perspective," she said. "It makes sense. The return on investment is solid. We're backing growing businesses, not shrinking ones."

He laughed. "Big oil is never going away, Whitney. Once you get a better understanding of the lay of the land, you'll see that."

Was he resistant to change because he wanted to protect his turf? Or was that a quality required to be part of the crowd?

This whole thing had been a mistake. She needed to back out before she got in too deep.

"Speaking of finance," he said, "I've put the word out that you're going to help us out."

"I didn't agree to anything," she said.

"Meeting me here today is agreement enough," he said, his expression slamming into neutral. "You said you wanted to climb the ladder. You're going to need to get your hands a little dirty to show you really mean it."

"I ..."

"The alternative means you'll be a one-term city council member."

Could she live with that? It would mean giving up everything that she had been working for the past ten years.

"What do you want?" she asked.

"The budget is coming up for review again," he said. "There's a couple of line items in the police department budget I'd like to see increased."

"But the budget has to balance."

"I'll point out a few places that could take a hit."

She stayed silent. It wouldn't be too bad. Just shift some money around. She didn't have to know what they were doing with it.

"Take it slow," he said. "Gradually shift your position. That way no one will really notice. Got it?"

She nodded.

"I've got your word?"

"Yes. Yes. I'll do it." For her community. That's what she had to remember. This was all for her community.

"Good girl," he said as he rose. "I think now is the time to spike that orange juice with a little champagne."

She sat quietly while he mixed mimosas.

Somehow she made it through the rest of the meal. As she was just about ready to leave, he said, "I'd really like to take you to dinner. Someplace quiet. How does Thursday night sound?"

"Um ..."

"Good. It's settled. I'll text you the name of the restaurant and time to meet." This time his kiss landed on her lips instead of her cheek. "I look forward to it."

She couldn't get out of there fast enough.

Chapter Sixteen

Elaine's day started off sultry, a tease of what summer must be like in the city. Maybe it was a threat instead. The summers in the south were notorious for their combination of heat and humidity. Screened in porches had been a necessity before air conditioning, and still were in places that hadn't been retrofitted. The image of Southern women fanning themselves—or more realistically having enslaved children fanning them while they sipped mint juleps and complained about the heat or what the neighbor's boy was up to—was a romance that totally ignored the hardships of most people's lives.

It looked good in pictures though. Maybe it was what she should paint today.

Elaine stepped out of her apartment and walked the block and a half to a small café. Once she'd tasted a beignet, she was hooked. This place served them hot in a paper bag. A shaker of confectioner's sugar allowed the customer to choose the perfect amount of sweetness. She was even becoming accustomed to the bitter coffee everyone seemed to drink.

She settled into a chair at one of the outdoor tables and pulled out her phone. She missed local newspapers. She and Jack had always had a pile of the *Whitefish Pilot* delivered daily. It had been long on nearby happenings and short on the blood and gore of national news.

She could buy a copy of the *Times-Picayune*—there was a vending machine just around the corner—but its size daunted her.

No, she'd sit here on the pleasant street with her breakfast treat and her phone, catching up on Montana's local news.

A few familiar people smiled as they walked by, daily walkers, people on their way to open up one of the local shops. She'd never seen the man who had looked at her over the newspaper again.

What was she going to do with Lance? His dinner had been amazing. But more than that, it was the way he treated her. There was an old-world charm in his gestures and manners. She'd always been independent, and Jack had never treated her like a hothouse flower, but whenever Lance touched the small of her back, it awakened something sensual in her.

If she had to name it, she'd call it femininity, the heart of a woman.

With her husband, she'd had to develop hard edges. Things needed to be done. He was a good man, but hadn't always thought things through. They'd bought the store with rose-colored glasses on. She'd placed more faith in Jack's ability to make a solid plan than she should have.

But that was in the past. She'd have some fun with Lance, go home, and that would be it.

Finishing up her breakfast, she stowed her phone in the back pocket of her pants, threw away the trash, and strolled back to her apartment. Because it was Thanksgiving week, special permits had to be obtained to paint on Jackson Square because of the heavy tourist traffic around the square.

She hadn't bothered trying to get one. In some ways, it was a relief. Maybe Lance had been right. Sitting there had been a romantic's dream, but had put far too much pressure on her to get the painting right the first time.

After straightening up her apartment and putting a light load of wash into the stacked washer-dryer, she scanned through the postcards she'd bought of New Orleans scenes. None of them satisfied her. They were of buildings, flowers, and the exorbitance of Mardi Gras. She wanted something more human. For the first time since she'd left her aborted college days, she wanted to draw people.

The image of the women on the porch came back to her. She picked up her sketch book and looked over the ones she'd done at the museum.

Yes. This was it. This was the right path.

Grabbing her purse, she went back downstairs. There was a small tourist shop that carried calendars and books of local history. Perhaps they'd have some inspiration.

It turned out to be perfect. They had a calendar based around women in southern gardens. The paintings evoked the style she had in her mind. Then she found a treasure, a used book depicting the scenes she'd sketched at the museum.

After paying for both her purchases, she headed back to her apartment. The day was beautiful enough to sit out on the balcony and paint, but first she'd take some time to create sketches.

Her heart beat excitedly in anticipation of creating something new.

LANCE CALLED WHILE she was setting up her easel on the balcony.

"Hello," she said, unanticipated joy filling her heart. "How are you doing? How was the aquarium?"

"It was great fun," he said. "My granddaughter is obsessed with things that bite like alligators and sharks."

Elaine laughed. "At least it's not dinosaurs. We always kept a few dinosaur items in the store during the summer. They were always gone by the end of the season."

"Must have been some happy kids," he said.

"Yes." She laughed. "They were always overjoyed to find them. But not as happy as their parents."

"I bet," he said, then chuckled. "What did your daughter play with as a child?"

"She liked coloring books as a kid, and any kind of book later on. She was a tomboy. A lot of the kids were back then, roaming the area, catching frogs and letting them go, exploring the woods. In the summer we could always find them at the beach. They'd swim, boat, and play volleyball."

"Sounds idyllic."

"It was. Sometimes I'd like to find Steve Jobs and shake him."

"Why's that?"

"Everything changed after cell phones," she said. "My granddaughter's childhood was different, especially once she became a teenager. Even in Promise Cove with all its beauty, they were glued to their cell phones. Every school has cliques, mean girls, and bullies, no matter how small the educational system. But cell phones make it worse. It's all done in private, away from the prying eyes of teachers and parents."

"I understand. Unfortunately, we cannot turn back time. My son missed most of it, although he seems to be attached to his phone now." Lance chuckled again. "But then, so am I. And here we are, using them to talk to each other which is a very good thing."

"Is it?"

"Of course. It's not as good as being together, but it is better than writing a letter knowing it will take days or months to get to you."

"Where are you?" she asked.

"City Hall," he said. "My friend, the mayor, has asked me to speak to a group about the problems restauranteurs have with the permit process."

"What kind of problems?"

"The usual difficulties one has with bureaucrats. They make things too complicated. Laws are passed without regard to what is already on the books. Then the pencil pushers ... or keyboard pushers these days ... simply add the requirements to existing forms. They never check for redundancy. Or even if the rules conflict with each other. It's a mess."

"But aren't some regulations necessary? I mean, I wouldn't want to eat in a restaurant with unsanitary conditions." The image of rat chewing on a chicken thawing on the counter that appeared in her mind made her sick to her stomach.

"Yes. They are. I'd like to think everyone will do the right thing, but I know from my years of working on the port, that the temptation to cut corners is too great. A few dollars can make the difference between a company's survival and failure. Then there are people with no morals, who think it is all about them. Nothing should stand between them and their greed, not even another person's life."

"You have a dismal view of humanity."

"No, cher, merely realistic." He paused for a moment. "But this is too depressing a conversation for such a beautiful day. What are you doing?"

"I'm going to paint," she said.

"In the square?"

"No. I thought about what you said. I'm setting up on my balcony."

"Isn't that still distracting?" he asked.

"Not really," she said. "I'm above it all."

He laughed, and the mood lightened.

Being with him, even on the phone, made her happy.

"Before I go back to my meeting," he said, "I wanted to make sure you were coming for Thanksgiving dinner. It won't be as good as it could be if you don't come."

He'd asked her several days ago, but she'd declined to answer. Dinner in his restaurant with all those people seemed overwhelming. Last year she'd shared it with Maggie, her friends, and their husbands.

But the alternative was eating alone. Nora and Owen were going to the home of distant relatives.

"Yes, I'll be there," she said.

"I'm glad," he said, his voice softening. "That gives me the strength I need to go back into my meeting."

She smiled. "Good thing I could help, then."

They chatted for a few more moments, then hung up.

After putting the phone down, she finished setting up and sat with the blank canvas for a while before leafing through her sketch book one more time. The image she originally had in her mind wouldn't fit on this canvas without being crowded, but if she used just one figure ... the one she'd added at the last moment ... it might work.

With a light pencil she began to outline the image of a woman languidly draped over a wicker chair, her arm draped to the floor, a mint julep on the table next to her, and a soft smile on her face.

The smile mimicked the one Elaine felt playing over her own face as she worked. It was a smile of contentment and a secret happiness not ready to be shared with the world.

Chapter Seventeen

How could it be Thanksgiving already? More importantly, why had she agreed to celebrate at Fontenot's where she knew no one besides Lance?

Elaine poured coffee and slipped a couple of pieces of bread in the toaster. Her morning go-to place was closed this morning, and her neighbors had already left to visit their relatives. She wasn't expected at the restaurant until two.

A whole morning to leisurely sit around and ... do what?

She didn't want to drag out her paints. Although she was pleased with what she'd done the past few days, it still looked amateurish to her eyes, as if she were trying to be something she wasn't. She didn't feel like struggling to uncover the missing element today.

Once again she found herself longing for a newspaper, only something more substantial like the Sunday *New York Times* or *San Francisco Chronicle*. Something with thoughtful articles about things she'd never even imagined existed.

Had running a general store atrophied her mind? Going to Paris for a few winters had shaken her awake for a while. She'd stumbled through the language, some of her high school French awakening from where it had lain dormant in her brain. There were constant adjustments to life: how to order coffee, a different daily tempo, learning how to operate one of the self-cleaning toilets on the street in an emergency without getting soaked or picking up some dreaded disease in the process.

Since then she'd nestled back into her own life, drawing the covers back over her head.

Coming to New Orleans had awoken her curiosity again, but she was coping, not going out and tackling learning head on.

Except for her painting.

She smiled as she pulled the toast from the toaster, spread the butter, and added a scoop of the jalapeno peach pepper jelly she'd purchased. At first she'd resisted the need these chefs had to add a bit of spice to everything, but she was coming to appreciate it.

She settled down with her current book, a recent thriller based in the city, and took her time eating her meal.

The phone rang just as she'd finished cleaning up and was about to head into the shower.

"Maggie!" she said, happy to hear her daughter's voice.

"Hi, Mom. Happy Thanksgiving!"

"To you and Tom too. And Teagan, if she's with you?"

"I just roused her and sent her to the shower. We've got cooking to do before we show up at Kelly's."

"I'll miss you all this year," Elaine said.

"You'd better be home for Christmas. We all miss you. Mike and Ruth are already planning a huge party for the town at the bar."

"We need a bigger place to put these things on in the winter, Madam Mayor," Elaine said.

"Don't I have enough to do?"

"You know what they say ... if you want something done, ask a busy person."

"Right."

"I met the mayor of New Orleans, and he has a long lunch at least once a week at my friend's restaurant." That was the best way to describe Lance, wasn't it?

"Is this the same restaurant where you're having Thanksgiving dinner?"

"Yes, Fontenot's."

"I looked that up when you mentioned it last time. Pretty fancy. And the mayor goes there once a week? I bet he's figured out a way to make the city pay for it too."

"I don't think so. The mayor and his wife seem to have money in their own right. And ... well ... I don't think Lance would go along with that scheme."

"Lance, huh?"

"Well," Elaine said, "I couldn't keep calling him Mr. Fontenot."

"I suppose not." Maggie's voice seemed troubled. "Mom, are you sure you aren't in over your head?"

"Of course not. I'm having fun. Why would you say that?"

"You're too trusting. I mean, this guy could be leading you on."

Elaine laughed.

"Mom! I'm serious."

Suppressing her laughter and wiping the tears from her eyes, Elaine said, "Sweetheart, I'm seventy. He's not going to take me off to a sex trafficking ring at my age. Women in their seventies—heck, earlier than that—we become invisible. They even call us up to rob us now because they can't see us on the street."

There was silence.

"But you trusted the man in France," Maggie said.

"He never lied to me," Elaine said. "I knew what was what. I simply forgot it. When he moved on, it hurt, but it was my own fault."

"I love you, Mom."

"Love you back."

There was noise in the back ground.

"Teagan wants to say hi, and I have to get back to my food prep. Don't forget to text me your flight arrangements. You already have your tickets don't you?"

"Yes, dear," Elaine said.

"Love you. Here's Teagan."

Elaine chatted with her granddaughter for the next half hour, before Maggie insisted it was time for Teagan to be put to work.

After ending the call, she poured herself another cup of coffee, flipped on the television, and watched the end of an old movie before taking her shower and getting ready for dinner.

AS ELAINE FEARED, FONTENOT'S was jam-packed.

Lance must have been watching for her, because he was by her side moments after she walked through the door.

"Let me take your wrap," he said. "I'll have someone put it in my office."

She turned slightly so he could remove the cloth shawl she'd picked up a few days ago. The weather was still far warmer than Montana, but sometimes she got a chill.

Lance held her shawl in his arms and snapped his fingers at a waiter and told him what he wanted.

"There are so many people," she said.

"Yes, but there are familiar faces too." Lance shook his head. "My son is over there, getting run ragged cleaning up. He'll learn this business isn't for him and go back to what he should be doing: business."

From the slight smile on Xavier's face as he worked, it probably wasn't going to be as easy as all that, but she kept her opinion to herself.

Lance guided her to the bar where Prosper was hard at work mixing cocktails. A younger version of the older man worked next to him, filling glasses with wine and beer.

"Hello, pretty lady," Prosper said. "Happy Thanksgiving."

"Happy Thanksgiving to you too. Is this your son?"

"You think I'm younger than I be," he said. "This my grandson."

The young man nodded, but kept working.

Prosper slid a drink toward her. "Your aperitif," he said.

"Thank you." She took a sip. "Delicious, of course."

"Yes, ma'am," he said with a smile.

She turned away from the busy man. "Thank you for inviting me," she said.

"It's my pleasure." Lance picked up the glass of red wine Prosper's grandson had set in front of him. "I'm glad you were able to come."

"Well, I did have a hot date with the National Dog Show, but I thought this might be ... um ... slightly less terrifying than watching over-pampered animals perform."

Lance chuckled. "This is why I like you so much. You make me laugh."

"I do my best," she said, holding out her glass to him.

They clinked.

"So what's on the menu?" she asked.

He rattled off a number of traditional Thanksgiving dishes, as well as a few New Orleans specialties with which she'd become familiar.

"And there is turducken for the main course," he said.

She puzzled over the name for a moment before she remembered. "Oh, yes! A chicken stuffed into a duck then stuffed into a turkey." She made a face. "I'm sorry, but that sounds revolting."

He laughed. "We also add sausage in the middle."

"I think I'll skip that."

"Oh, but you must try it," Lance said. "It would be a shame to have Thanksgiving in New Orleans without turducken. Have I ever steered you wrong?"

"It's good," Prosper said.

"Maybe a little piece. After wine." She imagined the dish again. "Lots of wine."

Lance laughed again.

"Come with me. I have you at a table with Thérèse and some others you've met."

She stood still. She couldn't do this. Have dinner—with strange food—with a bunch of people she didn't really know?

"Couldn't I have my usual table? Off in the corner?"

"No, cher. Not on Thanksgiving. This is a holiday for people. You have nothing to worry about. They will love you."

There was nothing to do except put on a brave face and deal with it.

"Everyone's curious about Montana," he said as he guided her to her table. "For people who've lived here all their lives, it's more foreign than Paris."

"Uh-huh."

Elaine smiled when she saw Thérèse.

"Ah, here you are, cher," Thérèse said as she enveloped her in a hug. "I was beginning to worry that I would have to go to your apartment and fetch you. You are missing all the fun! I see you have your drink. Let me introduce you."

The other people at the table, six in all, were of varying ages, but all beautifully dressed. That must be their connection. Lance had mentioned that one of Thérèse's many lines of business was a small, but very sought after, clothing line.

As Lance had predicted, they were all fascinated by her origin in "that wild place up north." One woman who looked even older than Elaine asked if the state had electricity yet.

Elaine let the woman know that not only did Montanans have that utility, most people had indoor plumbing, and some even had internet.

Several people at the table chuckled.

Elaine sat and took a sip of her drink.

"Promise Cove," a stylish young woman said. "I think I've heard of that. My aunt is a singer. She went through a rough patch a long time ago after her husband left her. I think she went there for a vacation or something."

"No, it wasn't a vacation," said a young man who must be related based on his facial features. "It was a retreat. Someone … what was her name …"

"Henrietta?" Elaine supplied.

"Yes!" the young woman said. "Do you know her?"

"I did," Elaine said.

Immediately, she was showered with questions.

Ten minutes later she'd forgotten why she had been so nervous about having dinner with strangers.

AS SOON AS ELAINE WAS settled with Thérèse, Lance got sucked into the busyness of a restaurant during a big holiday meal service. Most of the patrons today were friends or long-term customers, so he didn't have to deal with out-of-towners prone to complaining because what they really wanted was food they understood and a culture that made them comfortable.

New Orleans often delivered neither. It was an exotic flower that could only thrive where it did.

Elaine was still enjoying the difference from her hometown, as well as the warmer weather, but what would happen when she, too, inevitably tired of the strangeness?

"Kitchen needs you," one of the waitresses told him.

He strode to the kitchen, smiling at the diners as he went. It was a bit like acting in a play. No one needed to see the controlled chaos that went on backstage.

One of his recent hires stood by the stove, staring at a good-sized saucepan thick with a brown mixture.

"I ... uh ... put too much hot sauce in ..." the young man said, his gaze on the floor. His hands shook as he waited to be reprimanded or, more likely, fired.

Lance suppressed the flash of irritation. People made mistakes. He'd created his share of colossal ones.

"There is no such thing as too hot in New Orleans," he said, dipping a clean spoon in the mixture and tasting.

Apparently, he was wrong.

He turned to get to the sink, but someone had a glass of water ready for him.

Staring at the pot for a moment, he considered the possibilities. Wasting food in a restaurant kitchen wasn't an option.

"Here's what to do," he said. "Create a new base ... um ... two-thirds of all the ingredients *except* the hot sauce."

The young man lifted his head. "You're not going to fire me?"

"On Thanksgiving? Not a chance. Just follow instructions exactly from now on."

"Yes, chef," he said.

Lance finished giving him directions, then walked around the kitchen to check on everything else. Everyone was moving economically in the small space, and there was a lack of the foul language he knew would start up again as soon as he walked out the door.

There were few things guaranteed in a commercial kitchen, but swearing and someone trying to deal illegal drugs out the back door were two that could always be counted on to occur.

He navigated the tables in the restaurant, checking in with the wait staff as they made sure drink glasses were full, bread baskets refreshed, and orders delivered when they were ready. The bussers assured him things were going smoothly, but it was early for him to worry about them. He swung by the bar where Prosper was reminding his grandson to work slowly and steadily to make sure things got done.

"Haste makes waste" was still true no matter what century it was.

His glass of wine was on the bar before he'd had a chance to take a stool. Workers who spent time on their feet learned to sit whenever the opportunity arose.

"It going well," Prosper said.

"So far. But we have just started serving soups and salads." The Thanksgiving menu was limited to cut down on chaos.

"It will go well. Is your lady enjoying herself?"

"She's just a friend."

"So you say."

"So I mean." Lance made his voice firm. There were many reasons it was impossible for him and Elaine to be anything more than that. Beyond the physical difference in where they lived, there was the age gap. He told himself it didn't matter, but he sensed he might be lying to himself.

"Age be a number," Prosper said, as if he were reading his mind.

"What?"

"I heard you talkin' to Thérèse," Prosper said. "Sayin' how Elaine was older than you by some years. Some people, they old by the time they thirty. Others, like your lady, stay young all their lives."

"I told you."

"I know. I know. She's not your lady."

A waitress zoomed to the bar and rapidly delivered an order.

Lance took his glass and climbed the stairs to a balcony few people knew about.

The narrow ledge ran around the entire inside of the restaurant except for along the back wall. At both ends at that point, the space expanded, enough for a small table setting and a view out a hexagon window. Often, especially at the end of a particularly trying dinner service, Lance would sit and enjoy a glass of port as he studied the view. Although it was a small sliver of skyline, the architect had sited the window so Lance could see the river framed by iron lacework, tree leaves, and glittering lamps. It always made him feel he'd been transported to one of the fantasy novels he used to consume as a kid.

Now, however, he stood at the center of the balcony. Anyone who looked up couldn't see him, but he could see pretty much the entire floor. It calmed him to be up here, master of his universe.

He'd created this. His vision had been translated by the interior designer into a spacious, well-lit environment that throbbed with class. People rarely wore jeans to Fontenot's. At least not the locals. Sometimes a tourist missed the cues the outside provided. They weren't harassed, but pointed looks from the other customers let them know their mistake.

Studying the scene below, it appeared that everything was running like clockwork. Whenever he hired anyone new, they were explicitly trained in the methods he had developed to ensure everything ran smoothly. Then they shadowed another person for a day. Finally, they were let loose under a close eye of supervision by a more experienced member of his staff. Corrections were gentle, but consistent. Anyone who couldn't or wouldn't learn was let go after a few weeks.

Lance zeroed in on his son. He'd given Xavier the full training, and this was the first time he'd been alone. There was a person watching him, but given the stress of Thanksgiving, the attention wouldn't be as rigorous as Lance liked.

His son seemed to be holding his own. Lance smiled when he saw Xavier take care of a water glass that had been sitting empty as the regular busser dealt with a large table. As he put the glass down, he smiled at the customer who said something to him. Xavier nodded, then went back to the kitchen, emerging a few moments later with bread to add to the table's basket. Then he checked the baskets of everyone in his section and refilled as necessary.

Xavier was a natural. Instead of deterring him, Lance's bright idea to drive away the desire to work in the business was backfiring.

He'd have to think of something else.

His gaze shifted to the table where Elaine sat. She was leaning back in her chair, observing her fellow diners as she sipped her drink. Her body language said she was relaxed, and it made him smile.

As if by some sixth sense, she looked up in his direction, and he could have sworn she saw him. He turned away from the viewpoint and hustled back down the stairs to join the table for a while.

The rest of the day went as smoothly as could be anticipated. He had several short visits to Elaine's table and took her around a few times to introduce her to some of the interesting people in attendance. It was only after dessert had been served that he approached her about staying a little longer. Reluctantly, she agreed.

After instructing one of the bussers to set one of the tables in the upstairs alcove, he made sure that everything was running smoothly in the kitchen and with the waitstaff. Satisfied that everything was in control, he snagged a bottle of port and two glasses.

"I've come to steal my guest away," he said to the diners left at Elaine's table.

"She's lovely," one of the few women from his mother's generation told him. Murmurs of assent flowed around the table.

"Don't forget you promised to come to breakfast with me soon, cher," Thérèse said.

"Yes, I will," Elaine said. "Thank you for asking me." She looked around the table. "I enjoyed meeting all of you. It was one of the most interesting Thanksgivings I've ever had. Thank you for accepting me into your group."

"Keep coming back," one of the men said. "Beautiful women are always welcome."

Elaine's cheeks pinked as she said, "Thank you. You're too kind."

"See. She's learning already," the old woman said. "Soon she'll sound like a real southerner."

The pink on Elaine's cheeks deepened.

"We'll see you," Lance said as he tugged on her hand and led her upstairs to the alcove.

"How lovely!" she exclaimed.

A white tablecloth had been spread on the table and napkins laid out. A silver bowl full of pralines sat in the center.

Lance poured them each a glass of port. "To your first Thanksgiving in New Orleans."

"Thank you," she said as they clinked. "It was truly lovely."

"And how was the turducken?" he asked.

"It was good," she said. "Way too much, but the taste was better than I imagined."

"That's good, because I have all kinds of culinary treats for us to explore together." The slowly descending sun hit the window and outlined the bones of her face as if they were part of an artist's painting.

The man at the table had been right. She was a beautiful woman.

"Have a praline," he said. "They are wonderful with the port."

"Sweetness on top of sweetness," she said before biting into one.

"La dolce vita, as the Italians would say." He sipped his port. "And mine is all the more sweet now that you are in it."

Her gaze darted to him, and for a few moments they stared at each other, as his awareness of his growing attraction to her clicked into place.

Chapter Eighteen

Below them the diners slowly filtered from the restaurant. Shuffling feet and clinking plates were punctuated by bursts of laughter and loud voices. On the balcony, time stood as still as their bodies.

As she returned Lance's intense gaze, Elaine catalogued the features of the man: the intensity of the dark brown eyes softened by thick eyelashes, above them a pair of still-dark eyebrows leading to a strong forehead slightly covered by some of his thick salt-and-pepper hair. His nose had the slight bend at the end that had become familiar in her time in the city, a legacy of the French who'd been pushed from Acadia by the British and migrated south. Lance's long, slender fingers matched the rest of his slim frame.

His chin lacked the strong forthrightness of his Scandinavian ancestors, but the lips above it were warm and sensuous.

It had been a long time since she'd felt the pleasure of a man's kiss.

A crash of a glass below and the seconds of silence that followed broke the mood.

Grateful for the interruption, Elaine plucked another praline from the dish. The sugar-and-cream-coated nuts were addicting. She'd bought some in her wanderings to enjoy at home once. They hadn't lasted an hour.

"Was tonight a success for you?" she asked.

"I believe so, but it's not important. This is a gathering about connections, reacquainting ourselves with each other, I believe. Getting to know new friends." He picked up his glass. "I'm sorry I didn't get to spend more time with you. Did you enjoy yourself?"

"Yes, very much so," she told him. "Thérèse was, as always, a delightful companion. She's had quite a life, hasn't she?"

"Yes. We've known each other since we were children. Her parents were very poor ... she was a scholarship kid at our school." He grinned. "She and

I were constantly in trouble. It was amazing how many creatively destructive things she could think up to do."

"It's served her well. When did she start her business?"

His smile faded a bit. "Not right away. She was headed down a wrong path for a while. You know the drill; it happens even in small towns. She ran with the wrong crowd and picked the worst kind of boyfriend. After one of her girlfriends died of an overdose, she saw the writing on the wall and pulled out of it. She went to college for a business degree."

"And created an empire."

"Not quite." He sipped his port. "She met what she thought was a nice, steady man in college. He turned out to be an abuser, both emotionally and physically."

"Poor woman."

"Yes. I didn't realize it for a while. Like most abusers, he isolated her from friends and family. He was actually a great businessman, and they started the company together."

"How did she get away?"

"He was very adept at hiding the signs of his abuse, and she was too ashamed to tell anyone. But one day she went home to see her mother after a particularly violent episode. Her mother may have been poor, but she was sharp. She convinced Thérèse to stay with her and hired a good lawyer. Thérèse won the company and built it from there."

"And the husband?"

Lance shrugged. "He disappeared from New Orleans, probably not voluntarily."

Elaine shivered. "We had something like that happen in Promise Cove recently. A woman and her daughter were running away from her ex, also an abuser."

"Did it end well?" Lance asked.

"Very well." Elaine smiled. "The man is in jail. The woman and her daughter have stayed in our town and started a new life."

"It must be a very nice town."

"It is." A longing for Promise Cove washed over her.

"And you miss it."

"I do." She sipped her port and stared through the oddly-shaped window. The view was beautiful, but she was beginning to miss the mountains. There weren't views like Montana's anywhere else in the world. "It's a unique place. And I don't know. We kid each other about something being in the water, but an awful lot of people seem to fall in love in Promise Cove."

"Including you?"

"Oh, I'm not sure I'll ever fall in love again in my life," she said, almost automatically. "I had my love."

"And a person only gets one in a lifetime?" he asked.

"I've never thought it about it one way or another ..." That wasn't quite true. In Paris she'd started to think she was in love again, but the practicalities of having a foot in two separate continents didn't make sense. Even before her lover had called it quits, she'd realized the craziness of a long-term relationship with him.

"I understand," Lance said. "I had my love with my wife. It was a grand passion when we were young, and I thought we had mellowed into the steady romance and love of adulthood."

"The restaurant must have been quite a surprise to her."

"Not at all. I'd talked about it all my life. Even when we were younger, I had a grand passion for cooking. In fact, I did a lot of meal planning and prep for the family. She was happy to let me do it. When we married, I promised I would have a steady job until whatever kids we had were out of the home and our retirement was funded. Then I wanted to open a restaurant."

"And she agreed."

"She did," he said.

"And?"

He shrugged and popped a praline into his mouth.

Elaine waited while he chewed and swallowed. She'd supported her husband in his dream and understood how some passions weren't to be denied.

"I think she got used to the lifestyle we had and didn't think we could maintain it. She was probably right, although I had no regrets selling the house. I didn't need to deal with the maintenance of an old house while trying to build this restaurant."

Elaine nodded, then let the subject drop. The restaurant patrons seemed to have left, but the footsteps of the servers and kitchen staff still echoed on the floor below.

"But ..." Lance said after they'd been quiet for a while. "I'm not sure Camille was my last love."

"Oh?"

"Up until a few weeks ago I would have assured you it was true, but then I saw this beautiful woman painting badly at Jackson Square." He grinned.

"I was not painting badly!"

He gave her what her mother would have called the side-eye.

"Yeah," she said, the fight leaving her. "It was pretty bad." She emptied her glass. Now was the time to make her exit, before he got back to the topic of love, a subject she had no desire to discuss any further. "I should get home," she said.

"Wait a bit," he said as he recorked the bottle. "I'll finish up with the staff then walk you home. It's early yet. Maybe we can take the long way back to wherever you are staying. The walk will do us both good."

She wanted to protest, but having someone by her side while walking through the city in the dark would be nice. It wasn't a bad area, but after all the time in a rural town, she was more comfortable with the thought of a grizzly a few feet away than a stranger.

"Okay," she said.

They walked down the stairs, and he returned the bottle to Prosper. They wished the man and his grandson good night, then walked to the main part of the restaurant. The tables were cleared and fresh clothes put over them. The place looked ready for the next group of dinner guests.

Lance checked on the kitchen, then went into the office to get her wrap. After they left the restaurant, he turned toward Jackson Square.

For a while they walked in silence, then he once again became a tour guide, telling her about some of the things she was seeing and the history behind them. He was as proud of his city as she was of Promise Cove and Montana. They both had places that nurtured them, and they weren't the same.

But it would be nice if there was a way to compromise.

She almost stopped walking then. Was she falling for him? They'd only known each other a few weeks. There were a dozen reasons why it wouldn't work.

Ridiculous. A person doesn't fall in love at seventy. A woman should be beyond that.

Fortunately, he didn't notice her preoccupation.

About halfway into their walk, he took her hand, and she let him. It was nice to be holding hands as they walked. There were a number of other couples out strolling, some of whom Lance knew. Even when they walked by these acquaintances, he held her hand.

He could have anyone. That's what Thérèse had told her.

What was he doing with her?

When they finally reached her apartment building, he stopped to say his goodbye. The moment was almost as awkward as when the first boy she'd dated brought her home.

"I think you've bewitched me," he said. "You must have brought some of the Promise Cove magic with you."

"I think you're probably overtired," she said, trying to lighten the mood.

"No," he said. "I think not."

Then he leaned in, his gaze never leaving hers.

She didn't move away, and she didn't stop him.

The sweetest kiss she'd had in a long time, if ever, landed on her lips.

It was ... indeed ... magic.

Chapter Nineteen

Whitney slid on one of her favorite dresses, a sleek red dress that favored the color of her skin and showed off her legs to advantage. She added contrasting silver earrings and a matching choker. Droplets from a spritz of her favorite perfume fell gracefully on her bare shoulders.

But her shiny lips were in a frown. Her aunt's voice—the one who'd raised her after her mother had died in an accident perpetuated by a drunken white city council member—chastised her as if she were standing in the room with her.

"A gift from a bad man will only make you weep. Take your time, cher. Make sure he's worth it before you give it away. You remember that now, promise?"

Whitney had promised.

Was Vince a bad man? Or only a man with a cop's attitude toward everyone—guilty until proven innocent. In some ways she could understand it. A cop's life was in danger more often than not. But they tended to look at people of color with more suspicion than most.

That was the part that was hard to take.

What was she doing with a cop? She should cancel the dinner.

But that would be rude, and her aunt also brought her up not to be rude.

No, she'd go tonight and find out what was what. Vince had told her to take a good look at the proposed budget. She'd done that and asked questions about every aspect of the police budget until she felt she truly understood it. She'd jotted down the salient numbers and was prepared to discuss them with her date.

Not a date. They were having a business meeting, a business meeting she'd gotten all dressed up to attend.

Her heels clicked on the front steps of her apartment building. He was a good looking man. He was separated. Okay, so separated wasn't the same as divorced, but it almost was. Vince had told her he and his wife weren't going to make it this time.

It was—as the mob saying went—only business.

The drive to the restaurant was short and the traffic light. Too soon she was there. Was she going to be an equal negotiator for what she wanted or a lamb led to slaughter?

Taking a deep breath, she determined to negotiate.

Vince was at a table when she walked into the restaurant, a small venue with sturdy wooden tables and low-level lighting. Spicy aromas emerged from the back where the kitchen must lie.

As she made her way to where he sat, he rose to greet her. He looked comfortable in a pressed shirt and creased black pants.

"Mmm. Very nice," he said, looking her up and down before leaning in to kiss her, settling for the cheek she presented.

She wanted to be clear that this was not a seduction.

Then why had she worn one of her most sensual dresses?

They sat down, and the waitress took her order for a glass of wine.

"How was your week?" she asked.

"Good, for the most part. We hired some new recruits and started their training in various sections of my district. They spend half a year moving from one section to another. Gives them a perspective of what the district's all about and how the departments work."

"Must be a difficult time for a new person. There's a lot of difference from one area of the city to another."

"Right. That's why I'm focusing on consistency. Some of the department chiefs are resisting … used to doing things their own way. But we make it worth their while, and they come around."

She should probably ask what exactly made a department head stop resisting, but she didn't really want the answer. It skated too close to information she didn't want to have. They were making changes for the betterment of the city. Vince's district had the lowest crime rate of all the districts in New Orleans. That was what was important.

How he got there didn't matter.

Their drinks came.

"You see," Vince said after taking a sip of his whiskey. "It takes strong leadership to make this city work. An astute eye for the right kind of pressure to be applied. The carrot and the stick are still applicable. So is the saying, 'It's not what you know. It's *who* you know.'"

Should she say something? Although what words were appropriate escaped her.

"That's where you come in. The mayor and I ... well, let's just say he and I have never seen eye to eye. He's too much of a do-gooder if you catch my drift. You understand what's what. You didn't grow up expecting everything to be handed to you. You worked for everything, including your scholarship to Tulane."

How did he know these things?

"I've got my sources," he said with a grin, answering her unasked question. "I'm the same way ... pulled myself up by my bootstraps in a family full of cops. My dad was killed when I was twelve. Some drug-crazed coward just up and shot him for no good reason." Vince's hand tightened around the glass.

"I'm sorry," she said softly, trying to ease some of the tension.

His shoulders slowly relaxed and he released the glass, pushing it slightly away from him. "No, I'm sorry. I asked you here for a nice dinner, not to drag up bad memories." He reached across the table and grasped her hand. "Let's begin again. How was your week?"

His thumb caressed the skin on top of her hand. She wanted to pull back, but it didn't feel safe to do so. His flash of anger had unnerved her. Maybe she was the lamb after all.

"It seemed like there were lots of small emergencies this week," she said. "From water and electric problems, to some suspicious activity in one of the departments that needed investigating. I thought everyone would take the week off, enjoy the holiday."

He laughed. "Holidays can bring out the worst in people." He frowned. "The investigations didn't involve the police department, did they?"

"No, the tax department." Although she wouldn't have been surprised if the problem was in the police department, and neither should he. New Orleans police had the reputation of being one of the most corrupt law enforcement organizations in the country.

She knew that. Then why was she risking her own reputation to dance close to the flame?

The waitress came over and delivered their order. The next few minutes were devoted to tasting their meals and talking about how they'd spent their holidays. He'd spent some time with his estranged wife and kids, but assured her it didn't mean anything. She'd gone to dinner with extended family, like she had always done.

When their dinner wound down, he brought the conversation back to city business.

"How was the mayor this week?" Vince asked.

"I didn't see him," she said with a shrug. "He spent the first part of the week in meetings, made an appearance at the parade, and then he and his wife went to her relatives for dinner."

"Her wealthy relatives. His honor has always known how to line his coffers."

"Why don't you like him?" she asked. "He does a good job for the city."

"He's too smooth. Everyone thinks he's one of the good guys, but I know he does things on the sly, like everyone else."

"I haven't seen anything like that."

"That's because you're young. You've only started. Keep your eyes out, especially when the mayor dines at Fontenot's. There's a lot of wheeling and dealing going on at that place. It's exactly what Lance Fontenot wants. He even has a back room where private meetings occur. Only those on the inside know it's there."

"I didn't know."

"You aren't high enough on the food chain," Vince said. "Like I said. Whenever you're at the restaurant watch what's going on. If people disappear for a while, it's likely they're doing business in that back room. It would be interesting to know who's seeing who."

It was time to stop being so trusting and naïve. It was the way of the city. Even her aunt was a sharp bargainer when she wanted to be.

The waitress asked if they wanted dessert. Vince declined for both of them, and the waitress whisked the plates away, returning almost immediately with the bill folder.

Vince slid in his credit card.

"I thought we'd go back to my apartment and have an after dinner drink," he said. "That way you can show me what you have in private."

"I don't think that's a good idea," she said.

"Afraid I'll seduce you?" he said with a grin.

"Something like that," she admitted, feeling vulnerable.

"It'll only happen if you want it to happen," he said. "I don't force women."

"Good to know," she said with determination, trying to take back some of her equality.

He studied her as if he knew exactly what she was thinking, but also letting her know he'd never let her be his equal. He may not force women, but she suspected he didn't totally respect them either.

If she didn't watch her step, she'd wind up a pawn in his sophisticated game of chess with the mayor and the city council.

He leaned forward and once again took her hand, this time turning it palm up and tracing its lines with his fingertip. "We can also talk about how I can help you get what you want. I know you're ambitious. Being on the budget committee is a great first step. But there are other positions that can also give you leverage to work the system for what you want." He lowered his voice. "I promise nothing will happen ... not unless you want it to. We're simply going to have a business discussion in private." He folded her fingers back up over her palm. "Okay?"

"Okay," she whispered.

Chapter Twenty

He shouldn't have kissed her.

Lance scowled at the coffee pot. Since Thanksgiving night, he'd thought of nothing but how right Elaine's lips had felt. The age difference had dropped away, and all he could do was be in the moment.

It had gone on for a long while, until she'd gently detached herself. He'd opened his mouth to say something, but she'd put her index finger on his lips.

"Thank you for dinner, Lance. Dinner and everything else," she'd said before letting herself into the apartment building.

He hadn't seen her since, even though he checked the square every day. There was a different group of artists there at the moment. A lot of the regulars he knew hadn't been able to afford the increased holiday permit costs.

Something he'd need to mention to that young woman who'd come with the mayor a few times. When the mayor had introduced her, he'd said she was on the finance committee. Whitney ... that was her name.

He poured coffee into his mug and settled into his modern black leather couch to read the Sunday paper. Over the summer he'd hired a head chef and restaurant manager. Between the two of them, they could handle most of the traffic. He only *had* to go in on their days off or when he wanted to try out some new menu items.

But he was there most days. It was his restaurant and his reputation. Plus, he liked to keep his finger on the pulse of the city. A lot of what happened in government germinated in an atmosphere of good food and a discreet waitstaff.

That was something he made clear to every new hire. Any rumors had better not come from them. Only one person had ever broken that trust. Lance had fired him the moment the indiscretion had become clear.

When the mayor had asked him if he had a back room that could be used for private meetings, Lance had cleared out one of the small storage rooms and set it up. If food and beverage were delivered, either Lance did it himself, or it was done by the waiter who'd been with him the longest, a middle-aged man he trusted implicitly.

In some ways it was a dangerous game he played. The people he let use his back room with his full knowledge could be planning something illegal or dangerous. Regardless of the legality of the discussions, the participants definitely didn't want to be overheard.

The whole secrecy of it was what gave him a thrill. He liked being part of the "in" crowd.

Would Elaine understand? Or would she be horrified that some of the activities happening in his restaurant might not be entirely aboveboard?

He had to stop thinking about her. If he were smart, he'd stop seeing her too. There was no good outcome.

Except that he enjoyed her company very much. He could keep it friendly. It was simple. No more kissing.

He turned the page of the newspaper and got caught up on football scores. College games were entering their semi-finals and finals. Professional teams were taking aim at the Super Bowl.

A small advertisement for a new restaurant caught his eye. It wasn't far from Fontenot's, and it looked to be one of those Asian fusion places, an odd choice in the somewhat stodgy French Quarter. For a place that enjoyed an edgy reputation, the quarter could be remarkably traditional.

He should take Elaine there and get her reaction. It would be nice to dine somewhere other than Fontenot's. They should also take an outing to one of the old cemeteries. He had relatives buried in St. Louis, so that should be the one. There were plenty of intricately-carved above ground tombs. Maybe she could get some inspiration for her painting.

Without spending too much time thinking about it, he texted her to see if she was free on Wednesday.

His phone pinged with an incoming message, but it wasn't Elaine.

"Come over for brunch," Xavier had texted. "Avery is with her mother. I'm lonely."

It was definitely what he needed. The weather was predicted to be gloomy, that gray heaviness that made him always think it was going to rain, but never did.

Plus he enjoyed time with his son; he always had.

"I'll be there."

They arranged a time, and Lance finished his coffee, took a shower, and got dressed.

XAVIER LIVED IN THE Lower Coastal section of New Orleans. It wasn't far from Lance's apartment, but it was worlds away from city life. Tucked in a bend of the Mississippi River, it was made up of land that had once been part of three plantations: Stanton, Shamrock, and Delacroix.

It lacked the density of most of the rest of the city, where the young and ambitious, or older and wealthier people staked out their claims. It was a mixture of country people who'd been there for generations, sometimes in run-down "mobile" homes next to a ditch, sometimes in neat farms that would have easily transported to the Midwest; farms that had been in their families for generations.

For a long time, it had been a dumping ground for things no one wanted anymore, and sometimes a rusty pickup or bedspring coils could be found deep in swampy woods or hidden by tall grass and shrubs. A few gated communities had been built, a sign that property values were going to rise.

Xavier and Harper had bought a newly constructed ranch house not far from Audubon Wilderness Park when Avery was about six months old. They'd quickly realized the city life they so enjoyed as young adults didn't work well for a child, especially as they'd planned to have another.

Unfortunately, Harper had miscarried the next baby, and the marriage had taken a hit. Even though he'd never been his daughter-in-law's biggest fan, Lance had mourned with them, even venturing into a church and lighting a candle for the baby's soul.

Once the marriage began to crater, Xavier rented a smaller house on a treed lot on the same street.

After picking up beignets at his favorite place, Lance drove across the bridge over the Intracoastal Waterway to the district. The darkness of the sky was reflected in the channel of water below him. A few speedboats traveled down the waterway in spite of the weather. Boaters and fisherman weren't going to let the threat of rain keep them from their craft on a Sunday.

Lance parked in his son's gravel driveway and climbed the freshly built steps to the roofed porch, a porch that could really use some screens for summertime. The front door was open, the screened door keeping outside critters of all types where they belonged. This part of New Orleans was as far from city as a person could get. In addition to the more appreciated wildlife of songbirds, snakes, hogs, and bobcats were also neighbors.

"Hey there," he said as he opened the door and walked in.

"Hey, Dad."

Lance enveloped his son in a big bear hug. No matter their occasional disagreements, he loved his son and was proud of the man he was becoming.

"Coffee's on," Xavier said. "You know where the mugs are."

Lance grabbed a coffee cup from the hanger and poured a cup. "I brought beignets," he said. "Also the paper." He indicated the kitchen table where he'd left both.

"Thanks." Xavier moved around the kitchen efficiently, exactly as he'd learned from Lance.

Aromas of crab and rich hollandaise sauce tickled Lance's nose. "Crab benedict?"

"Yep. Guy found a mess of them while he was out and brought them in. Not peak season, so crabs are rare. I snapped them up. Shucked them all morning."

"Guess that's one of the benefits of living all the way down here. People always catching more than they need."

"It's not all that far," Xavier said as he pulled English muffins from the toaster. "You just like to complain."

"Maybe." Lance grinned.

Xavier pulled together the benedict and slid plates onto the table. "Let's dig in while it's hot."

Over breakfast, Lance listened to his son's stories of the week, his work at the port—which bored him to tears—and the antics of Avery. He also talked a bit about the work he'd done at the restaurant.

"What's the deal with the back room, Dad?" he asked.

"Why?"

"Seems to be such a secret. And someone asked about it."

"Who?" Lance's antenna went up. People didn't ask about that room unless they wanted something.

"Don't know her name. Pretty, probably Creole. She comes in with the mayor. She was there last night."

"Whitney Goodwin," Lance said. "What did you tell her?"

"Did exactly like I was taught. Told her you were the only one to answer questions about that."

"Good." It shouldn't mean anything, but the spot between his shoulder blades, the one that had always been his tell of danger, was itching.

"But what's the big deal?" Xavier asked again.

How much should he tell his son? He wasn't doing anything wrong necessarily, but he'd promised people privacy. But telling him made him uncomfortable.

He plunged ahead anyway.

"I keep it for meetings that people want to have away from the public eye. It started with the mayor, but others have heard about it." Lance shrugged, trying to rid himself of his discomfort with the topic. "It's business."

"The business you've built by catering to the rich and powerful," Xavier said. "I've never understood why that was necessary. Fontenot's serves good food in an exceptional venue. That should be enough, shouldn't it?"

"Old habits," Lance said. "In my position at the port I had to work with the city to get things done. It was the usual case of getting to know the right people in order to succeed. I never crossed the line. It was how projected were completed." He cut another piece of the benedict, but didn't pick it up. "A lot of those people, like the mayor, I'd known for a long time. When I wanted to build clientele for the restaurant, I reached out to them. It's as simple as that."

Xavier eyed him sharply. "I hope so."

"There's nothing to worry about. I've got it under control," Lance said, finally forking the piece of English muffin. "This is really good."

"Thanks."

"We should add it to the menu for brunch," Lance said. "In fact, let's talk about the brunch service. I think it could use some shaking up. I'd like to hear your thoughts."

Xavier was apparently chock-full of ideas. He started talking and didn't stop until Lance left a few hours later.

As he pulled out of the drive, the discussion about the back room floated back into his consciousness. Maybe it was time to pull back from the city's politics.

Chapter Twenty-One

Elaine was going back to painting at the square three mornings a week, even though she'd become aware she wasn't producing her best work there. The fair thing to do would be to call the city and tell them to resell her permit and give someone else a chance. She wouldn't get her money back, but she'd be free of the obligation.

"How was your holiday?" she asked Delilah.

"Like everyone else's." She took the cup of coffee Elaine handed her. "I ate too much, quarreled with one of my more obtuse relatives, and we pretended it never happened when the gathering ended."

Elaine laughed.

"How was yours?" Delilah asked.

"One of the most fascinating Thanksgivings I've ever had. I even tried turducken."

"Hate that stuff. Too rich. Too much meat. And way too much effort to make."

"Totally agree." Elaine set up her easel and arranged her work space.

"I take it you went to Fontenot's. I hear they put out quite a spread."

"That they do. And the people I met were so interesting. They have so many different experiences. My brain was as stuffed as my stomach when I was done."

"And the owner?" Delilah said with a smile. "How's that going?"

"Uh … fine."

"That means he kissed you."

"Not necessarily."

"Definitely."

Elaine's cheeks reddened, and she tried to concentrate on the painting she'd started earlier in the week. The painting was an adequate depiction of a woman on a porch, even evoking the feeling of languid heat that she was going for, but it looked like every other painting of the genre.

How did artists do it? How did they make their artwork stand out? Or maybe she was trying too hard. She was no longer a young woman with her life and possibilities in front of her. This might be as good as it got.

If so, she should pack it in and head back to Montana.

"That's different from what you were painting earlier," Delilah said.

"I decided to try something different."

"It's nice. Something that people might buy as a souvenir."

"Could be." But Elaine couldn't find it within herself to care. She needed to satisfy herself first, and she wasn't anywhere near satisfied.

She soldiered on. It was good practice.

An hour later she'd completed the painting. A few tourists had stopped by, and one had expressed pleasure in what she was doing, but that was all the interaction she had. Her romantic idea of being an artist around Jackson Square was losing its luster.

"I like that," Lance said.

She dropped her brush and it clattered to the sidewalk.

"Where did you come from?" she asked.

"The coffee shop." He handed her a cup and a second to Delilah before bending down to pick up her brush. "There is a chill in the air, and I thought you might need some warming up."

"Thank you," she said.

"I also want to invite you to dinner. There's a new restaurant that has just opened up, and I want to try it out."

Elaine hesitated. After their kiss, she'd given herself a good talking to and planned to end whatever was going on between them. There was no future, and she wasn't someone who was capable of committing herself to casual relationships. She'd already proved that in France.

But she wasn't about to turn him down with Delilah sitting next to her with a big grin on her face.

"I'd love to," she said. She'd let him down gently after dinner.

They made arrangements to meet at the restaurant. He left, and she put a blank canvas on her easel. For the rest of the morning, it remained empty.

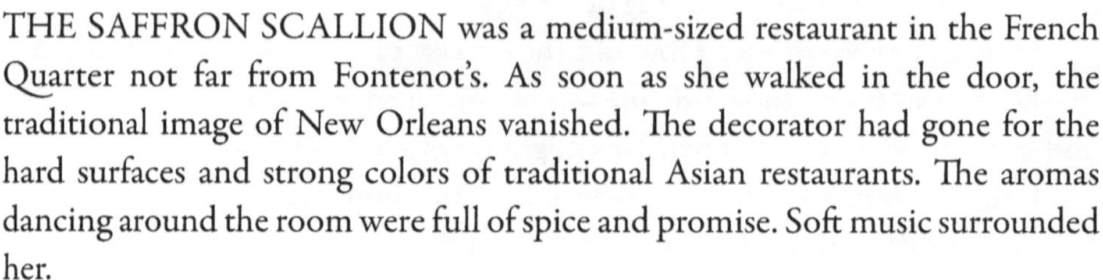

THE SAFFRON SCALLION was a medium-sized restaurant in the French Quarter not far from Fontenot's. As soon as she walked in the door, the traditional image of New Orleans vanished. The decorator had gone for the hard surfaces and strong colors of traditional Asian restaurants. The aromas dancing around the room were full of spice and promise. Soft music surrounded her.

She gave her name to the hostess who led her to where Lance was already seated.

He rose to greet her and kissed her cheek. "It's good to see you. I feel like it's been ages since I had you to myself."

"It was only last week," she reminded him.

"It was too short a time after a very crazy day," he said.

A day that ended with a kiss she was still trying to process.

The waitress came by, and Lance suggested they order some sake to begin their meal.

"One glass," Elaine said. She had a dim memory of sake and a throbbing headache.

"Or maybe none?" Lance asked. "We don't have to have it if you don't like."

"You're right," she said, warming to his perception. "I don't really want sake. A glass of white wine would be fine."

He ordered a sake for himself and suggested a Riesling for her. "The sweetness will blend nicely with the spice of the food," he explained.

It took her a moment to process what had just happened. Her husband, like most men, would have asked the question then ordered the drinks without giving it a second thought. Lance had taken a moment to really check in with her, to make sure she wasn't simply going along.

How odd ... and wonderful ... to have her feelings considered so thoughtfully.

She smiled at him.

Drinks out of the way, they spent the next few minutes catching up on the events of the week.

"It looks like you are trying a different kind of painting," Lance said.

"Yes. I took your advice and did some painting on the balcony at home."

"Still a public place."

"It's the best I could do. I don't think the rental agency would appreciate drops of paint on their beautiful floors."

"Probably not. You need a proper studio."

"I have one at home," she said, thinking longingly of the large space her husband had created in the top story of the general store. Skylights let in the sun's rays even in winter. "Had," she amended. "When my daughter and I decided to sell the store, I lost my studio."

"That's sad," he said.

"We needed out from under the pressure of the business," she said. "The new owners said I can continue to rent my apartment from them, but it's not the same." Sorrow blanketed her. This stage of life seemed to be about giving up things, ideas, and people. She was no longer young with her life in front of her. That was why any sort of relationship, especially one as strewn with complications as this one, was out of the question.

The only problem was how much she liked the man. Apparently, her libido wasn't quite ready to give up the ghost either. It wasn't so much a desire to leap into bed and tear off his clothes, as it was a desire to kiss him again in a more private place, where no one would pass by and wonder what this old lady was doing with this attractive man.

He was staring at her, his dark eyes concerned. Sliding his hand across the table, he covered hers with his.

His touch was warm, a soft caress in an often harsh world. Her heart beat a little faster. She should pull her hand back, tell him this was ridiculous. Instead, she let it be, returning his gaze with hers.

"What do you want from me?" she asked.

"This moment. There doesn't need to be more than that right now, does there?"

She shook her head.

For a few moments longer they sat like that, simply being in the same space with each other, connected by the simple act of holding hands.

His eyes were limpid pools of depth. Who was he really? Even what little she knew of him had so many layers, it would take a while to go through them. He was as exotic to her as the city around her.

The approach of the waitress interrupted the moment.

"Do you know what you'd like to order?" she asked.

"I'd like the chef to choose for me," Lance said. "Elaine?"

Since everything on the menu was unfamiliar, Elaine nodded. "That sounds like a wonderful idea."

"Very well," the waitress said and walked toward the back.

"I would never think to do that," Elaine said.

"This is a new restaurant so I have no idea what's good. There are a few reviews, but not enough of them to indicate a trend. I always like to see what a chef feels are his best dishes. It gives me an idea of the man ... or woman."

"And to scope out the competition."

Lance shook his head. "Asian fusion isn't my competition. If someone wants Asian food, they're not even going to consider Fontenot's. A French restaurant is a more likely candidate."

"So many things I hadn't considered before," she said. "You must have put a lot of thought into this business."

"All my life I wanted a restaurant," he said. "But it's a risky business, and I wanted to make sure my wife and son were cared for. But once Xavier was on his own, I started doing deep dives into the business, particularly the New Orleans scene."

For all his seeming casualness, Lance was a methodical man. How very differently they'd lived their lives. She'd given hers over to her husband's dreams, even after he was gone. She hadn't even begun to think of a life without obligations when Maggie had gotten pregnant and become a single parent.

What did she want out of the final chapter of her life? Wasn't that what she was supposed to learn while she was away from Promise Cove?

Yet here she was, becoming tangled up with a man again, a man who would have his own priorities and his own strong sense of self.

He'd crush her fragile beginnings.

"What do you want from me?" she repeated. "I don't live here, we're very different people, and I'm probably a decade older than you are. There's no future for us."

"Why can't today be enough?"

She considered the question.

"Because I'm not a day at a time person. I need to know where I'm going, what the future holds. All my life I've had to plan for the winter. Well, the winter of my life is upon me, and I need to make plans."

He frowned, then opened his mouth to speak.

The waitress placed two steaming bowls in front of them and described what they were about to taste.

ALL THE WHILE THE WOMAN was talking, Lance was contemplating what he'd just heard. He didn't consider himself in the winter of his life, far from it. He'd just embarked on a new adventure, one that would keep him going until he was ready to quit. He figured that was decades away.

"How old are you exactly?" he asked without thinking as soon as the waitress left.

"I'm seventy." She looked down at her broth.

"Hey, none of that," he said. He hadn't meant to make her feel bad.

"And you?" she mumbled without looking up.

"Sixty-two." He took a deep breath, not sure what to say that would make it any better. He'd known she was older, but hadn't considered it a problem.

Eight years was a lot, especially if she considered she was entering the winter of her life.

On the other hand, he thoroughly enjoyed her company. Everyone she'd met during the Thanksgiving dinner had loved her. Thérèse said she was the hit of the table because she'd made people feel good about themselves.

"She was one of the few people who wasn't babbling about themselves," Thérèse had told him. "Instead, she was curious about the lives of everyone around her."

"Let's not worry about that right now," he said. "Age is simply a number. It's how you act and feel that matters."

Cautiously, she looked up.

"You're right. I know people in their thirties who act as if they were born in the horse and buggy days." She gave him a tentative smile.

"You're not one of them," he said. "I mean, here you are, trying out a new restaurant with a man you've recently met, daring to eat whatever the chef puts in front of you." He picked up his spoon and took a sip of the soup.

"Try it," he said. "It's really quite good."

She dipped her spoon, tasted, and smiled. "You're right."

He let the moment pass. As they ate their soup, he took the conversation to sights in the city he thought she might like.

"Like I said, one of the old cemeteries is a must. I'd love to take you, like I mentioned, but it might be good for you to explore one on your own. You know, take your easel or sketchpad and have fun exploring."

"I might do that. Maybe after Christmas."

"You said you were going home for the holidays. Is that still true?"

"Yes. I'm afraid my friends and family would be very upset if I'm not there. They still haven't forgiven me for spending two Christmases in France."

"Very demanding family," he said.

"And you?"

"I'm not sure yet. I'll spend it with my father. Whether Xavier can be there or not depends on how many hoops his wife makes him jump through to see Avery."

"How is that going?" she asked.

"I wish they'd pull the plug and move on."

"No hope, then?" she asked.

"I don't think so, but Xavier can be stubborn." He caught the look on Elaine's face. "I know, a lot like his father."

"You said it, not me." She grinned.

His shoulders unclenched. They were back to an easy give and take. He should leave it that way and leave the discussion of what season of their lives they were in for another time ... or never.

"Are you looking forward to going back to the cold?" he asked.

"Not really," she said. "I'm not as willing to deal with cold and snow as I was when I was younger, so I stay inside too much. I almost feel trapped."

"A good reason for you to come back soon. Besides, Mardi Gras is early this year. You can't be gone for Fat Tuesday."

"I'm hoping my daughter and granddaughter will come join me then," she said.

"That would be fun for them. You can show them all the wonderful things you've found. I'll prepare them something special at the restaurant."

"Not turducken," she said with a look of mock horror.

He laughed. "We only make that once a year, so you're safe."

"My daughter's safe. You've already inflicted it on me." She grinned.

He laughed again. "Next year I'll remember you're not a fan."

Her smile faded at the words.

"If you're here next year, that is," he added quickly.

The waitress, with her impeccable timing, took away the soup dishes, then placed an array of platters in front of them, describing their contents as she did so.

The chef came out midway through their meal to ask how they were enjoying it. Lance introduced himself and told him he was very impressed. As he and the chef discussed techniques and the local restaurant scene, Elaine watched them with interest, occasionally asking a question.

Once the chef left, they went back to their meals. He told her tales of growing up in New Orleans and his escapades at school. All the time they talked, he kept searching for the closeness he'd felt with her at the beginning of the meal, but it seemed to have vanished. Their dinner was friendly enough, but he missed the closeness.

He paid the check and wished the chef good luck before they left the restaurant. It was another beautiful evening, cool but not cold.

"People are starting to put up Christmas decorations," he said. "Would you mind taking a stroll and looking at them? I've always enjoyed the quarter at this time of year. The lights are amazing."

"Not too long," she said. "It's a bit chilly out here for me."

"Losing your Montana blood already," he said with a grin.

"I think I lost that a while ago," she agreed.

He held out his hand.

After a split second, she took it.

"Do you know about the concerts?" he asked as they walked.

"No."

"They put them on at the cathedral in Jackson Square. They last about an hour. All different kinds of music: jazz, indie folk, zydeco, gospel ..."

"Zydeco?" she asked.

"Surely you've heard of zydeco," he said.

She shook her head.

"It's bayou music—Cajun music. Accordion, washboard, that's all you need. It sneaks up on you. First your foot starts tapping, then your leg. Soon you'll find yourself clapping and snapping your fingers. Then your whole body has to get up and dance." He did a little two step to the music that was dancing in his head.

She laughed.

"C'mon. You'll have to try it." He pulled her along with him, close in, then out, and a twirl around the sidewalk before letting her go.

"Good thing there's no one around," she said.

"Good thing," he agreed, pulling her close again.

Her face was within inches of his. The exertion in the humid southern air left a sheen on her cheeks, and her eyes were bright with laughter.

This time he didn't hesitate. Slipping his hands into her soft curls, he guided her the final distance to his lips.

She didn't pull back, but instead leaned into the kiss that lasted several moments. It was only when they finished that she took a step back.

"I shouldn't ... we can't ..." she stammered.

"Yes, we can," he said. "And no one else besides us gets to decide whether or not we should."

"I'm not sure ... it makes no sense."

"Does it have to?" he asked.

"It's not how things are supposed to work," she said. "Everything has its season, and I'm in—"

"I know. You think you're in winter." He took her hands. "But you aren't. Not in the least." He caressed her cheek with his fingers. "You're beautiful, Elaine. Yes, no one's going to think you're twenty, but they won't believe it of me either. There is beauty in age. This country tries to think it's perpetually young, and that doesn't do us any good. We need to embrace all our people, including us older folk. We have something to offer."

"That makes sense. In general," she said. "But I'm not talking about philosophy. I'm talking about me. And you."

He took a deep breath. "So am I." He took her hand and guided her to a nearby bench where they sat down. "Tell me. Did you enjoy that kiss?"

"I did."

"So did I. But more importantly, I enjoy that it's you I'm kissing, not some twenty-year-old. I like that you're older, more experienced."

"I'm older than you are," she said. "By a lot."

"I told you. It doesn't matter."

She was quiet.

"I think it does to me," she finally said. She looked up, her beautiful green eyes liquid with emotion. "Here ... in New Orleans ... it's a bit like being in Disneyland ... not that I've ever been in Disneyland. It's a dream world. People have different ways of looking at things, different values. I'm a Midwesterner. We're a bit more rigid, I'm afraid." Her smile was sad.

"Don't give up on us yet," he said. "It's all new to you. I understand. We've had good times together, haven't we?"

"Yes."

"Then let's have more good times. I understand what you're saying about the bubble. It's worse if you're on vacation in the French Quarter. We work hard to create and keep that illusion going. But underneath, we're the same. We grow up, get married, have children, work hard, and grow old. I think the difference is we're equally focused on finding the joy and play in our lives and maybe less on—I'm not sure what to call it—duty?"

"That's a good word, I think," she said. "What you're saying makes sense to me. I'm not sure it would be possible to get over that difference."

"Then we celebrate it," he said. He took her hand again. "So are you with me? Shall we have fun for a little while longer and not worry about the rest of it?"

She pursed her lips as she thought, but finally nodded.

With a big smile, he stood.

She followed.

He held out his hand again. Once she took it, they continued their stroll down the streets together.

Chapter Twenty-Two

So much for telling Lance she didn't want to see him anymore.

Elaine rolled to her other side in another vain attempt to get back to sleep. All night she'd been going over what had happened after dinner. In her dreams she could come up with all kinds of more appropriate answers than the ones she'd given him. Answers that would have made it clear that they needed to call things off.

Instead, she'd told him she liked his kiss.

Well, she couldn't lie, could she? She had enjoyed the kiss, just like she enjoyed her times with him. He was interesting. Their lives had been so different that it seemed like they never ran out of things to talk about.

Their lives were *too* different. She belonged in a small town in Montana where people did what needed to be done, said what was what, and didn't sneak around making back room deals. She'd been raised by practical Nebraska parents who laid out their clear expectations. It was old-fashioned, but she'd grown up on the cusp between the 1950s and 1960s. White gloves and formal attire was still required at social events, and girls were expected to be homemakers. A well-worn copy of *The Feminine Mystique* was passed around behind closed doors. She'd seen her mother hide it at the bottom of her lingerie drawer once.

When her mother had seen her, she'd made Elaine promise she'd never say anything to her father. She'd sworn never to tell, thinking the book must have something to do with what happened in the bedroom. Elaine had put the book in the same category as erotica, and still hadn't read it, even after she'd realized what it was.

She was fine being a traditional wife, supporting her husband, and nurturing her child.

It had been a good life, but was that all there was?

Was the New Orleans lifestyle less traditional because it seemed more exotic?

She was never going to get back to sleep.

Fingers of daylight were slipping through the louvered shades.

Tossing back the covers, she headed to the kitchen area to flip on the coffee maker.

An hour later, she was staring at a book of Georgia O'Keefe paintings she'd picked up at a used bookstore and drinking her coffee. The paintings were beautiful and sensual, even the ones of skeletal trees in the desert. It had to do with her use of line and color. She used her palate in the same way that Maggie used the colors of flowers that would bloom in Montana to advantage.

Elaine rose and looked at the painting she'd done of the woman sitting on the porch. It was good and would probably sell, but it was inauthentic. She wasn't a Southern woman, and no matter how much time she spent here, she never would be. She could observe the sense of history and sense the sultry heat, but she'd never feel it in the marrow of her bones.

The lush flowers of the south appealed to her, in the same way those of O'Keefe had delighted women for decades. In the early days of operating the store, she'd insisted they carry some O'Keefe day planners, items which had gone the way of the dodo bird in the cellphone age.

Somehow, painting the flowers of the south seemed more authentic than the people of the south. That's what she'd try when she went to the square today.

As for Lance, she was going to have to find another time to end it unless she did as he'd suggested, and enjoy it for as long as it lasted.

ELAINE GOT TO THE SQUARE before Delilah and settled in. She propped the painting of the woman she'd completed on the fence that surrounded the square. She'd shipped her few Montana paintings home. Delilah had been right. They weren't going to sell here.

She'd snapped a picture of a piece of a lush garden and had the photo printed. Using that, she began to sketch. The curving lines of the flower petals instantly felt natural to her, and her conviction grew that this was the right thing to paint. She was so absorbed, she was startled when Delilah tried to hand her a cup of coffee.

"New painting?" the other artist asked. She gestured to the one Elaine had propped against the fence. "That one turned out pretty well, I think."

"I like it too," Elaine said. "And thanks," she added, holding up the cup of coffee.

"Are you going to paint more like it?"

Elaine shook her head. "I don't think so. It doesn't feel like me."

"I can see that," Delilah said as she set up. "Definite lack of snow."

"It doesn't snow all the time," Elaine protested.

"I know. Just joshing." Delilah settled down to work and for a while they painted in companionable silence.

As it got closer to noon, the crowds began to pick up, and a few people browsed the paintings. A man picked up her porch scene, examined it and put it down. He didn't make eye contact as he walked away.

She ignored him and continued to work on the flower she had created in front of her, a white magnolia blossom with a bright yellow center. The shading of the white needed to be delicate yet clear to make it stand out from the white paper beneath it. After mixing various shades of creamy white, she picked one to use as a background color, over which she'd add other layers of subtly different hues.

For the first time in a long while, she was deeply engrossed in her work.

"Excuse me," a male voice said.

Startled, she almost let her brush slip, but caught it before she marred her painting. "Yes?"

It was the man who'd been by earlier.

"I looked at your painting and thought my wife might like it." He gestured to a short stout woman holding up the painting. "She loves it. How much?"

Elaine did quick calculations and named a price.

He nodded and pulled out his wallet.

Once the transaction was complete, the couple walked away, taking her work with them.

It was the oddest feeling.

"First one since you got here?" Delilah asked.

"First one."

"Really?"

"I never got around to marketing them when I was younger," Elaine said. "I was caught up running a business and tending a family. Since I started up again, I've been painting just for me. We have an art co-op in town, and I've wanted to put some there, but I couldn't take the shifts because of the store. So I never sold any."

"Congratulations!" Delilah said. "You'll have to get that handsome man you've been seeing to buy you a drink."

"I can celebrate on my own," Elaine said, then realized how curt that had sounded. "Unless you want to celebrate with me." She smiled at her neighbor.

"Do you mean a double espresso?" Delilah said with a grin.

"Absolutely. My treat."

Delilah nodded, and Elaine went across the street for a couple of double espressos, happy to pay the exorbitant price for the drinks in this tourist section of town.

She'd sold her first painting!

Lance would be thrilled.

She stopped at the edge of the sidewalk. Even though she'd told Delilah she didn't want to invite him for a drink, she found she suddenly needed to let him know.

He would celebrate with her. Her late husband, Jack, would have praised her, told her she'd done a great job, then switched the conversation back to what needed to be done for the store. It wasn't that he didn't care; he simply believed the acknowledgement was enough.

The traffic ceased, and she walked across to the square.

She touched the paper rim with Delilah's cup, and they talked a bit more about the impact of making a first sale. It was a conversation unlike any she had had in Promise Cove. There were plenty of artists in the small town, but they didn't see her as an artist. She was the widow of the man who'd created the general store.

Or the mother of Her Honor, the mayor.

When she returned to her easel, she chatted with Delilah for a few moments before returning to her flower. As she stroked the paintbrush on the emerging petals, she had a glimmer of an idea of how she could make this painting unique, and not a clone of dozens she saw every day.

Like the painting, she'd almost been a clone of the people she'd known when she'd grown up. Life had thrown her curveballs, and as she'd adapted to them, she'd changed. Maybe it was time to consider something else.

If she ignored the little voice in her head that told her she was too old to become someone new, what were the possibilities?

She played with ideas the rest of the time she painted. Halfway through her time, she put aside the magnolia blossom she'd been working on. It wasn't finished, but she wanted it to dry before adding detail. Picking up a blank canvas, she contemplated the possibilities, then started again with a dramatic vermillion hue.

As the day wore on, more people stopped to talk with her than had ever done before. Maybe she was finally getting it right.

"Those are looking really good," Delilah said. "They suit you."

"Thanks."

Delilah packed up and left before Elaine.

A half hour later, Elaine pulled together her easel and canvases and prepared to wheel them back to the apartment on the small trolley she'd purchased for the job.

Before she left, she made one last call.

"Hello?" Lance said when he answered.

"I sold a painting!" she blurted out.

"That is fantastic! We must celebrate. It's a grand occasion. Come by the restaurant and I will buy you the drink of your choice."

"That would be lovely," she said. "Let me go home and change first."

"I'll be ready."

After they ended the call, she grabbed the trolley and strode back to her apartment, a smile on her face and joy in her heart.

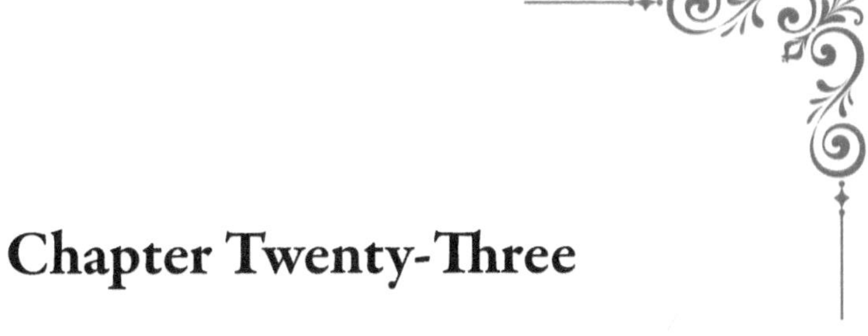

Chapter Twenty-Three

Whitney buttoned her blouse. She'd crossed a line and wasn't happy with her choice.

She glanced over at Vince. He was fully dressed and watching her.

"You're very beautiful," he said.

"Thank you." She ran her fingers through her hair, trying to smooth away the evidence of what she'd done. "I need to get back to the office."

"No need to rush. It's NOLO. Long lunches are fine."

Not if they involved what we'd been doing.

"Look," she said, turning to him. "This was a mistake. I can't do this again."

He quickly crossed to her and pulled her close to him. "Sure you can. We're good together. Tell me you didn't enjoy yourself."

She couldn't lie. She had. He was good, very good, but her nerves couldn't stand the secrecy. If everything was over with his wife, why couldn't they be open about their relationship?

He was probably lying. He was a high-ranking member of a department known for its ability to slide along the edge of the law. If someone crossed over, it was explained away as a simple mistake.

"Come here," he said, taking her hand and leading her to the couch. "There's something I want to discuss with you."

"What?" she asked as they sat down. All she wanted to do was get out of that apartment and never come back. He'd been all sweet talk before he'd gotten her into bed. Now there was an edge to his tone she didn't like. She was being led down a slippery slope.

First, she'd gotten him the numbers he'd asked to see from the budget negotiations which were supposed to be top secret. From the number of items the local press reported, there were already plenty of leaks so she didn't feel badly about that.

He'd looked over the numbers and asked her to make some suggestions, decreasing funding in a few places so more could be added to one specific account. He'd even supplied arguments for doing so.

The committee was still in discussion, but it looked like he was going to get his wish.

What was so important about that one account? She'd asked, but he'd waffled on the answer which disturbed her even more. Where money flowed, power followed.

She waited to hear what he wanted now.

"What did you find out about the back room at Fontenot's?" he asked.

"It took me a while," she confessed. "Everyone's been told to deny its existence. They all pointed to Lance for answers."

"Good little soldiers," Vince said with a smirk.

"I didn't know if it was a good idea to approach him," she said. "Lance, I mean. What if he thought my asking was suspicious? What if he told the mayor?"

"You worry too much," Vince said. "Nobody even notices you."

That stung.

She tried to move away from him.

"Sorry, hon," he said, stroking her arm. "I didn't mean that the way it came out. Everyone notices how pretty you are. They know you do something in government, but they aren't sure what."

She wasn't sure that was totally true. Being on the financial committee made her the target of everyone who wanted a piece of a rapidly shrinking pot. With all the anti-tax movements, corruption, and climate disasters the city had faced over the last decade, the committee needed the skills of a coupon-clipping housewife to make it work.

But it wasn't a discussion she wanted to have with him.

This time she managed to maneuver out of his range. She stood and walked to the small kitchen area where the coffee was still mercifully hot. She poured herself a mug and turned to face him.

"I did talk to Lance. I made some noise about a girl's night out and not wanting to disrupt his restaurant," she told Vince.

"And?"

"He pointed out that Fontenot's was made for celebrations and a little noise never hurt anyone." She looked into the coffee, a little ashamed of what she'd said next. "I kind of said we might want to play some games that might offend some of the older patrons."

Vince laughed. "Clever girl."

"Not clever enough. He admitted he had a back room, but it wasn't for parties like that, but for business meetings. He told us if we wanted to be risqué, we'd need to find another venue, like a bar."

"So, nothing." Vince's look was beyond frustrated; it almost looked threatening. "You failed."

"Not entirely. I took some clues from where he looked as we were talking. When I left, I made sure no one was watching, and I went down the corridor where the restrooms are. This time I walked past them. Lance's office is down that way and clearly marked, but beyond it is another door, also locked. I'm betting that's where the room is."

"Locked?"

"Locked."

Vince looked thoughtful. "How sturdy did the lock look?"

"I didn't examine it. I only tried the door."

"Those old buildings have pretty flimsy locks. The kind that can be opened by a credit card."

She shrugged and drank her coffee. What was he after? What did he want from her now?

He stood and walked to where she stood. "I want you to take another stroll down that corridor. I'll give you something that should open that door if it's as easy as I think it will be." He reached into a drawer and pulled out a small box. He opened it to reveal two small disks.

"Once you're in there, I want you to stick one of these under the table. Then put the other on something that doesn't get moved around much. A picture on the wall is perfect. Or even on top of the door jamb."

She had a good idea what the things in the box were. "You want me to plant bugs? You're out of your mind! That's illegal. I'm not doing that."

"Look. We know the mayor is corrupt. We can't prove it yet. You'd be doing your city a service. Isn't that why you entered politics?"

"I entered politics to … never mind why I ran for office. I've never seen the mayor do anything illegal in my time in office. I don't believe you."

"Such a loyal little follower." Vince's tone was mocking. "I love how you are all so trusting when you start. It doesn't take long before you see the truth for what it is, though. Like I said, we know he's been doing things against the city's interest." He put his index finger under her chin and gave her a light kiss.

Against the city's interest? Or against his?

She needed to get out of here. Turning out of his embrace, she put the mug on the counter.

"I have things to do," she said, walking toward her purse.

"You forgot these," he said. He rummaged in another drawer. "And here's something that will help you get into the room."

"I'm not doing it," she repeated. "Even if I believed you, which I don't, I'm not getting involved in something so obviously illegal."

"How about immoral?" he said, his smile no longer friendly.

"What do you mean?"

"Well, I'm a married man," he said. "What would your friends … your aunt … think if they found out what we've been doing?"

"You told me you were separated, that there was no hope?"

He shrugged.

"You aren't?" Her stomach turned with nausea.

"Let's just say we're in negotiations. In the meantime, we can still have some fun." He took a step toward her.

"No. We can't." She picked up her purse.

"I'd advise you to play along," he said.

"Or what? My friends don't care what I do. Most of them are doing worse things than being with a married man who said he was separated. And I'll tell my aunt ahead of time. She'll be disappointed, and make me do penance, but in the end, she'll forgive me."

"And the mayor?"

"You wouldn't."

"Not me, personally. He doesn't trust me at all. Which is why when the gossip gets to him, he'll banish you from the inner sanctum. You'll never win another election in this city again, Whitney."

She sagged against the wall. If she didn't do what he wanted, he'd ruin her.

If she got caught, she'd be prosecuted.

"Take these." Vince handed her the small box and thin metal plate. "Get it done. Soon. Then let me know it's done." He smiled, but it was no longer an expression that did anything at all to her heart. "We could always meet back here to celebrate."

"Never." After a few more seconds of a staring contest, she admitted defeat and took the objects he was holding out, stuck them in her purse, and walked out the door.

SOMEHOW SHE MADE IT through the rest of the afternoon at work. The bugs were heavy in her purse when she picked it up to go home. For the first time in a long while, she declined an invitation to go out for drinks with the others, claiming she felt like she was coming down with something.

It wasn't far from the truth. She'd felt sick to her stomach all afternoon.

As soon as she got home, she took a shower, but it wasn't enough. She still felt dirty.

What was she going to do? She was trapped. There was no doubt Vince would make good on his threats if she didn't do as he wanted. Then everything she'd worked for would be gone.

Somehow she had to do what he wanted ... and not get caught.

What would he do with the information he received? It couldn't be good. Now that he'd revealed his true colors, whatever his intentions might be, they wouldn't be beneficial to anyone. The corruption wasn't in the mayor's office. It was right where it had always been, with corrupt cops like him. Vince was the kind of man who made the majority of people in the police department, people who were dedicated to providing safety to all people in the city, look bad.

But there was no choice. Not for her.

Chapter Twenty-Four

Elaine arrived at Thérèse Designs at the time Thérèse had told her to be there. She hesitated at the door, a beautiful creation with dark wood and heavy-leaded glass fronted by iron grillwork. Overhead an arched awning bore the name of the company.

She rang the buzzer and announced herself. When the door buzzed, she pulled it open and climbed the stairs to the offices over the main showroom. A receptionist greeted her and showed her to the main conference room where a full breakfast had been set up.

"Welcome, welcome, cher!" Thérèse said as she pulled Elaine into a hug and air kissed one cheek. "Please, make yourself at home. These are all my employees. We make sure they work with a full stomach, right?"

There were murmurs of agreement from the half-dozen people in the room.

Thérèse handed her a sturdy plate, then presented her choices of hot breakfast foods, breads, juices, and the inevitable beignets. Elaine served herself, then joined her hostess at one of the few round tables in the room. Some of the employees sat at the other tables, while some took their food and went back to their desks.

"You do this every day?" Elaine asked.

"Every day." Thérèse's features softened. "I know what it's like to be hungry. I pay my workers the best the company can afford." She shrugged. "But it is an expensive city. And many of them are providing for others. If they can count on one good meal a day, it keeps them going."

Elaine nodded, a little bit overcome by emotion as she placed her fork into an eggy dish that was almost guaranteed to have more heat than she was used to. Kindness to others always impressed her. She never would have expected it from the hard-nosed businesswoman Thérèse appeared to be.

Throughout their breakfast, Thérèse chatted with the employees. In between conversations, she told Elaine about the business, including its inception at her grandmother's kitchen table.

"I made and sold doll clothes to my classmates," she said. "The school shut me down when they found out I was making deals on the playground." She shrugged. "I took my store to the streets and set up shop on a street corner. When the cops chased me away from that, I went underground. I created small coupons for a discount and used friends and family to distribute them. Eventually, I convinced our local store to carry them."

"Sounds like you were unstoppable."

"I wanted more from life than what my mother and grandmother had," Thérèse said. "They worked all their lives at hard jobs. My grandmother was a hairdresser in someone else's salon. My mother waited tables. They made do, but once my grandmother died, things got really tight. Sometimes we didn't eat. I decided two things then and there."

"Which were?" Elaine asked.

"I was never having any kids, and I was going to own my own business."

"Don't you miss having kids?"

"Every once in a while ... Mother's Day ... that kind of thing. But I made the right choice. I'm driven. A kid would have taken second place. And there were times money was thin. If I had a kid, I wanted to give them the best. By the point that came around, the time for having a family had passed me by." She gestured to the employees. "These are my children. It's good enough."

By the time she finished, Elaine had eaten her fill.

"Come, let me take you to the showroom," she said.

Elaine followed the woman down another set of stairs to the store below. The place was full of beautiful dresses, hand-woven table linens, and homemade lotions, candles, and soaps, all bearing the Thérèse Designs brand. Thérèse explained how she worked with local producers on the design and quality. If the standards were met, the product was marketed and sold under her label.

Next to some children's clothes in a separate section, there was a selection of doll's clothes.

"Wow!" Elaine exclaimed. "This is wonderful!"

"I couldn't abandon my first love," Thérèse said. "I have a few others assist me, but I still keep my hand in. And I design the bulk of the clothes as well."

"This is amazing. Do you sell anywhere besides the city?"

"I have two more upscale places: one in San Francisco and one in New York. I don't know if I'll expand beyond that. Brick and mortar stores have taken quite a hit lately. I have a substantial online store."

Elaine nodded. "It's how the artists in our town have been able to thrive," she said as they started up the stairs to the office space.

"Oh?" Thérèse said as they entered her office. "How is that?"

Elaine's answer was interrupted by a familiar-looking man in a police uniform who knocked on the door, then stepped into the space. He flicked Elaine a glance, but didn't appear to recognize her.

"Hey, Thérèse, got a minute?"

"I have a guest, Vince. Surely even you could see that." The tone of Thérèse's voice indicated she didn't hold the man in high esteem.

"Sorry," he said to Elaine. "I wouldn't bother except it's important."

"I can't imagine anything we need to say to each other is that important," Thérèse said.

Vince frowned. "It would be worth your while to hear what I have to say."

What was going on between the two of them? What would a businesswoman like Thérèse need with, based on his uniform, a high-ranking police officer?

This town definitely ran on rules Elaine didn't understand and wasn't sure she wanted to learn.

"Later, Vince," Thérèse said.

"You're treading on thin ice ..."

"I'll take my chances." Thérèse made a shooing motion. "Give me a call around eleven."

"Yes, ma'am," Vince said sarcastically.

But he left.

"A thoroughly annoying man," Thérèse said. "Unfortunately, he's got a good amount of power in this district so I sometimes have to play nice with him."

"Why?" Elaine asked.

"Why what?"

"Why do you need to play nice with him? In Promise Cove, it's pretty straightforward. Someone needs help, we help them. No questions asked."

It used to be that way across the whole state, but people from outside had moved in, people who decided people needed to earn the right to services, even the sovereign nations of Native Americans within Montana's borders.

"It's never been that way here," Thérèse said. "Remember, this is the south. There were people who were regarded as property." She shook her head. "It's a town founded on bargains and secret deals. How much for that bale of cotton? Well, if you throw in a guarantee to look the other way the next time I slip over to your manager's wife, I'll let you have it real cheap, yessah, real cheap." Thérèse's voice drifted into a southern drawl by the time she got to the end.

"I'll never understand it." Elaine shook her head.

Thérèse's laugh was low and sultry. "I'm not sure I could deal with all that forthrightness either."

Elaine gave her a rueful smile.

"Now, cher, tell me about these thriving artists."

With enthusiasm, Elaine told Thérèse about the website the talented webmaster had set up for the artists who were part of the co-op that ran ART, the gallery in town. "She's driven a lot of traffic and convinced them to hire a PR person who's gotten the group in all kinds of upscale magazines and featured as feel-good pieces on daytime television."

"But what about shipping?" Thérèse asked. "I've always found logistics the most miserable part of the whole business."

"We've got that nailed. A firm in a nearby town gets the order, picks up the pieces, then ships them out. They truck to most places in Montana and Idaho. The rest we use one of the national carriers for the rest."

"It sounds like things work very well."

"They do." Elaine grinned. "And without any intrigue at all."

Thérèse laughed. "I like you. I'm getting used to your ability to 'tell it like it is.' That is what they say, isn't it?"

"Yes."

Thérèse sobered. "So what are you doing with my friend, Lance?"

"Me? Nothing. We're having fun. Nothing serious."

"Maybe for you it's nothing serious, but it isn't the same for my friend. I've known Lance all my life, and I've never seen him this taken with anyone since he fell for Camille."

"Believe me. It's not that way. We've talked about it. There is no way I can spend my life here. I have a family in Montana. And he can't exactly move Fontenot's to Promise Cove."

"No, I suppose not. But there are many ways to make a relationship work." Thérèse tapped a beautifully magenta-painted nail on her chin. "Have you slept with him yet?"

"What? No!"

Thérèse laughed. "I forgot. You aren't from the Big Easy. Things like that are not such a big deal here."

"It's not the idea ..." Elaine's cheeks heated. "It's talking about it ..."

Thérèse's laughter increased. "You are too much, cher."

"But I have no plans either to talk about it *or* do it before I leave. Lance is safe with me. We're just friends."

"You keep telling yourself that," Thérèse said. "I know you believe it, and maybe even he believes it, but it's not what the stars have planned for you."

"Well, the stars are going to have to work on someone else."

"As you wish." Thérèse's phone buzzed. "I'm afraid I'm going to have to do some work. I have an appointment in fifteen minutes. And this one is business, so I must let the gentleman in." She stood.

Elaine gathered her things and stood as well.

With the now familiar hug and kiss, Thérèse sent her on her way.

As she walked down the stairs, Elaine felt like she was in a surreal dream. How did people live like this all the time? All the intrigue was exhausting, not to mention the underlying tempo of constant seduction. It was too much. She needed a break.

When it was time to fly home for the holidays, she was going to be ready to go.

Chapter Twenty-Five

Lance stood in front of the mirror and examined how he looked. It was ridiculous to be worried about how he looked to a woman who wasn't going to stick around, but he couldn't seem to help himself.

He wanted to impress her.

She was unlike any woman he'd ever met. He'd loved Camille with all his heart when they were young, but if he was truthful, they'd grown apart long before he brought up the idea of the restaurant. He wasn't in love with Elaine though. That would be impossible. She had no idea how NOLO worked, and even if she did, she'd disapprove.

He could skip the age difference. The few times he'd kissed her had proven to him that the fire was still there. There would be other consequences, but he could deal with them when the time came.

Except the time would never come.

He should stop seeing her, but he couldn't manage to help himself. He was having fun, and it was a long time since he'd had fun.

He pulled on his jacket, more for the chill than any sartorial reason. After letting himself out of the building, he walked down to Elaine's building to pick her up.

She'd said she could meet him at the club he had in mind, but he'd insisted on picking her up.

"You look pretty," he said when she came out of her lobby to great him. She had on a white blouse with one of those wide round necklines, decorated with embroidery around it. The skirt swirled in an array of colors and picked up the deep blue of her heels. "Very artsy."

"Thank you."

He leaned in to kiss her cheek and caught a whiff of her perfume, a soft citrus scent that seemed to float around her wherever she was. Every time he'd squeezed a lemon for a drink or dish, he'd found himself thinking of her.

"Have a good week?" he asked.

"Yes. I haven't sold any more paintings, but I'm playing around with some ideas. I think working away from the square has given me the ability to work in the square without the tourists bothering me."

"That's great!"

"And you?" she asked.

As they walked to the place he had in mind, he entertained her with stories from the kitchen and some of the bizarre requests of patrons. Working with the public was always an adventure.

It was so easy to talk to her; she was genuinely interested. Even when he was working for the Port of New Orleans, Camille had never wanted to hear much about his job. After a few years he'd begun to time it.

Ten minutes of his news was about all she would tolerate.

It hadn't bothered him at the time. Most of his friends noted the same thing, so they'd started into the rituals of after work drinks and Saturday morning golf. He'd never liked the sport, but he tolerated it to get what he'd really craved: companionship.

Elaine shivered.

"Chilly?" he asked.

"A little. I should have worn my warmer coat, but I didn't think I needed it. Besides it screams mountains, and I'd like to look like I belong here ... even if it's all fake."

"It's not fake. You *do* belong here." He put his arm around her slim shoulders. "Come closer. I'll keep you warm."

She nestled close, and they walked the remaining block to the small neighborhood jazz club.

"It's a place for locals to play," he said as they sat down. "Sometimes the acts are less than impressive, but every once in a while you hear someone who you know will make it in the long run."

The décor of the place wasn't much to note: badly painted brown walls, mullioned windows that were never quite clean, and neon lit signs with at least one bulb blown out. A faint scent of smoke lingered from the previous night when the bartender had enjoyed a cigarette or two while he cleaned up.

Along with the jazz, the menu was hit or miss, but he'd been there enough times to know which was which. He indicated the best choices to Elaine while they waited for their drinks.

Once she'd told him her choices, she looked around the room.

His gaze remained on her.

She was beautiful, not in a youthful twenty-something raw prettiness that any girl could achieve, but in the way that only some women could. By the time a person was in their sixties, their genetics and character combined to create sublime beauty ... or something that came nowhere close. Elaine's beauty came from deep in her creative, loving soul.

Being around her for the last month had been like a balm for his spirit. With her, he felt ease. He didn't have to protect his back because she'd never go on a sneak attack. If she had something to say, she'd tell it to his face, not whisper it to a gossipy girlfriend who'd make sure it got back around to him.

The Midwestern honesty was a fresh breeze in his heart.

And what about his heart?

He covered Elaine's hand with his.

Her gaze darted back to him.

"I enjoy being with you," he said quietly.

She nodded.

"I know it's only been a short while," he continued. "But I'm coming to care for you a great deal."

She shook her head and tried to pull her hand back.

He let it go, but kept his hand where it was. She stopped the backward motion, leaving their fingertips touching, sparks of energy connecting them.

"Even if you leave come summer, I hope you'll plan on coming back in the fall. I'll still be here." He smiled, realizing he wanted more, but had no idea how that could ever work.

They sat like that for a few moments. On the stage, the musicians who'd been setting up began to riff with each other, the soft brush of drums transitioning to the low notes of a bass which led to an arpeggio on the ivories.

"It's not that easy," she said.

"As long as the planes are running, I'm sure it is."

"There's the cost. I'm going to need to find a new place in Promise Cove now that the store is sold. It's not comfortable for me to be with the new owners. They're lovely people, but I need my own space. I don't think I can afford rent in Promise Cove and still pay for everything here."

For the first time since he'd sold it, he wished he still had the house in the Garden District. There would have been plenty of space for both of them there, and they could have gone hours without running into each other.

If wishes were horses …

The waiter brought their drinks and took their order.

For a while they sat in silence listening to the music and sipping their drinks. Elaine was an engaged listener, nodding in time to the music with her lips upturned.

He leaned back in his chair and closed his eyes, the better to hear the music. He let the melody roll through his body, like the Mississippi River rolled through the city of his birth. He could never leave here; who was he to ask that of Elaine? She must feel the same as he did about her adoptive home. Everything she'd told him about the town had made it seem special and unique.

It would be good to see it someday.

The song ended, and he looked across the table. Elaine's gaze was on him, and a strong connection pulsed between them.

There had to be a way to make this work … at least for a little while.

Halfway through the set, their waiter brought their meals, but there was little conversation as they continued to enjoy the music.

They finished about the same time the set concluded.

"That was really interesting," Elaine said.

"Interesting as in good … or bad?" he asked.

"Interesting … as in interesting. I liked some, but some I didn't relate to. My late husband was a country buff so that's what we listened to. Jazz was for the rich east coasters who came to Montana to ski in the winter and fly fish in the summer."

"I'm going to have to expand your horizons," he said. "Jazz is so elemental in the Big Easy. Everyone who came here added their influence. It began with the Creoles, and as time went on Sicilians and Cubans added new flavors. Even marching bands influenced New Orleans jazz."

"Fascinating," she said. "You must like it a lot."

"I do. And when I like something ... or someone ... I need to know everything about them."

"Everything?" She arched an eyebrow.

"Everything."

"Oh."

They stared at each other.

"It's not only the distance," she said. "It's the culture. I had breakfast with Thérèse yesterday, and this guy, Vince, showed up. Based on the uniform, I'd say he's someone with power in the police department."

"I know who he is."

"And you don't like him."

"It's more I don't trust him," Lance said. "What was he doing at Thérèse's place?"

"I'm not sure. I think ... well ... it sounded to me like he was threatening her a little. I hope she's not in trouble."

"Thérèse can take care of herself," he said. It would be interesting to know what was going on, though.

"I can see the wheels spinning," Elaine said. "That's what I mean. There are all these secrets, and I don't do secrets." She smiled. "Unless they're good surprises, like birthday parties."

Lance nodded, but he hadn't really heard her. What was Vince up to? There was that woman—someone on the city council—Whitney, that was her name—who had asked him about the back room. He could have sworn he'd seen her having lunch with Vince once, but he wasn't sure.

The crash of a cymbal brought him back to the moment.

Elaine's smile had turned to a frown.

"Dessert?" he asked with a forced smile.

Chapter Twenty-Six

Lance was still mulling over the news that Elaine had given him when he arrived at the restaurant the next day. Approaching Thérèse wouldn't be a good idea. She kept her business, and her political efforts, to herself. The few times he'd tried to discuss anything with her, she'd shut him down faster than a scalded cat.

But he did have a source with an ear to the ground. He made his way to the bar.

Prosper was already there, prepping for the lunch crowd. Tourists always wanted to try a mint julep; the regulars wanted something stronger. Any effort the government had made to shut down the three-martini lunch had, like most things, failed utterly in the Big Easy.

"Club soda?" Prosper asked.

"Sure."

Prosper streamed the liquid into a tumbler, then added a wedge of lime just like Lance had told him the first time he'd gotten the man to pour him a glass of fizz.

"You hear anything about the deputy superintendents of the police department?" Lance asked.

"My daddy taught me early to stay away from cops; that's what I know."

Lance grinned. "Good advice."

"Yessir."

"I think there might be something going on in our restaurant. Something that wouldn't be good for us if it came out."

"You tempting fate with that back room," Prosper said.

"How's that?"

"Word spread. People want to know what's goin' on in that room."

"Nothing bad's happening," Lance protested. "I'm not importing call girls or anything."

Prosper laughed. "I don't mean that." He held a glass up to the light, then polished it a little more with a thin towel.

Lance waited.

"Mayor's here a lot," Prosper finally said.

"He likes the food."

"He like you always have a big table for him and treat him real good. He also like that back room."

"He was the one that suggested it in the first place."

Prosper put the glass away and picked up another. He rubbed that one clean before he spoke again. "Just makes me wonder what he need with your back room when there be a whole big office for him in city hall."

"Guess he wants to keep some things private."

"Probably. An' that be what people are wondering. We elected him. We should get to know his business. No good havin' secret business."

"Huh." Lance sipped his soda. What Prosper said made sense. What did His Honor need to discuss that couldn't be done in his office? It had to be something real close to the line that politicians love to skate next to.

Was Vince one of the good guys? Was he trying to reveal a scandal that the public needed to know about?

Lance didn't think so. The mayor may skirt close, but he was one of the good guys. Just as sure as Vince was not.

"Thanks, Prosper."

"No problem."

Lance left the glass and went to the kitchen to see to last minute prep.

OVER THE NEXT FEW DAYS, he thought more and more about that back room. The mayor had been into the restaurant a few times, and once Whitney had been in that group. Another time she'd eaten alone.

Vince had also been there. Lance had caught him exploring the hallway past the restrooms, but when he asked Vince why he was there, Vince had shrugged.

"Just curious," he'd said. "Nature of a cop. Sorry." Then he grinned. "I hear you have a back room. Got a hot poker game going back there or something?"

According to Elaine, there was a connection between Vince and Thérèse. He wouldn't put it past Thérèse to have a spoon in the jambalaya of New Orleans politics, and she wasn't above dancing close to the edge of the law. She'd clawed her way to the top and that never came easy.

Whatever was going on, he wanted no part of it. Especially if it meant a strain on his relationship with Elaine. He couldn't do much about the physical distance between their home bases or her imagined problem about an age difference, but he could make sure whatever was going on in the restaurant didn't cost him the chance at her love.

Love? Where had that come from?

He looked at his watch and told the hostess he was going out for a while. Then he walked—the long way—to Elaine's perch in Jackson Square. For a while he stood in the shadows and watched her.

Unlike the first time he'd seen her, she'd acquired an ease. She laughed and chatted with the artist sitting next to her. Tourists no longer avoided her and seemed to enjoy looking at her work. She'd told him she'd sold a few more paintings of what she called her double flowers.

He still hadn't seen one.

Did she consider what they had a friendly flirtation?

Of course.

He'd failed to make himself clear, mainly because he hadn't been clear to himself about what he wanted.

Now he knew. The only problem was he didn't know how to convince her to give him a chance. She was right. Their potential relationship was beyond the Facebook status of "Complicated." Still, he'd be an idiot if he gave up without really trying.

Other than slowly closing down the back room, what did he need to do to win her over? He'd already cooked his best meals for her, although he hadn't been able to create the dish she'd told him was her favorite: a freshly caught trout.

He walked over to her.

"Hello, Elaine," he said with a smile that she couldn't see because her back was to him.

Her weeks at the square had also given her time to adapt to people coming up on her unexpectedly because her brush continued its soft strokes.

"Give me one more minute," she said. "I want to get this paint on while everything is still wet."

A stalk of yellow flowers was emerging under her skillful hands, one he recognized from many gardens around New Orleans. The image was a close-up, the petals lush even in the painting's beginning stages.

She finished whatever she wanted to do and plopped the brush in an enameled tin of water, rinsed it, then stood it brush up in a pot containing many other brushes. She stood up and turned to greet him.

He stood there like a dolt. Somehow the traditional New Orleans' brief hug and air kiss deserted him, and his posture became the same as it had been when he'd asked his first girl out.

She seemed equally at a loss.

He cleared his throat.

"Are you ... um ... busy for lunch?"

"I brought a sandwich," she said.

"Oh."

They stood, staring at each other.

The artist next to her watched them. "I'll eat the sandwich," she said. "So you can take her to lunch if that's what you want to do."

Elaine turned to her. "But you always bring your lunch, Delilah."

Delilah shrugged. "Forgot today."

"I don't believe you for a second," Elaine said.

"You make better sandwiches," Delilah countered. "I'll have mine for dinner. Just go, would you? You're killing him. Put the poor man out of his misery."

"There's a good vegan place a few streets over," Lance said. "You like vegan. I remember that."

"Yes. I've been there a few times with my neighbor."

"So you must like it." He smiled. "Come with me."

Elaine gestured at her easel. "I can't leave—"

"It's okay," Delilah said. "I'll watch it. While I'm eating your sandwich." She held out her hand.

Elaine bent down, picked up the insulated bag that had been sitting next to her easel, and handed it to Delilah.

"Now go." Delilah made a shooing motion.

"My hands ..." Elaine said, looking down at her paint-splotched fingers.

"They have a washroom. Now *go*."

"I guess we're having lunch," Elaine told him.

They were quiet as they walked down the street, the life of the quarter swirling around them in bright colors and street musician riffs. He reached to take her hand, but she shook her head and held up her colorful fingers.

He let his arm fall back to his side.

There was so much to say to her, but he didn't want to talk about serious matters on the street. Besides, what was he going to say? "I'm falling in love with you," was too big a bombshell to drop casually.

It was a stupid idea to tell her anyway.

What if she were nowhere near feeling that emotion? He'd sound like a fool.

She didn't provide any of her easy chatter either.

After what seemed like an eternity, they finally reached the restaurant. He held open the door and she walked inside.

"Let me go to the restroom," she said before dashing off.

"I'll find a table," he told her retreating back.

He claimed a table and scanned the menu a fast-moving waitress had slapped down. All the words blurred in front of him.

This was an idiot's errand. There were too many problems—real and imagined—between them. He'd treat her to a nice lunch, they'd have an interesting conversation about the people she'd met. He could tell her about the group from Germany who'd come to his restaurant and demanded he serve one meal for every two people.

"Americans waste too much food," one had declared.

He'd complied. In his restaurant, the customer was always right.

As he saw her walking back from the restaurant, though, he knew he was wrong. The problems didn't matter. No matter how irrational or how short the time he'd known her, he wanted her in his life. There had to be some way to make it work.

But he couldn't tell her here. No, he'd have a table set up in the nook above his restaurant. As the sun set over the river, he'd tell her he was falling in love.

LANCE HAD AN ODD EXPRESSION on his face, Elaine thought as she sat down. He'd been staring at her as she walked back from the restroom, but he hadn't been smiling. He wasn't frowning either.

The only comparison that came to mind was of someone run over by a truck who was just beginning to realize what had happened. The idea sent a shiver up her spine.

"Have you looked at the menu?" she asked. She didn't want to spend too long at lunch, leaving Delilah responsible for her stuff. It was an imposition.

"Um ..." He picked it up and frowned at it. "What are you going to have?"

She held out her hand for the single menu the waitress had left. Scanning it, she told him she'd have one of the bowls full of lentils, vegetables, rice, and a curry sauce.

The waitress stopped by.

"Sorry. I didn't realize there were two of you," she said. "Do you need another menu?"

Elaine looked over at Lance.

"I'll have what she's having," he said.

The waitress looked at Elaine, pen poised over the pad.

Elaine gave her the order, trying not to laugh at Lance's phrasing, the perfect imitation of a line from one of her favorite movies, *When Harry Met Sally*.

After the waitress left, Lance tried to tell her some story about Germans in his restaurant, but the anecdote fell flat. There was something he was keeping from her.

"What's up?" she asked, sipping the iced tea the waitress had dropped off. "You don't usually drop by and invite me for lunch."

"It's a beautiful day, and I needed a break from my restaurant."

She frowned. That's all she was? A distraction?

"No, cher. No. That's wrong. I wanted to see you. To be with you for a while."

"Why?"

"Why? Do I need a reason?" he asked. "I ... um ... I like being with you. I've told you that."

She gave him the same stink eye she used to give Maggie when she'd thought her daughter was hiding something.

"Is there something wrong?"

"No. Not at all." His smile was bland.

The waitress brought them their bowls and quickly hurried off.

Over lunch, Lance steered the conversation to inconsequential matters in a very determined manner. Every time she tried to get to the heart of the matter, he skillfully diverted her.

It was only when their meal was finished and the check delivered that he stopped trying so hard.

"There is something I want to discuss," he said.

"Yeah. I kind of thought that."

He laughed. "There's no fooling you."

She tried to laugh with him, but she was getting a sense of foreboding about what he wanted to say. Did he want to stop seeing her? If so, that was inevitable anyway. She'd get over it.

After a bout of crying, that was. Even in the short time they'd been together, she'd begun to like him ... a lot. More than she should. It didn't feel the same as what she'd felt with her late husband. This was more relaxed and fun, not so prescribed by family traditions and rituals.

Nor was it like her brief fling in Paris. That had been irrational, a consequence of all the stress she'd been under for years. It had been a grand passion, undergirded by nothing substantial or long lasting.

This had the qualities of both with a lot more compassion, not only for each other, but for themselves. They knew who they were.

She steeled herself for the worst, then asked, "What do you have to tell me?"

To her disappointment, he shook his head. "I thought I could tell you here, but it's too busy ... too real." He slid his credit card into the folder and stood it up so the waitress could see it was ready. "Come by the restaurant later. We can have a small supper on the upper level."

She remembered the last time they'd been there, the time that had led to their first kiss.

He probably wasn't going to dump her then.

What was the alternative?

The waitress picked up the folder.

"I'm not sure. Can't you tell me here? Or on the way back to the square?"

He shook his head. "I can't. I have to ask you to be patient."

"I guess I'll just have to wait then."

"Thanks," he said. "It will be worth the wait, I promise."

SEVERAL HOURS LATER, she'd changed her outfit to one that was more fitting for an intimate dinner for two. As she walked to the restaurant, she was filled with a sense of anticipation. What was he going to tell her?

And if he told her something crazy, like he was falling in love with her, what would her reaction be? All the problems they'd had before were still there.

But how did *she* feel? She'd come to New Orleans to find out who she was. How could she do that and still be in any kind of relationship, even one that wasn't going to go anywhere?

She opened the door to the restaurant.

"Hello, Elaine," the hostess said. "I'll take your wrap and then show you upstairs. Lance will join you shortly."

As she waited farther into the restaurant, Elaine could hear loud words coming from the corridor where the restrooms were. It sounded like Lance. He'd told her his office was around the corner.

He must be giving a waiter a good talking to.

But then she began to make out some of the words. As if they had a will of their own, her feet turned toward the corridor.

"I could have you arrested," Lance said.

"I didn't do anything wrong." It was a woman's voice, sounding close to tears.

"Breaking and entering is a crime. What were you doing with these? Who put you up to this, Whitney?"

"No one. I just wanted to see what the room looked like."

"You can't be that naïve."

Elaine reached the pair who were standing just outside the closed door at the end of the hallway.

Even though he was shorter than most men she knew, Lance seemed to tower over the small, dark-skinned woman. The age furrows on his face had deepened, and his eyes were intense orbs.

Whitney shrank against the wall.

"You're scaring her," Elaine protested.

"That's my intention." He gave her a brief glance. "I'm sorry, but I'll have to catch up with you in a bit. Have Prosper give you a drink. I need to take care of this."

"I won't let you browbeat her." Elaine took a step toward him.

"She was breaking into a locked room. Who knows what she was up to. It's not your business, Elaine. Go to the bar."

"What is going on, Lance?"

The woman—Whitney—pressed her body against the wall. Her gaze darted between the two of them.

"I'll handle it. Go to the bar."

"You're too angry. Let me call the cops."

"There are three of them in the restaurant. I don't need them. Besides ..." His attention focused back on Whitney. "It was Vince, wasn't it? He put you up to this."

Whitney looked at the floor.

"Yeah. I should have guessed. No cops. They're involved."

"There must be someone ..."

"You don't get it, Elaine. In your world, everyone is who they say they are, and all your problems are easily solved and tied up with a neat red bow. It's not that simple here."

He was right. It wasn't.

She didn't belong here.

Leaving was the only option.

Except ...

"You're not going to hurt her, are you?"

His gaze snapped to her. "You think that little of me? I'd never hurt a woman."

They stared at each other for a few moments.

Then she nodded and walked back down the corridor. On her way back to the entrance of the restaurant, she passed the mayor who barely acknowledged her.

She didn't go to the bar. Instead, she asked the hostess for her wrap and walked back out the front door.

It was over.

As she walked away from the restaurant, she noticed a familiar figure across the street. He turned away when he saw her, so she didn't get a good look at his face. Her mind tumbled through its memory. Halfway down the next block she realized why he seemed familiar.

It had been Vince, the man who had barged into Thérèse's office. Lance must be right that he was involved somehow.

Did that make Thérèse part of whatever was going on? That would hurt Lance immensely. Thérèse was his oldest friend.

It was best if Elaine went home, back to Promise Cove. Lance was wrong. There were plenty of secrets in Promise Cove, but they were secrets about love and longing, not power and money. Maggie couldn't even find someone to take over as mayor.

For the first time since she'd walked into the restaurant, Elaine's shoulders relaxed a small amount and her stride shortened. She knew Promise Cove. As exotic—and warm in the winter—as New Orleans was, she didn't fit.

Was that the truth?

She'd enjoyed her friendships with Delilah and Thérèse, even with Nora, although she was from the Midwest. After a while, chatting with tourists in the square had become easier, and she was nodding acquaintances with many of the artists.

Most important, she'd begun to come into her own as an artist here.

Even Lance ...

No, she couldn't think about him right now. The pain was too fresh. The same agony that was telling her she'd fallen for him.

Only this time, she was going to be the one to walk away.

Chapter Twenty-Seven

"Your guest left," Lance's hostess informed him.

He wasn't really surprised. There'd be no declaration of love tonight, if ever. The ache in his heart had already started, but he didn't have time for that right now.

"I see. Have someone clear the alcove table. And, could you ask the mayor to come back here? I saw him at his usual table this evening."

The hostess nodded and walked off.

"Who are you working with?" he asked Whitney again.

"No one," she whispered, the whites of her eyes more visible because of her fear.

The mayor came around the corner.

"Whitney," he said. "I'm disappointed."

"I didn't *do* anything," the woman protested again.

Lance held up the thin shim and the tiny bugs.

"Looks like we'll have to put a stronger lock on that door," the mayor said.

Although he nodded, Lance had a different thought. Maybe Elaine was right. It was time to do away with the room all together. Make it into a small dining room that groups could rent, all on the up and up.

He was tired of secrets.

"Shall we go into your office?" the mayor suggested.

Lance nodded.

Her head down, Whitney followed His Honor into Lance's office. The mayor seated himself behind Lance's desk. His Honor was in charge, in spite of the fact that it was Lance's restaurant that had been attacked.

The situation proved how much of a fool Lance had been. In his excitement to be part of the crowd of people who seemed to make things run in this city, he'd jeopardized some of his values. Secrets were exciting, but they were also dangerous.

Trying to be part of the in-crowd always had a cost.

He'd put the reputation of his restaurant, the thing he'd worked so hard to build, at risk. People might view him as someone who had the mayor's ear, but that didn't make him a good human being. Worst of all, he'd lost a chance with the woman he loved.

He was going to have to make changes. Whether or not that would be enough for Elaine remained to be seen.

"These are not items an innocent person would carry," the mayor said, pushing the shim and bugs toward Whitney. "What was the plan? Bug the room for someone? Then that person could listen in on conversations—private conversations?"

Whitney sat straight in her chair, her expression neutral.

The mayor shook his head. "To say I'm disappointed is putting it mildly. I went to bat for you. I endorsed you, Whitney. You owe me an explanation."

Whitney still sat silently.

With a sigh, the mayor looked over at Lance. "I guess it's time to call the cops," he said.

Whitney stirred.

"I can do that," Lance said. "Definitely an attempt to break into what was obviously a locked room, no matter how flimsy the lock was."

"Don't call the cops," Whitney said. "Please."

"Then tell us what was going on," the mayor said.

"I can't." There was raw pain in the woman's voice.

"You must. Or we have no choice."

"My aunt ... she'll be devastated. You can't tell her. But ..."

"But what?" Lance asked.

"I'm afraid."

"Yes, we can see that." Lance moved his chair closer to Whitney's, naturally falling into the role of the good cop.

"Someone must have told you something to make you cross a line like this. Help us get him, and we can help you."

Whitney shook her head.

"You came to me," the mayor said. "You told me you had ambitions. You wanted to be in a position to help the people of color in this city, to show them that the government cared about them too. What kind of example are you showing them?"

"I know ..." she whispered.

"Do you?" The mayor's voice was hard. "Do you know what will happen, even if we don't arrest you? It's over. Your career in this city, in this state, is done."

"You don't have to tell anyone."

"Oh, but I do, Whitney. I do."

There was silence in the room. Whitney shifted uneasily in her chair while the mayor studied her.

"You see," the mayor said. "By taking this action, you've broken my trust. Not only that, the people's trust. You can't be in charge of our financial well-being. If it was this easy for you to break the law, what would you do with our money? You're a smart woman. You could easily manipulate our funds."

She looked at him with misery in her eyes.

"You've already done that, haven't you?" he asked softly.

She nodded once, then dropped her head in shame.

His phone buzzed. Elaine.

He couldn't help but look.

I saw Vince on the way out of the restaurant, the text said.

Interesting.

There was nothing more.

His heart felt a pang of regret.

He couldn't deal with that right now. He needed to straighten out this mess first.

"You know Vince Landry, don't you?" he asked Whitney.

She took in a sharp breath.

Lance looked over at the mayor.

"I suspected as much," the mayor said. "He put you up to this, didn't he?"

"I can't ... my aunt ... he said he'll tell her I ..." Whitney descended into tears and stared at her hands.

The mayor leaned back in Lance's chair. "I can't say I'm surprised. The chief came to me a few months ago, telling me he suspected there was a group on the take. It seemed to be very well organized, which meant there was some upper brass involved. Then when we got the latest proposed budget—the one Whitney's committee created—we noticed some money had been shuffled around. Items that had always gotten the same percentage were suddenly getting less, and a line item we didn't know anything about had a matching increase."

"Corruption."

"At the highest levels."

"He asked you to move the money, didn't he?" Lance touched Whitney's arm.

She nodded.

"And to break in here?" the mayor asked.

Again she nodded.

"Why would you do that?" the mayor asked. "Why risk everything for that man?"

Whitney raised her head. Tears were streaming down her face.

"I thought I'd done the right thing ... that you were corrupt. That's what he told me. I ... I believed him."

Lance felt sorry for her. When a manipulative man decided he wanted something, there was no limit to the damage he could do.

"Do you want a chance to redeem yourself?" the mayor asked.

She nodded with tears still glistening on her cheeks.

"Good. Here's what I want you to do."

ONCE WHITNEY WAS GONE, Lance asked, "What's going to happen to her?"

"She's finished here no matter what, which is a real tragedy. She's sharp and committed to making things better for all the citizens."

"Maybe after some time in exile as punishment, she can try again," Lance suggested. "People have run for higher offices with more baggage."

The mayor's smile was brief. "Could be. Not on my watch though. Rumors to the contrary, I try to run a clean office."

"Then why did you need the back room?" Lance asked.

"I didn't need it to make deals that were against the law," he said. "I gave that impression because I didn't want people to know what I was actually doing."

"Which was?"

"Working with a task force to root out corruption in the departments. The exact opposite. People like Vince are exactly who I was hunting."

"Will Whitney's testimony be enough?"

"No. And that's where you come in."

"Why me?" Lance asked. "I'm done with all of this. In fact, I'm closing down the back room. As of tonight."

The mayor shook his head.

"I need you to keep it open." He held up the bugs. "I'm going to have one of my guys plant these. In a few days, I'll have an interesting conversation with the police chief. The topic should draw Vince out."

"Are you sure you can trust the police chief?"

"He's my poker buddy." The mayor shrugged. "I know his tells when he's lying."

Lance hated doing it, but if it would bring Vince to justice, he would. The man deserved to suffer for the pain he was causing Whitney.

"Well, you figure all of that out. I've got a restaurant to run."

The mayor nodded.

Lance walked out onto the floor and found everything was still running smoothly. He checked in with the head waiter.

"We almost had a problem, but then your son smoothed it over," he said.

"What happened?"

"Wrong order. Well, it was the right order, but the customer claimed it was incorrect."

"But the customer is always right," Lance said.

"Except when they aren't. I was busy with something else when it happened. Xavier stepped in. He has the same magic you do, boss. Customer was eating out of his hand in five minutes. He tried the dish we'd brought out, loved it, and agreed to keep it. Of course, the extra scotch and water on the house and agreement to comp the meal didn't hurt."

Lance looked across to his son, nodded, and smiled.

Xavier gave him the same grin he used to as a child when he'd actually made it all the way around the bases in T-ball.

Lance's phone buzzed.

He stepped away from the head waiter and checked the message.

It was the one he'd been dreading all evening.

I don't think we should see each other anymore, Elaine wrote. *New Orleans is too much. I'm going home to Promise Cove.*

His gut twisted with pain.

A second text followed.

Don't contact me. Please. It will be easier for both of us.

Lance shoved the phone in his back pocket.

It was over before it had had a chance to begin.

Chapter Twenty-Eight

Elaine set up the canvas where she'd already started a hibiscus flower. It was her third floral creation, and the first two had sold immediately. She'd finally found her subject matter: the deep colors of nature in all its glory.

She'd decided to give herself one last week—a week without Lance—in New Orleans. She was never coming back, so she may as well enjoy the city on her own and give it a proper farewell. She had a few more days at the park, then she'd begin packing. Some of her stuff she'd ship back to Maggie as it was too cumbersome to bring on the plane.

Her flight arrangements were already made, and her daughter had agreed to pick her up at the airport in Kalispell. Maggie must have sensed the sorrow in her voice because she hadn't asked too many questions about why Elaine was coming home early.

Delilah handed her a cup of coffee and settled in next to her.

"You've really found your niche," she said, gazing at Elaine's painting.

"It's just a flower."

Delilah shook her head. "No, there's something about it ... It sounds weird, but I'd call it an experienced flower. Kind of like you." She smiled at Elaine. "Beautiful, but a little worn around the edges."

Elaine laughed. "That doesn't sound like a compliment."

"It's meant to be. There's something very beautiful about a woman who's had experience and learned from it, don't you think?"

"Maybe." Elaine mixed some darker red paints together to begin adding contrast to the petals. "But plenty of people have experiences and don't seem any wiser afterward."

"True."

Elaine turned Delilah's remark over in her head as she layered more color onto the petals. When she'd finished with one hue, she turned back to her friend.

"I think a person has to examine the experience they've had to get smarter about it. Then after a while they may get to the wisdom you're talking about. My friend, Henrietta, was excellent at analyzing experiences and reactions. She helped other people with it too. In fact, women artists of all types came to Promise Cove to go on one of her retreats."

"Sound amazing," Delilah said. "Does she still do them?"

"No. She passed a while ago. Her granddaughter seems to have inherited the gift though. She's running them now and building quite a reputation for herself."

"Probably pretty pricy."

"Yes. But she often holds a slot open for a local."

"Have you ever gone?"

"No. I've never felt the need," Elaine said.

Until now.

"I'm leaving," she told Delilah.

"But you just got here. Don't you want to work more on that flower?"

"No, I mean leaving New Orleans. This is my last week."

"But you'll be back after the holidays."

Elaine shook her head. "I'm not coming back."

"But what about the guy who owns the restaurant—Lance? I'm pretty sure he's fallen hard for you."

"Why?" Elaine asked.

"The puppy dog expression on his face," Delilah said.

Delilah was probably right. She was an astute observer of people which is what made her portraits of characters from around the city so popular with the tourists.

Lance would get over it, though. They hadn't been together that long.

"We're not right for each other," she told Delilah.

"That may be," Delilah said. "But it seemed like you made each other pretty happy. In my experience, it doesn't get much better than that."

"Too many differences," Elaine said and turned back to her painting.

A FEW DAYS LATER, SHE was ready to pack up for the last time. She'd miss being here, no matter how difficult it had been to paint at first. She learned a lot by observing other artists, not only the many different styles of painting, but how to interact with tourists. She'd dealt with the odd stranger coming through the general store all her life, but never this many with such a varying range of personalities.

"Could you do me one last favor?" she asked Delilah.

"No problem."

"Could you take this to Fontenot's for me?" She handed her friend the hibiscus picture.

"You don't want to do it yourself? Say good-bye?"

"No. We've said all we need to say." Thankfully, Lance had respected her wishes and hadn't come by the square.

"If you're sure ..."

"I am."

"I'll take care of it." Delilah stood and wrapped her arms around Elaine. "I'll miss you, girlfriend," she said. "Keep in touch." They'd exchanged phone numbers and emails.

"I will. And thanks for all the help you've given me."

"No problem. It was nice to have someone to share coffee duty with." Delilah frowned. "Now I'm back to having to get it myself." She gave a wink.

"I'm sure you'll make friends with the next person that has this spot."

"And I'm sure she won't be nearly as good as you," Delilah said.

They hugged one more time, then Elaine set off back down the street to her apartment. As she walked, she said mental goodbyes to the people and places she'd come to know. She almost stopped when she saw the man she'd spotted one of the first days she was here. He was looking at her over the top of his paper, like he had been that day. Once again, as soon as she looked at him, he quickly raised the paper so she could no longer see his eyes.

New Orleans was full of strange characters. It would be good to get back to Promise Cove.

She ignored the flat feeling inside her, the sense that she was going to miss New Orleans more than she thought right now, almost as much as she'd longed for Promise Cove.

Had she outgrown the small town?

She shoved the idea aside and picked up her pace.

"I CAN'T BELIEVE YOU aren't coming back," Nora said. "I'll miss our Friday walks."

"Me too. But I'm sure someone fabulous will rent this apartment, and you'll have a new friend."

"Could be."

Elaine continued to pack as she chatted with her neighbor. They'd done a lot of exploring together, from the city's cemeteries to an old brothel in Storyville that had just been opened to tourists. Nora had become a friend, not just a neighbor.

"You should come visit me in Promise Cove," she told Nora. "Glacier National Park is amazing."

"I'd love to, but it took me a lot of effort to get Owen to winter here. Now he's settled into a routine of winter here and summer at home. Asking him to go one more place would take a lot of heavy lifting." Then Nora cocked her head. "But I could go by myself. Wouldn't that be an adventure!"

Elaine laughed.

Shortly after, they hugged each other good-bye.

When she finished packing and had made arrangements with a carrier to pick up her items and ship them to Promise Cove, she decided to take one last walk around the neighborhood.

The sky, matching her mood was overcast. As she strolled by the familiar shops and cafés, she took mental snapshots to remember them: the place where she got her morning coffee, a shady bench that was perfect for people-watching, the bookshop and poster store with its odd assortment of hot sauces for sale.

Her footsteps took her to the levee overlooking the river. She sat down on another favorite bench and watched the river traffic, as well as the people who made sure the boats and ships navigated safely, had all of their papers, and were headed to the right spots for loading and unloading. Farther downstream, she could see the clusters of cruise ships. Far up the river, a steamboat casino was permanently anchored, somehow skirting the betting laws by being on water instead of land.

The Port of New Orleans was busy. No wonder Lance's job had been stressful.

She allowed herself to think of him. In spite of her words to Delilah, she wasn't sure she should leave without saying goodbye. But what was the point? He wasn't going to change. He was born and bred New Orleans, raised on intrigue and innuendo.

Promise Cove was where she belonged. She knew the rules and the people. There were flowers in Montana, too, although they were few and far between in the winter. She'd have to take lots of pictures in the warmer weather to get her through the winter.

Her phone buzzed.

Safe trip home, Lance had texted. Nothing else.

She was definitely doing the right thing. Promise Cove was her home, where she belonged. It was time to accept the fact that her life's adventures were over. They were fine for Nora who was a decade or so younger. Lance needed someone more his own age if he was going to have one more romance in his life.

Standing up from the bench, she took a last look around, then headed back to the apartment. Her flight was before noon the next morning, so she'd need to get up early and take care of last minute things before taking a taxi to the airport.

When she got home, she'd have to find a place to live. Maybe Fiona would let her have her cabin, at least for the rest of the winter. She'd settle into her proper role as mother, grandmother, and one of the town's artists. There were finally pieces to put into the gallery.

It would be a nice, quiet life for her remaining years.

She was too old for anything else.

Especially romance.

Chapter Twenty-Nine

"**G**ood morning, your honor," Lance said to the mayor as he greeted him at the hostess station a few days later. "We have the room all ready for you."

"Good. Please bring my guest there as soon as he arrives."

"He already has," Lance said.

"Oh, good. You've made him comfortable?"

"Quite. Shall I bring you your usual drink? Your guest has already been served."

Lance hadn't felt comfortable with the high-strung man he'd let into the back room about ten minutes ago, but the mayor had assured him the man was a trusted confidential informant. The police chief had chosen him as the most convincing person for the job.

The man—his name was Donat—had ordered a beer, that Lance had had one of his most trusted waiters bring to him.

Now he led the mayor down the corridor.

"Bon appetit. The waiter will be in shortly with your drink and to take your order."

"And no one else will disturb us," the mayor said.

"No. I've made sure of that."

"Good." The mayor closed the door behind him.

Lance stood there for a moment, unsure what to do next. He was supposed to act naturally, but for the first time the machinations of what was going on were as glaring as neon lights.

He'd treated it as a game in which he was a minor, but important player. In his mind, he could pretend that no one got hurt.

The image of Whitney in tears rose before him.

He walked away from the room.

These were real people who were affected by this corruption. Business people had lost thousands in protection money, and never felt quite safe anyway. The mayor had confided there had been several murders they'd tried to connect to Vince and his cronies, but the cops and their friends had covered their tracks well.

If they got anyone at all from the sting they were trying to run, the charges wouldn't be enough to do serious damage to the group. They were hoping for a way into the morass, a crack they could work to their advantage to pry the thing wide open.

"Corruption never totally goes away," the mayor had confessed. "As long as there are people willing to bend the rules to their own gain without considering the consequences for anyone else, it will exist. All we can hope to do is keep it at a reasonable level."

The statement had depressed Lance. So different from the idealism that Elaine had held dear. She'd recognized the difference between them before he had. For her, there were always rules. In New Orleans he had to accept that there were people for whom rules were only a suggestion to be ignored.

Laws didn't apply to them.

While he would never be willing to leave the city permanently—it was his home—he could see the appeal of never having to figure out who was playing by which rules.

He reached the podium as Thérèse arrived.

"Hello," he said, pulling her close for their traditional greeting. "I didn't expect to see you here today."

"Last minute thing, cher," she said. "I'm meeting someone. Business. Hush, hush." She smiled. "Is your back room free?"

"I'm afraid not."

"Oh. Busy day for secrets," she said.

He nodded. "There is a table on the opposite side of the kitchen that is away from the rest. It's quiet."

"Sounds perfect. Will you seat my guest when they arrive?" she asked the hostess.

"Of course. What is her name?"

"Him. Vince Landry."

Lance had to bite back his exclamation.

"You know him, cher," she said to Lance. "The deputy superintendent."

"Yes, yes. I do. Let me show you to your table." He brought Thérèse to the table at the far end of the restaurant. It was in a quiet nook, with a small window overlooking the courtyard behind the building. Men who were about to propose often asked for it.

Lance left his old friend, went to the bar, and asked for wine.

"Troubles?" Prosper asked.

"You could say that."

"Lotsa intrigue happenin'," Prosper said. "Can feel it in the air."

"Does it ever end?"

The old man shrugged. "Not really. All them lies and secrets swirling around us, like currents of water in the bayou. Some days it hard to keep our canoe on a steady course."

"Truth." Lance took a sip of the wine, the liquid warming the inside of his mouth, promising relief from the reality around him.

He'd best be careful with the stuff today. He put the glass on the counter.

"What about your lady friend?" Prosper asked.

"Ah ... well ... she's not my lady anymore. She went home. Back to Montana."

"She went back to all tha' cold? You must notta done a good job of keeping her warm, boss."

"She wants a life with rules."

"Ahh." Prosper handled some drink orders.

Lance stared into the garnet color of the wine. He could almost see Elaine's face in it. The ache of missing her was becoming a familiar companion.

"You need to talk to her," Prosper said. "Convince her you'll play by her rules."

"Her rules?"

"All women got rules. Don't you know that by now?"

Lance had to smile.

"Yeah," he said. "I suppose. But she won't even answer my texts."

"Don't mean she don't read 'em."

Lance nodded, but he knew the conversation was one that couldn't be had via text, even if he had any idea what to tell her. He had to see her face to face, which meant braving the cold in that far-off state.

Which was impossible.

He took another sip and went back to work, all the while keeping an eye on Thérèse and Vince, who had arrived while he was talking with Prosper, and waiting for a text from the mayor.

It was exhausting. Once this was over, the back room was out of business. He'd still be welcoming to the movers and the shakers—he wasn't foolish enough to think he could totally live without the adrenaline—but he'd keep his distance.

He was going to get back on the straight and narrow.

Vince's and Thérèse's conversation appeared to grow tense, based on his closed fist and the tightness in her neck.

Lance turned his back on them and went to greet a couple he didn't recognize as they came into the restaurant. They informed him they were tourists from Indianapolis and had heard this was the best place in town for fish. He explained he was the owner and would be delighted to recommend some dishes.

After he took them to their table, he learned more about them and got them two complimentary glasses of wine while he made some recommendations. They were interesting people. He was a scientist that worked for Eli Lily, and she was an executive director at a philanthropic organization.

They probably played by the rules too.

During their conversation, he began to relax. This was how he'd started with the restaurant: getting to know his guests and experimenting in the kitchen to please their palates. Somehow, he'd lost his way. He thought he was missing the power and excitement he'd had at his old job.

But maybe what he'd been missing was something else.

As he walked to the kitchen to check on how things were going, he glanced at the table where Thérèse and Vince sat. The pair were more relaxed.

In the kitchen, things were moving swiftly but in the well-organized manner he'd instilled in his head chef and employees. He leaned against the wall and watched for a while, noting little efficiencies that could be made, but also seeing which dishes were most popular and which were sent back for some adjustment or other.

There were improvements to be made, more dishes to create.

He felt a little bit of excitement as he mentally took notes.

His phone buzzed. The mayor was finished with the meeting.

Lance left the kitchen and worked his way to the back room. He unlocked it and checked for the bugs. As promised, the mayor had taken them with him. Then Lance closed and locked the door. He studied the lock for a moment. Flimsy didn't begin to describe it.

He walked into his office and called a locksmith. A second call was made to his interior designer. The back room was going to get a complete overhaul. Business was out. Subdued elegance was in.

Taking out a pad of paper, he wrote down all the thoughts he'd had about the food and restaurant while standing in the kitchen. Then he pulled up his payroll. There had been people who'd carried the weight of the restaurant while he was playing politician. It was time to give them a raise.

He'd received good reports on his son. As much as he hated the idea of Xavier giving up a steady job for the business, his son definitely had a talent for it.

It was time to give in. He'd come up with a formal training plan for Xavier.

That left him with two problems: Thérèse and Elaine.

Two women.

Of course.

At some point he'd need to confront Thérèse, but instinct told him he'd be better waiting for whatever the mayor was doing to run its course. No need to tip off Vince by discussing him with his friend.

That left Elaine.

Someone knocked on the door.

"Come in."

The hostess stepped in, a canvas in her hand. "Someone left this for you. She said it was a gift from Elaine."

Lance held out his hand. "Thank you."

The woman gave him the canvas, then left, closing the door behind her.

Only then did he look at the painting.

All breath left him.

A striking lavender peony stretched across the canvas, the profusion of petals artfully captured. A one-word signature anchored the lower right corner.

Elaine.

Chapter Thirty

"Hi Elaine," Sage, the general store's manager, said to Elaine. "Good to have you back for Christmas. How is New Orleans? Are you returning there soon?" Sage gave a mock shiver. "It must be nice to be warm this time of year."

"I'm not going back." Elaine pasted a smile on her face. "I missed Promise Cove too much."

"Yes, it's a special place. Anything I can help you with? Our lunch hours are passed, but I'm sure Henry can whip you up something. He's still in the kitchen."

"No, I'm not hungry. Thanks." Elaine wandered away from the counter. She wasn't sure why she was here. Habit, probably.

It had only taken her a day to confirm that she wasn't comfortable sharing the upstairs with people other than her family. Fiona had come through, and Elaine had moved into her cabin. It was only temporary, unfortunately, so half her stuff was still upstairs.

She was paying rent on two places, a situation that wasn't viable, even though neither of her landlords charged her very much.

After wandering up and down the aisles, she picked up a locally-made pie to bring over to Maggie's place. Her daughter had been badgering her to come to dinner. Even though Elaine didn't feel like seeing anyone in particular, she'd finally relented.

Best to get it out of the way. Then she could go back to brooding about Lance.

She'd thought he would be easy to get over. After all, what had they shared? A few outings, a lot of dinners ... some kisses.

Magical kisses. Kisses that had left her wanting more in a way she hadn't felt for years, if ever.

Pushing the thoughts from her head, she paid for the pie and left. She descended the outside stairs of the store and walked to the car. After depositing the pie in the passenger seat, she looked around, trying to anchor herself in the reality of where she was.

Diagonally across the main two-lane road from the general store, the ART building looked the same as it always had. Built of logs, the aging building had been used for many things since it was built, including a bar. Its last reincarnation had been as an art gallery, but somewhere along the line the letters for gallery had fallen off, so now it was simply ART. Local artists had created a co-op to run it. A co-op she hoped to join soon.

Next to ART, on the road leading out of town, stood the new performing arts center, Maggie's pride and joy. It was only open in the summer, but was already proving to be a good draw for tourists, so much so that finding a bed for the night was becoming impossible, even though several residents had offered AirBnB rentals. There simply weren't enough people in town to handle the surge of tourists who came in to see the acts at the center.

Fortunately, it wasn't her problem to solve.

"Elaine! I'm glad to see you," Kelly Svoboda said as she approached her.

They hugged, then Kelly stepped back.

"You're looking ..." Kelly frowned. "Sad? I thought you were having a good time in New Orleans ... that's what Maggie said. You were only home for Christmas."

"I'm not going back. I ... uh ... missed Promise Cove too much."

Kelly shook her head.

"I'm not buying that at all. Something happened." She raised her hands in surrender. "But I'm not going to pry. It's your business."

Elaine felt a sense of relief. Like her grandmother, Kelly saw too much in people. She had a kind of sixth sense that enabled her to ask the right question to get to the heart of whatever was wrong. That trait was part of her growing success in running her grandmother's business: a series of retreats for women artists of all kinds, some of them quite famous.

"Anyway, welcome home," Kelly said.

They chatted for a few more minutes, then Kelly started toward the general store to pick up her supplies. She'd only gone a few steps before she turned back.

"I have an idea. I'm running a retreat in mid-January. I don't have a local participant. How would you like to join us?"

"I'm not stuck on anything," Elaine said. "In fact, I had an artistic breakthrough in New Orleans."

"These retreats aren't only about art," Kelly said. "In fact, they rarely are." She paused. "Something's bothering you. I can see it in your eyes. I'm offering you a safe place to explore it."

The idea was terrifying and comforting at the same time. But what was the use of rehashing her time in the Big Easy? It was a nice break, but it was over. There was no point in dwelling on it.

Kelly waited, her gaze steady on Elaine.

It was eerie how much her presence reminded Elaine of Henrietta, her grandmother. She'd never been able to hide from Henrietta either.

"I'll think about it," she told Kelly.

"Good. I'll email you the information." Kelly nodded, then walked back to the general store with a small wave.

All Elaine had said was she was going to think about it. As soon as she'd gotten whatever Kelly was going to send her, she'd let her know she wasn't interested. She wasn't going to be browbeaten into navel-gazing or whatever went on in those retreats.

She walked around the mounds of snow that edged the general store parking lot, crossed the street, and went into the ART building. Stomping the snow off her shoes, she unzipped her coat-length parka and stepped into the main gallery.

"Elaine!" Ruth Anderson, a fantastic knitter and sweetheart of the town's bar owner, bustled from behind the counter to greet her.

Once again, she found herself enveloped in familiar arms.

This is why she'd come home. She knew who she was here.

Blinking back tears, Elaine pasted a smile on her face. "How are things going?"

"Amazing. This has been a very strange winter so far. The snow came heavy at the end of October, lasted a few weeks, and then the ground was bare again by mid-November. Lots of people came up from Kalispell and Whitefish. Things are selling like crazy over the internet. Business has been very good, but my fingers are aching from trying to keep up."

"I'm glad business is going well. Sorry about your hands."

"At some point I'll have to stop and say that's all there is. But what about you? How was New Orleans? Was it as marvelous as they say?"

"It's different from any place I've ever been," Elaine said. "I met some nice people, had some fabulous meals, and I painted a great deal. In fact, that's why I'm here. Is the procedure to join the co-op the same as it's always been?"

"Yep. You submit three pieces, and the board plus a group of the older members review them. If they accept them, you're in. And I'm sure you'll be accepted. I can't wait to see what you've done."

"I'll have to paint two more while I'm home. I only brought one back with me. The rest of them sold while I was still in New Orleans."

"How wonderful for you!" Ruth clapped her hands together. "I can't wait to see them."

"Thanks." Elaine looked around the large room. Things were pretty much the same as when she left.

It was good to be home.

Maybe if she told herself that enough, she'd believe it.

"IT SURE SMELLS GOOD in here," Elaine said as she walked into Maggie and Tom's cabin on the shore of Whitefish Lake.

"Elk stew," Maggie said. "Tom got a good-sized buck this year. The freezer is over-flowing. I'll be sure to get you some steaks once you're settled in."

"That would be nice." After they'd been in Montana a few years, Elaine's late husband had joined several others who went out during the appropriate season to get their deer or elk. It was one of the things that kept them afloat during the lean years.

"How are things going now that you're back?" Maggie asked. "Are you settling into Fiona's place?"

"Everything's fine," Elaine said.

"That's good." Maggie poured a glass of wine and handed it to her. "It's good to have you back. We're coming up on the Valentine's Day Fireman's Ball, and I'll need your help with that. Before you know it, the snow will melt, and it will be time to get the performing arts center open. They've got a great line-up this year. Many more name acts as well as some great ideas to get the locals involved."

Elaine sank into one of the chairs in the great room that served as kitchen, living room, and dining room in the small cabin. They'd built a master bedroom addition over the summer, but according to her daughter, there was still work to be done to add an office for her business as well as a small guest room.

"Do you think you could run the Summertime Celebration?" Maggie asked. "It's my busiest time for the garden design business. We're also doing more renovations, and you know how that goes with only a few short months of good weather."

Elaine was exhausted simply listening to her daughter. The celebration was more than she wanted to take on. All she really wanted to do was find a nice warm place to paint.

She missed her balcony ... and Delilah's companionship ... and Lance.

Why had she left?

"Mom?" Maggie asked. "Are you okay?"

"Yes, dear." Elaine smiled at her daughter, stuffing her own worries away with well-honed skill. "I think I'm tired. Listening to all your plans and ideas definitely wears me out."

"But you will help with the celebration and the ball, won't you?"

"I'll think about it."

From the look on Maggie's face, her daughter was about to launch into another cycle of persuasion, but just then Tom said, "Dinner's ready."

Elaine stood and walked to the table. Somehow, she needed to figure out what to do with her life in Promise Cove or Maggie would fill her days with noble busywork.

Chapter Thirty-One

Elaine studied the shooting star on her canvas. The delicate purple petals of the flower were slowly coming into focus as she layered on shades of paint. But it was missing something.

The dreary early January light that filtered through the thick windows didn't inspire her to the same type of lush painting that the bright light of the south had done. Shooting stars were beautiful, especially when they carpeted the high mountain pastures in late May or early June. To survive in the high elevations, though, the plant had adapted, its few small petals pointing upright to catch the sun, its dark anthers and bright yellow style pointing to the earth.

The hardy little plant was a survivor. It didn't have time to develop the lush petals and exotic interiors of the flowers she'd begun to paint in New Orleans.

That could probably describe her as well. She was a survivor. She'd always done what needed to be done, starting with coloring inside the lines as a child. The attitude had served her well as life threw its inevitable curveballs.

Given the choice, though, was that the life she wanted to live now? Instead of cutting up hard little apples into exact wedges, wouldn't it be fun to bite into a ripe peach and let the juice run down her throat?

She applied another layer. The painting would be able to convince the committee that she belonged as part of the ART family, but would it be enough to bring her joy?

Her phone buzzed. Another attempt from Lance to reach her.

She didn't answer, but a part of her wanted to pick up the phone and hear his voice.

When the phone rang again, it was Maggie. After a few pleasantries, she got to what she wanted.

"I hate to be a pain, Mom, but I could really use your help with the ball. People have been dropping out left and right with all the nasty bugs going around. It seems like every year there's a new variation of a respiratory disease."

"No problem," Elaine said absently, still staring at the flower on her canvas, trying to figure out how to make it come to life. "I told you I'd help. Just email me a list of what you want done, and I'll take a look."

"Okay. Mom, are you all right? You don't seem to have much energy. Maybe you should see a doctor."

"I'm fine."

"When was the last time you had a checkup?"

Maybe if she added a little halo around the upper petals?

"Mom."

"Oh, what darling?"

"When was the last time you had a checkup—you know—with a doctor?"

"I go every year at the same time. You know that. May. That's when I go. And there's nothing wrong with me."

Except the gloom. Why hadn't she ever noticed how dark December and January were?

"If you say so. Come to dinner tonight. Tom's grilling up some chicken, and I've made a couple of side dishes."

"Thanks. But I think I'd like to spend the night at home. Snuggle in with a good book or an old movie." Then she remembered. "I forgot. I promised Ruth we'd get together tonight."

"Well, that's good. At least you're getting out."

"I'm fine, Maggie. Really. Now let me get back to my painting."

"I can't wait to see it."

"Bye, Maggie."

Her daughter finally hung up, and Elaine picked up her brush.

SHE WAS FINISHING UP a few hours later when another phone call came in. This time it was Kelly, another person who wanted her to do something, although attending a retreat sounded a lot more fun than chasing people to make sure they were supporting the Fireman's Ball, a major fundraiser for the volunteer fire department.

Except that if Kelly was too much like Henrietta, Elaine would be required to face some hard truths she wasn't sure she was ready to deal with.

"Have you thought any more about coming to the retreat?" Kelly asked.

"I don't think it's the right time for me," Elaine said.

"Oh? Why is that?"

"Maggie's got me working on the ball, and I've got these paintings to finish up. I want to join ART, you know. It's about time. And I need to look for a permanent place to live. Fiona said they plan to use the cabin this summer. There are a lot of acts booked at the performing arts center they want to see. They already have their subscriptions."

"We all have those kinds of things in our lives," Kelly said. "Especially with Maggie around. I've got my list of tasks too."

"I bet. That daughter of mine is really good at telling people what to do."

Kelly chuckled. "But the thing is, we all need to set aside time to take care of ourselves. I'm not talking about our physical selves, although that's important, but our inner work, the kind that helps us find our ultimate paths and peace as we travel this human journey."

"I don't know. It sounds a little airy fairy to me."

"I know, but you were one of Henrietta's closest friends. You must have heard it before."

Elaine's heart ached. She missed her lifelong friend, who'd died way too early as far as she was concerned.

"I always let it wash over me," she told Kelly. "I had practicalities to deal with, like a daughter who was pregnant with no man in sight. And a store to run."

"Yes," Kelly said. "You held it together. You, Henrietta, and a few others built this town. You created a vision of what it could be, then slowly built it. You're the one Maggie gets her drive from."

Elaine hadn't ever considered it that way, but it was probably true. Once Jack had his store, he was content to be a storekeeper for the rest of his life. He had no dream beyond that.

Whereas her dreams had been deferred ... no, more than that ... they'd been abandoned. Once Teagan had been ready to go to college, Elaine had tried to resurrect her decades old ambitions, but they no longer fit who she was. She'd thought Paris would be the catalyst, but she'd felt like a fish out of water, trying to become someone that wasn't in her DNA.

Kelly seemed to sense when she ran to the end of her thought process.

"And what now, Elaine? Do you know?"

"I'll figure something out."

"I know you will." Kelly's voice was calm. "What I'm offering is a chance to take some time off and do the thinking in the company of a few other women who are also at a crossroads in their lives. Plus some good food and great wine, of course. I've even arranged for a body worker to work with each of you. Sometimes our muscles remember things our minds have buried too deep."

"I don't know." It was tempting. If she kept going to places and then running away when things got too complicated, she was never going to face what was holding her back from having her last years be the best they could be. The art was beginning to come together, but what about the rest of her life?

She didn't think she'd miss Lance, but she did. His calls and texts were becoming less frequent, but her longing to answer had increased.

"When is it again?" she asked.

"Next week. We begin Sunday."

"When do I need to let you know?"

"Now would be good," Kelly said. "But I can wait until tomorrow morning. If I don't hear from you by noon, I'll assume you aren't coming. I really wish you would, Elaine. Not only for yourself, but for the other women who will be there. I find sometimes a dose of Promise Cove reality helps them look at their lives from outside their artistic bubble."

"I'll let you know tomorrow. It will probably be a no, but ..."

"Think about it. It did good things for Alex and Maggie."

"I know." But her daughter and her friend had their whole lives ahead of them.

"By the way, one of the women, a dancer, is in her late sixties," Kelly said. "It's never too late to examine your life and see how you can make it better."

"Thanks. I'll talk to you tomorrow."

The woman may be in her sixties, but there was no way Elaine was going to be able to relate to a professional dancer.

She'd call Kelly tomorrow and politely decline.

"YOU SHOULD GO," RUTH said when Elaine explained Kelly's invitation. "Everyone who's gone to those retreats raves about them. They make changes, significant changes."

"I don't want to change," Elaine said. They were seated at Ruth's old oak table eating chili that had simmered all afternoon and huge hunks of homemade bread.

"Then why did you go to New Orleans?" Ruth challenged.

"Snow. Cold."

Ruth laughed. "I'm with you there. I'm trying to convince Mike to let Larry run the saloon in the winter so we can go to Florida. He's told me so much about Key West I can't wait to go."

"It would be good to get there before it's swamped by rising sea levels," Elaine pointed out.

"I know. It's sad to think of one of the icons of easy ocean living is under threat. Sometimes it feels like everything is changing beneath our feet. Everything familiar is shifting."

"Yes. I went back to my hometown a while ago, and I didn't even recognize it. My elementary school was an assisted living facility, and big box stores were everywhere."

"That's the worst part about getting old," Ruth said. "Things don't remain the way they were in our memory." She sliced off another piece of bread. "That's why we have to keep moving forward."

Was Ruth right? Was she trying to recreate something that had been a dream when she was in her late teens, before Jack had swept her off her feet? She wasn't young anymore. The vision of a New York City art career wasn't going to come true.

Jack was gone. He'd been gone for a long time.

She loved Promise Cove and had always envisioned spending the rest of her days here, but she hadn't counted on the loneliness.

"Didn't you meet a guy down there?" Ruth asked.

"Lance. He owned a restaurant. It was nothing ..."

She was lying. It hadn't been nothing. Not if her heart still ached the way it did.

"Lance ... like Lancelot," Ruth mused. "Lancelot and Elaine."

"Who?"

"It's one of the Arthurian legends," Ruth explained. "Unrequited love. She loved Lancelot, but as we all know, he had eyes only for Guinevere. Sad story."

"Sounds it."

Except in this case, it wasn't Elaine being spurned.

"Something happened in New Orleans," Ruth said, putting her bread on her plate. "And it sounds like it isn't finished. You know, I tried to tell myself I was too old and set in my ways to fall in love again. But when I stopped telling myself that, I found the man I didn't even know I was looking for."

"You and Mike make a great couple."

"I know." Ruth smiled. "But it wouldn't have happened if I didn't open myself up to it. That's why I think you should go to the retreat. Find out what you may be missing."

Elaine stirred her chili. Ruth was right. She had unfinished business with Lance. She hadn't really given him a chance to explain.

"Okay," she told Ruth. "You've convinced me. I'll call Kelly in the morning and tell her I'm going."

Chapter Thirty-Two

Lance knocked on Thérèse's door with trepidation. When he'd called to tell her he needed to talk with her, she'd asked him to meet her at her home.

As he stood in front of the modest house on the edge of the French Quarter, he couldn't help but admire the home Thérèse had made for herself. Blue paint was highlighted with bright white trim. Even on a chill mid-January late afternoon, the well-tended garden hosted beauty as her guest. Lance knew from experience that one of Thérèse's favorite things to do was to spend time in the spacious back garden, tending to blooms in the small greenhouse she'd had built. The size of the garden in the cramped quarter was what had led her to buy the house.

The door finally opened, and Thérèse greeted him with a warm smile.

"Come in, cher. I have drinks ready on the back porch."

The back porch was glassed in to maintain both the view and deal with the heat. Thérèse had had solar panels put on the back of the house, getting most of her electricity off the grid.

He settled into the comfortable chair as she poured him his usual drink and prepared him a small plate from the chacuterie that lay on the coffee table. He knew from experience that nothing would happen until she'd finished her preparations. Thérèse believed the graciousness of the Old South served a purpose. It was the way she ran her business and her life.

"Now, what has you so worried?" she asked as she sat down in her own chair, an aperitif in her hand.

"Why do you think I'm worried?"

She laughed. "I have known you too long for you to hide your feelings from me." She was quiet for a moment as she studied him. "But I see that it is not only worry that brings you here. It's sadness as well. We have much to talk about."

It was the thing he hated the most about his old friend. She saw too much.

"Was it a good week?" he asked. Two could play the delaying game that good manners provided.

"Yes, but that is not what you wish to discuss. Unfortunately, like I told you, I have someone coming for a late supper, so we have only an hour or so to talk before I must prepare for him."

Lance arched his eyebrows. "He?"

"I think the old-fashioned term is gentleman caller," she said. "And it is none of your business."

He nodded. Initially he'd been jealous when Thérèse took new lovers, but once he'd realized there wouldn't be anything between them but friendship, they'd begun to amuse him.

"What do you know about Vince Landry?" he asked.

"I thought that was what you wanted to know," she said. "I heard he has been arrested."

"Yes." The mayor's idea for a sting had gone well. They'd been able to trap Vince into committing a crime along with one of his partners. Vince had maintained his innocence, but the young man with him was all too willing to talk.

Unfortunately, they hadn't been able to hold onto the pair for long before the Feds swept in to take control of them.

"Your friend must have mentioned she'd seen him at my office. How is she, by the way?"

"Back in Montana so I wouldn't know."

"Ah ..." Thérèse said. "That's the reason for the sadness."

"Vince," Lance prompted.

"You weren't the only one who was undercover," she said. "Someone from the FBI contacted me a year ago. They asked me to cultivate a relationship with the man and report back to them."

"And you agreed? That was insane."

She shrugged. "I didn't really have a choice. My business ... well, let's say I may have cut some corners now and again, done business with people I shouldn't have. I cleaned it all up years ago, but they still found something to hang over my head." She popped a black olive in her mouth and chewed. "Prison would not have suited me," she added after she'd swallowed.

He half smiled. "I'm not sure about that," he said. "From what I hear, prisons have thriving businesses in black market items and information. Right up your alley."

"That's cruel, Lance. And it's not like you to be cruel."

"Sorry." He slid some slices of salami and mozzarella onto toasted bread and topped it with a marinated red pepper. After placing the delectable morsel in his mouth, he slowly chewed, exploring the flavors with all the taste buds at his disposal.

Somehow, in his urge to make his restaurant the premier place in the Big Easy to see and be seen, he'd forgotten about his first love: the food. When this was all behind him, he'd refocus on that. It had been a long time since he'd spent hours creating dishes in the kitchen.

"I hear the feds have Vince," she said.

"Yes. According to the police chief, they've got him in some secure location and are trying to get him to reveal the rest of the people on the take. Apparently, Whitney wasn't the only one he recruited within the city government."

"Good luck with that," Lance said.

"Yes. I think Vince will be more concerned about what his fellow cops could do to him than the feds," she said. "What will happen to Whitney?"

"She cooperated, and there were no charges filed. Her party has barred her from running for office again for two years."

"At least they did something. Most people turn a blind eye, even when there's a conviction. No wonder there's so much corruption in our government. Instead of working for us, some politicians spend their time figuring out how to run a better con."

"I didn't know you'd become so cynical," Lance said.

"Realistic," she said. Then a soft smile appeared on her lips. "But I still believe in love. That is something I'll never give up. So tell me, why did you chase the woman away to Montana?"

He laughed. "I think I was aided and abetted by the very corruption you mentioned."

"They don't have corruption in other places?"

"I think in the Western states they're much more blustery about it. We conceal our weapons. They wear them where they can be seen. I think it's the same with corruption. They say the dirty part out loud and dare anyone to come after them."

"So crass," she said.

He laughed again. "They think they're being out in the open."

Thérèse shuddered. "I'll take back room deals any day." She sipped her wine. "But that still doesn't explain why she's run away. She must have thought you weren't worth the effort."

"I'm crushed," he said, thumping his fist on his chest. He thought for a few moments. "I think she convinced herself it couldn't work. Anything became an excuse: the climate, our age difference, the city against the small town ..."

"Age?"

"She's eight years older than I am."

"Why does she think that's a problem? Men have adored older women for centuries."

"I don't think it's a problem. It's all in her mind."

"You must have done something to put it there."

"I swear, I didn't do anything to imply her age bothered me. In fact, the opposite. I told her it didn't matter."

"Cher," Thérèse said. "You're an idiot. Once you told her that, it was all she could think about."

He threw up his hands. "Women! I'll never understand them. Even my granddaughter ties me in knots."

Thérèse laughed. "You must get Elaine back. You've never been so happy as when you were with her."

"And how am I supposed to do that?"

"Go after her ... give her what she wants most in the world. Woo her. *Mon dieu*, have you forgotten the basics?"

"I've cooked for her," he said in his defense.

"Have you? Or have you served her meals in your restaurant. It is not the same. What's her favorite dish?"

He groaned.

"Grilled fresh trout from a Montana stream."

"So get her one."

"It's winter. They have snow up there. Lots of it. Besides, I don't think it's fishing season."

"A problem." She tapped her elegantly tipped finger on her lip for a few seconds, then waved her hand. "You can overcome it, I'm sure. You need to go after her and convince her to come back."

"And what am I to do with my restaurant? We just finished one busy season, but Mardi Gras will be on us soon this year."

"Then you had best get working. Train Xavier to handle the business while you're away. It's what he wants to do."

"He needs to get a real job, not play around in my restaurant."

She laughed.

"It isn't the way of these young people. They want to have careers and lives that they love. With so much uncertainty around us, I can't blame them."

He had to agree with her. Between climate change, endless war, and politics, there didn't seem to be stability anymore. Perhaps he should give his son the chance to live his life the way he wanted while he still could.

"I'll think about it."

"Wonderful." She rose. "Now you must be gone, Lance. I have things to prepare. An older woman may be just as attractive as a younger one, but we must work a lot harder at it."

He took a last sip of wine and put his glass down before standing up. She walked him to the front door and air-kissed him goodbye before shutting the door behind him with a thud.

Who was her caller? Anyone he knew?

Thérèse had always kept her love life behind closed doors, so he knew better than to pry. It had been difficult when they were younger, before he met Camille, when he thought he was in love with Thérèse. Then he'd realized what she'd always told him was true: they were better as friends.

She was right again. He was in love with the artist from Montana, and he needed to figure out how to get her back.

Chapter Thirty-Three

Elaine sat in her chair in Kelly's living room and glanced at the other participants on the retreat to fix their names in her mind. Martha was a dancer trying to figure out her next act, Imogene a comedy writer whose mourning for her husband was destroying her career, and Virginia, a writer who hadn't written a word in two years. When it had been her turn to speak, she'd stumbled through her reason for being there. With Kelly's help, she'd settled on "dissatisfied," without having a good reason why that was.

A fire burned in the stone hearth Kelly's grandmother had had built decades before. There were so many of Henrietta's touches still in the room: a painting done by a local artist, a quilt the local quilt maker—and Kelly's husband—had made when Henrietta had begun to ail, and a shawl Henrietta had knit up draped over the back of the small couch facing the fireplace.

"We're going to do some exercises this week that will help free up your imagination. We'll also have some discussions," Kelly said. "I've found the power of a small number of women to get to the heart of a matter quite amazing."

"All I seem to be able to do is cry," Imogene said. "I can't come up with anything coherent to say."

Kelly nodded. "That's what you said when you wrote me. I've scheduled the body worker to meet with you in your cabin tomorrow morning first thing after breakfast."

"I'm afraid I'll cry then too."

"And that's fine," Kelly said. "In fact, better than fine. Our bodies sometimes retain trauma far longer than they should. Releasing that may give you the breakthrough you're looking for. And the woman who will be working with you is totally used to people falling apart under her hands."

With small tracks of tears running down her face, Imogene nodded.

Kelly handed out small notebooks. "One of our local artists makes these. They're for your use while you're here. Tonight I'd like you to write about your dreams for the future and what you think is keeping you from achieving those dreams."

Dreams? Elaine was seventy years old. What right did she have to have dreams anymore? Her job was to avoid being a burden to anyone in her life before she passed on.

Virginia smiled at her. "It can be tough to think about dreams at our age," she said. "But I've found it's important to keep moving forward, keep our minds engaged with new thoughts and experiences. Otherwise, we risk becoming grumpy old folks who never see the good in anything that isn't exactly the same as it always was." She looked around the group. "It's why I'm having so much trouble with my writer's block. I'm so used to moving forward that's it's painful to be stuck."

"I've been dancing all my life," Martha said. "But my body can't do what I want it to do anymore. I'll never stop dancing, but I can't reach the positions or leaps I see in my mind's eye. If I attempt them, I risk injury that will put an end to my dancing days forever. I know I need to change direction a little, but not so drastically that I'd feel like I was done with dancing. That would destroy me."

It was Elaine's turn.

"I haven't had a career like any of you," she said. "I gave up my art before it even got started for my husband's dream. I've spent my life running the general store he wanted, raising my daughter, and later on helping her with my granddaughter." She shrugged. It wasn't much of a life compared to the resumes of the women sitting around her. Even Kelly had trained as a concert pianist before becoming a music teacher after she got married.

"Is your husband still alive?" Virginia asked.

"No, he passed a long time ago."

"And you're still here," Imogene said softly. "Running the store."

"Not anymore. My daughter and I sold it last summer."

"So you're free," Martha said. "And you don't know what to do with it."

The dancer put the truth so simply.

Elaine nodded.

"Are you painting?" Virginia asked.

"Yes. I was stuck with that for a long time. I was in New Orleans until before Christmas. I thought I had a breakthrough there, but ..." She wrapped her arms around her chest. "Now, I seem stuck again."

"It's no wonder," Imogene said, pulling the sweater she had on tighter to her body. "I don't know how you people stand this weather up here. It's so cold and damp ... and gray."

"You're spoiled," the dancer said. "All that California brightness."

"It rains in southern California," Imogene said.

"Nope," Virginia said. "But it pours ..."

Elaine joined her on the rest of the old song lyric. "Man, it pours."

The women laughed together.

She smiled. These women were wonderful. Maybe she could break through to new joy with their help.

THE NEXT MORNING THEY met in the great room in what had been an old barn. Coffee, fruit, yogurt, and breakfast rolls lay on the pass-through counter from the kitchen. Elaine had already had her breakfast at home, but she still took a cup of coffee and roll. The others, who were staying in small cabins on the retreat property, filled bowls and plates.

"Dreaming is hard work," Virginia confessed when she sat down. "I've always known where the next book was coming from, so I've never had to worry about it. When it all dried up, I had no idea what to do."

"What did you write down?" Elaine asked. She'd barely been able to come up with anything, except finding a studio. But every time she tried to nail down details, images of flower-filled gardens took over.

It had snowed during the night, so she'd had to shovel and clean off her car. She hated winter.

Her vehemence had surprised her. She knew she didn't like winter, but hated?

She'd dumped the question with the next shovelful of snow. Right now, it was reality.

"I thought a lot about what Kelly suggested," Virginia said. "I pushed myself to be outrageous. I went beyond the safe things like a daily massage—"

"Ooh ... that sounds wonderful," Imogene said.

"It did to me too," Virginia said. "But then I thought about a massage in one of those grass-roofed things built over the water ... you know ... the ones you always see for those high-end island hotels?"

"I know what you mean," Elaine said. Her body relaxed at the thought of a masseuse with strong hands digging deep into her muscles as the surf whooshed its way to the shore.

"But then I realized that wasn't bold enough," Virginia said. "I've been to islands. But I haven't been to ... Australia."

"Wonderful place," Martha said. "I had a residency once there. They make the arts so much more accessible to people. No need to pay a few hundred dollars for a ticket."

"Exactly," Virginia said. "I realized what I really wanted was a residency, a chance to sit and write ... or just think ..."

"That's a luxury," Imogene said.

"Yep," Virginia agreed. "Someplace with a bad wi-fi connection. Enough to email, but not stream. A nearby library, and an old-fashioned turntable on a shelf with a good record collection."

"Parrots outside the window," Martha said. "They're big on parrots."

"Lovely!" Virginia clapped her hands together.

The group laughed, and Elaine's spirits were buoyed.

Virginia was dreaming about a place she'd never been.

Was Elaine selling herself short because she didn't dare imagine herself in a place she'd already been? In a place with an attractive man ready to spend time with her?

Was it because she thought she didn't deserve it? Or that it was a sinful desire at this time of life?

The conversation drifted to the most exotic places people had been. Elaine was surprised to learn that Imogene had hiked in Nepal when she was younger and also gone on a safari in Africa with her late husband. For the first time, she smiled when she talked about her husband.

After breakfast, Kelly gathered them together and had them share their dreams. Martha wanted to win a Tony Award for choreography. Imogene surprised them all by saying what she really wanted to do was stand-up comedy.

"I'm tired of working in a group, coming up with ideas for the same comedy show week after week. I feel I really need to break out of the pack. It's what my husband wanted me to do." As soon as she finished talking, she started crying. Kelly put her hand on her back and handed her a tissue box. Virginia rubbed her shoulder from the other side.

"Why don't we take a break?" Kelly asked.

Martha and Elaine nodded. Both stood to refill their coffee mugs.

Of all of them, Martha was the hardest for Elaine to relate to. The woman was already well-known as a dancer. Truthfully, she intimidated Elaine a little. She was about the same age but had accomplished so much more.

"Stop comparing," Martha said sharply.

"What do you mean?"

"I can see it in your eyes, your body movements. Every time one of us speaks, you measure your life against ours." The dancer shook her head. "There's only two results that come from comparisons, and they both lead to dissatisfaction. Either you think you're better than the other person—probably not true in your case—or you think you're less than them. So stop doing it."

Martha walked back to her chair, each step a graceful movement.

Elaine looked at the small group. She didn't belong here. She'd make her excuses to Kelly and leave.

Virginia got up with her coffee cup. After she refilled it, she linked her arm through Elaine's. "Your turn," she said and guided Elaine back to the table.

ALL WEEK LONG ELAINE forced herself to dig deeper. As Martha had challenged her to do, she tried to think of the other women as inspiration, not competition. It made her realize that she'd been taught at an early age to view people as better than or worse than herself. It had been an unintentional result of her parents' method of child-rearing, but they hadn't been alone in the tactic.

Her grades were always compared to the other girls she knew—never the boys because, by default, they were going to be better than any girls. It had been a subtle point that she hadn't been aware of at the time, but it was clear now that it had had a powerful impact on how she'd lived her life.

Girls were always in competition for the boy of their choice. They weren't taught to go after a career ... not yet ... so the MRS was their aspirational degree. In fact, her father had expressed his relief when she'd given up her dream of being a New York artist in order to follow Jack to Montana.

When they'd had to draw the gremlin that represented the inner critic that lived in their heads, Elaine had drawn a composite: mother, father, aunts, preachers, and teachers. She gave the gremlin a glossy women's magazine to carry.

So many voices ...

Martha's eyes had widened when she'd seen it. "Oh my!" she'd shouted. "It's perfect!" She'd beamed at Elaine.

Later that night, Martha had instructed Kelly to put on some music and led them all in a dance. She gave them all long scarves and told them to simply move themselves to the music. Then she came around and offered small suggestions. At the end, winded and tired, they'd gathered in a circle for a mutual hug.

Elaine had never felt so in tune with other women.

But, in spite of it all, she wasn't any clearer on the direction she should take than she'd been before.

It was only when they had a session on internal rules that some ideas began to shake loose.

"Many of us believe things because we've been taught them as children," Kelly said. "Some of them are useful, like looking both ways before crossing the street. Others may serve us well at the beginning of our lives, but fade out of usefulness as we age."

"Like the idea that women should defer," Marsha said. "I got that one in spades. Ballet teachers ruled my life as a little girl, even though I realized early on that I was no one's ideal of a fairy tale princess. I wanted to make bold leaps. Choreographers wanted me to dance pretty pirouettes on my toes."

"Exactly," Kelly said.

"Like staying quiet as a child," Virginia said. "Because it was what kept me safe." She glanced at the others. "My dad was an alcoholic who beat my mother and brother."

"I'm so sorry," Elaine said.

Virginia shrugged. "It was a long time ago. I've had enough therapy to put it in perspective. But it took me a long time to find my voice." She frowned. "And now I'm being quiet again. Maybe it's time to think about who is blocking my words and not what."

"What about you, Elaine?" Imogene asked.

"There were all kinds of rules growing up, that's for sure," Elaine said.

"We kind of got that from your gremlin," Martha said with a grin.

Elaine nodded. "And they've served me well through most of my adult life. I worked hard, was a good wife to my husband. My daughter turned out pretty well, although she had a few lapses of reason along the way."

"Don't they all?" Kelly said with a smile.

"Sure do," Virginia said with a grin.

"But now ... well, I'm not sure what the rules are. My parents stayed together all their lives and passed within a few months of each other in their early seventies. The rest of the families are also together. Some are happy. Some aren't." She had a mental image of one of her uncles who spent his retirement watching television, drinking beer with his buddies, and serving on the church council. His wife lived a totally separate life, doing crafts and gardening with her lifelong friends.

They didn't even have dinner together anymore.

It had always struck her as impossibly sad.

"Maybe it's time to invent your own," Martha said.

Elaine barely heard her. She'd continued down memory lane, remembering that same aunt explaining exactly how many years older the man must be for a woman to have a successful marriage.

"Oh!" she exclaimed.

"I think she realized something," Imogene said.

"Looks like it," Virginia agreed.

Elaine nodded. "I've got some thinking to do."

"Good," Kelly said. "Because that's your assignment for the night. Brainstorm about the internal rules that govern your life and make a conscious decision about which ones you want to keep and which ones you want to try to give up. I say 'try' because internal rules can be stubborn."

There was murmured agreement.

"But, Elaine, your work will have to wait. You're scheduled to be with the body worker in a half hour. We've warmed up the Athena cabin, and she'll be waiting for you there."

"Really? I hadn't expected ..."

"Everyone gets the same experience," Kelly said with a smile.

"Thank you." Hiring a body worker wasn't cheap, and since she hadn't paid anything for the retreat, Elaine hadn't expected the same treatment as paying guests.

She approached the cabin with trepidation. She'd had a few massages, but hadn't enjoyed them as much as others. The idea of someone she didn't really know touching her naked skin didn't sit comfortably.

Probably another one of those conservative Midwestern rules she'd been indoctrinated with.

Once inside, she was greeted by soft music and a spicy aroma. A young woman emerged from the attached studio.

"Welcome," she said in a soft voice. "I invite you to sit here for a few moments while I finish my preparations. Then I'll be back to talk with you."

Elaine sat down, every muscle in her body tense. She looked around the room. As befitting the goddess of wisdom, there was a bookshelf of old texts from different cultures and religions, from books by the current Dalai Lama to an annotated Bible. Women authors were well-represented.

"I'm Suri," the young woman said as she re-entered the room and took a seat. "We will be working together today to increase your creative energy and joy. I understand you're a painter?"

"Yes."

"Women come to this retreat because they feel they are stuck or at a crossroads. Can you tell me a little bit about what may be preventing you from having a life of joy and creativity?"

"Uh ..."

"Take your time. We aren't on a schedule."

Elaine thought for a moment. "The closest I can come is that I feel discontented with pretty much everything, including myself."

"That can happen when we don't allow ourselves time to grieve," Suri said.

"But I don't have anything to grieve. No one's died ... at least not recently."

"It's not only death that causes us to grieve. Since I've been working with Kelly's clients, I've realized that most of you are at a major crossroads of one type or another. It's like the Tarot Death card coming up in a reading. It doesn't mean death, literally. It means a major phase in your life is ending, and a new one is about to begin. Our society encourages people to keep plowing ahead, when what we need to do is take some time to grieve the ending of that part of our existence."

"We've recently sold the general store, the one my husband and I bought decades ago." Elaine's voice trailed off. That store had been her whole life. Everything had revolved around Maggie and that store. Now one was gone, and the other was well into her own life.

"Let's go into the other room. I'll step out and you can disrobe as much as you feel comfortable."

As if in a trance, Elaine followed the young woman. After Suri left the room, she stripped down to her underwear and lay on the table, face down as instructed.

When the woman returned, she turned down the lights, and said, "Feel free to let go. There's a tissue box within reach if you need it. I'm going to start with light touches on your back, neck and head. Where I go next depends on what I feel from you. Okay?"

"Yes." She felt safe with Suri, although she couldn't exactly explain why.

For the next hour, Suri worked on various points of her body, sometimes with a light touch, sometimes digging deeper. Elaine almost fell into a trance, one that was painfully interrupted when Suri's fingers pressed into her lower back.

What she'd thought was pain, however, quickly transformed to tears.

"Let it go," Suri said softly.

So she allowed herself to cry. It was ridiculous, lying on her stomach while a stranger massaged her lower back. But it was also freeing, letting herself go without being concerned about taking care of anyone else or what she'd look like when she was finished.

By the time Suri was done, Elaine was exhausted, but somehow freer. She couldn't put the difference into words, but Suri assured her that was part of the process.

"Sometimes," she said. "Our grief and trauma are stored in our muscles. It's only through work like this we're able to release them. It's important work." She stepped out to allow Elaine to get dressed, then encouraged her to lie down on the bed and nap.

"I'll clean up and exit by the side door."

"Thank you," Elaine said.

Suri clasped her hands and looked into Elaine's eyes. "Remember. Once you fully let go of the past, there's room for your future to come into your life."

Elaine's throat tightened. All she could do was nod.

Then, as Suri had suggested, she lay on the bed and went to sleep.

Chapter Thirty-Four

How did people deal with this for months on end? And why weren't there more cars lying in ditches? Especially the way these people drove?

Lance's white knuckles gripped the steering wheel of the rental car as he followed the directions from the airport built on flat land next to towering mountains. The scenery was beautiful, especially now that he was on the ground—that plane had come far too close to those peaks for his comfort.

To his relief, the two-lane highway was mostly clear of snow, but every once in a while a hard piece of snow remained, and the wheels seemed to slip just a little.

This was a fool's errand. Why had he let Thérèse and Xavier talk him into it? Thérèse had assured him he'd have nothing but regrets if he didn't make some grand gesture to win back Elaine, and Xavier had guaranteed he'd keep the restaurant running while he was away.

The problem was that Lance wasn't sure he believed either one of them. And what was he supposed to do for a grand gesture? All he knew how to do was make sure ships dealt with the Port of New Orleans correctly and run a restaurant.

And even that was going through a change. The mayor had not been happy about his decision to close the back room for clandestine meetings, instead opening it up for small parties. Some of his clientele, as if sensing they could no longer feed their need for gossip at Fontenot's, no longer came.

As a result, his receipts were down.

Thérèse assured him a little marketing would take care of that problem.

Somehow they'd convinced him to buy a ticket to this frigid place. But neither of them had the faintest idea how to impress Elaine. They patted him on the shoulder and said he'd figure it out.

Right.

Finally, he pulled into the parking lot of the hotel in Whitefish where he'd made a reservation. He'd rest, find a restaurant for dinner, and desperately try to come up with a plan.

In the end, he decided on pizza and beer. A number of restaurants were only open on the weekends when the skiers decided to descend from the mountain and the locals came out for date night.

He found a table and placed an order for a local beer.

When the waiter brought it back, he asked, "What do people do around here in the winter?"

The waiter, a thin young man with a scraggly beard and longish hair, smiled. "From your accent, you're not from around here."

"No. New Orleans."

"Always wanted to go there. Anyway, people ski." He pointed in one direction. "Or they ice fish." He pointed in the opposite direction. "A lot of folks cross country ski or snowshoe in the park. Some folks just hunker down and wait for spring."

That would be Lance's choice if he lived here.

"What do they fish for?"

"Lake trout, whitefish, that kind of thing."

Trout. It wasn't out of a flowing mountain stream, but it might do. Over the rest of the night he quizzed the waiter on the particulars of the sport.

When he went to bed, he thought he might have a great idea.

LATER THE NEXT DAY, reality struck.

Lance sat on a camp stool on a frozen lake, staring into a small hole where his fishing line sat still in the water. He'd been fishing all his life, but this experience was totally alien. The clothing the clerk had assured him was totally adequate seemed to have myriad small slits that let in the frozen breeze that was constant on the lake.

He'd been there for an hour when he got a nibble on the equipment the clerk had also sold him. He played the fish for a while, but then his line went slack. He muttered under his breath, stood, and reeled the line from the water.

"Bad luck," another fisherman said. He held out a beer. "Helps keep you warm. Your first time?"

"Yes." And hopefully his last.

"Wow, man. You're from the south somewhere. What are you doing up here?"

Lance shrugged. "I like to fish. I thought I'd give it a try."

"Got it," the man said. "Mind if I give you a few pointers? My name's Jim, by the way."

"Lance. And no, I don't mind. I'll take all the help I can get."

"Good man." Jim grinned, allowing Lance to discover the man's mouth in the midst of his bushy beard.

Jim gave him some tips, then went back to his own hole, where he turned up the radio so Lance could hear it too. A half hour later, he shared a roast beef sandwich, then suggested they toss a football for a while to warm up.

After another beer, Lance was feeling a bit mellow. That was when his fish decided to bite. Jim helped him haul out a fish that weighed about eight pounds. Good enough for a nice dinner. He asked Jim where he could get it cleaned and filleted, packed up his gear, and left, promising Jim he'd contact him the next time he decided to go out on the ice.

Which would be never.

He dropped off the fish, went back to the hotel, and stood in the shower until he ran out of hot water. For dinner, he settled for a hamburger and whiskey at a restaurant around the corner, went to bed, and slept the night through.

The next morning, he picked up his fish and headed to Promise Cove.

The town was just as Elaine had described it, and the young woman at the counter of the general store was only too happy to give him directions to the cabin Elaine was renting.

The people up here were entirely too trusting.

"COMING!" ELAINE YELLED toward the front of the house as the doorbell rang for a second time. She wiped as much of the fresh paint off her hands as she could, then strode to the living room, ready to give the person who'd interrupted her a piece of her mind. She'd finally gotten back into the flow and didn't need anyone bothering her.

She yanked open the door.

Lance stood there with a shopping bag and a bouquet of flowers in his hand.

"I've come to win you back," he said. "Trout dinner." He held up the bag. "I caught it myself."

The poor man looked frozen, and his cheeks had the raw red of skin that had been out in the cold for much longer than it was used to.

What was he doing here?

He cleared his throat. "Would you mind if I came in? It's way too cold out here."

"I'm sorry." She stepped aside.

"Kitchen?" he asked.

She pointed, still trying to figure out what he was doing here. Although he had said he was going to win her back, apparently with trout he'd caught himself.

A vague memory floated up.

She'd told him her favorite meal was grilled, freshly-caught trout.

He'd gone out ... in winter ... and caught one for her.

And he'd left his beloved restaurant in someone else's control.

For her.

She gasped. No one had ever done anything approaching that kind of effort for her. Not even Jack.

Slamming the door closed, she hustled into the kitchen.

Lance was laying things out on the counter, but when she entered, he picked up the bouquet from where it lay on the table and handed it to her.

"It's nowhere near as good as the one I would get you in New Orleans, but it's hard to find flowers in this frozen wasteland." He held them out. "It's good to see you. I've missed you."

"I've missed you too," she said, stepping closer and taking the bouquet.

He pulled her close and greeted her the way he'd always done in New Orleans. After the obligatory air kiss he held still for a moment and looked into her eyes for a few seconds.

Then he kissed her on the lips.

His mouth was so right on hers. She wrapped her arms around him and returned the kiss, deepening it, allowing her feelings to be free from the rules her family had imposed on her so long ago. While she wasn't in love with him yet, she was open to the idea.

More than open.

She released him and searched the room for something for the flowers.

"I think there." Lance pointed to the top of a cabinet.

She pulled the vase down and took it to the sink where she washed it and filled it with water.

"You went fishing?" she asked, still incredulous that he was here and that he'd caught a trout to please her.

"Yes. It is an insane practice you have here ... sitting on a huge lake, freezing, to get a fish. A man named Jim was very helpful."

"Oh?"

"Yes." Lance soon had her in stitches as he explained his adventures on the frozen lake. "Did you know they even drive on top of this lake? It's insane!"

She laughed. "It takes a special kind of person to live in Montana."

"I'm afraid, cher," he said with a sad expression on his face, "I can never be that person. I thought I might be able to adapt, but ..." He shivered. "It is too cold. I would miss walking down the streets of my city." He faced her. "I'm hoping I can persuade you to return to New Orleans." He reached out and took her hands in his. "I would very much like that."

He gestured to the supplies on the counter. "This is not all. I heard what you said about the politics of the city." He shrugged. "I can't change that, but I've taken myself and the restaurant out of the middle of it. The back room is only for parties now. I've told the mayor, and others, they are welcome for a good meal and friendship, but politics must stay where it belongs, at city hall."

He'd upended his life for her, so that she would feel comfortable with him. The ice fishing almost paled in comparison.

"That's a huge change."

"I know it," he said. "But you're worth it. You're more than worth it." His voice dropped to a whisper. "So, what do you think? Are you willing to return to New Orleans with me and give us a chance? A chance to fall in love?"

This was the moment. She'd spent the time at the retreat putting the past behind her. Now she had to decide where she wanted to be during the next phase of her life. It was all she'd been thinking about since the retreat had ended.

She'd followed a man once, and didn't want to do it again, but New Orleans had been her choice first. To be truthful, she'd grown to love the freedom of living without winter. Yes, there were other problems, but no place was free of natural hazards of all kinds.

Promise Cove had given her a good life, and she'd always want to come home to see her daughter and friends.

But now it was time to live her life for herself. Time to find out exactly what the man in front of her was offering.

"Yes," she said. "I will go back to New Orleans with you."

This time their kiss awoke desire.

Dinner was served later.

Much later.

THE NEXT FEW DAYS WERE a lesson in living with snow and cold, but more happily, Lance was shown the importance of community and deep friendships. Relationships were often convoluted messes in New Orleans. Everyone was polite, but what wasn't said could be lethal.

Here it was pretty clear who was friendly and who wasn't. But all of that went by the wayside when someone needed help.

Elaine's daughter turned out to be almost as gifted in getting people to do what she wanted as the mayor of New Orleans. Lance found himself promising to ship back a box of pralines and Mardi Gras beads for the all-important Fireman's Ball. Elaine pointed out that Maggie could ship them herself since she and Teagan had promised to come to his city for Mardi Gras.

Maggie had waved that aside, informing her mother that if Lance was going to be a part of their family, he could pitch in like everyone else.

Her husband, Tom, had given Lance a look of sympathy.

And so, even in the brief amount of time he was in the small town, he'd been knit into the fabric of Promise Cove life. The local saloon owner, Mike, had even thrown a small party so everyone could meet the man who was taking their beloved Elaine away.

Not everyone had been happy.

Mike had proudly delivered a burger to Lance, declaring it the first of the New Orleans style hamburgers he was going to promote.

Lance looked at it warily, but it turned out Mike understood the essence of heat and had added the right amount of hot sauce. Lance had nodded, and quickly finished off the meal.

Just when he felt he couldn't endure meeting another person, accepting another handmade gift, or shoveling another foot of snow, it was time for him to leave.

Elaine promised to join him in a few days.

He'd never been happier in his life.

Chapter Thirty-Five

New Orleans, a few weeks later

"Grandma, this is amazing!" Teagan said to Elaine as they watched one of the many Mardi Gras parades thread through the French Quarter from their perch near the fence around Jackson Square. Maggie stood on the other side of Elaine. Lance had gotten them grand stand seating near the Hotel Lafayette. He would be joining them as soon as the lunch rush at Fontenot's was complete.

There was no shortage of parades to view, he'd told them. There were over eighty of them throughout the city in the weeks leading up to the final day of Mardi Gras. In between, Elaine had taken her daughter and granddaughter to many of the most popular sites in the city.

Her neighbor Nora had joined them several times, ecstatic that Elaine had been able to re-lease the apartment next door again. Although Elaine hadn't taken up her spot on Jackson Square again, she'd introduced her daughter and granddaughter to Delilah.

Delilah was also growing tired of being on the square, and they were talking about renting a studio together.

Elaine had a lot of friends she'd left behind in Promise Cove, but she was making new ones in the city. Once she'd realized that her life as a store-owner's wife and mother were in the past, she'd embraced the idea of creating a future for herself.

As much as she understood, Maggie had played the guilt card once or twice.

When she'd had enough of Maggie trying to get her to stay, Elaine pointed out it was time for younger people to take over the soul of the town. "We did the heavy lifting while you were all finding yourselves," she told her daughter. "Henrietta's gone, Fiona and Ruth have started their new lives, and even Betsy is talking about retiring from the post office. I've found something I love to do, and maybe a man to do it with. I'm not sure how it will all turn out, but I'm not going to let the opportunity to find out pass me by."

Eventually, Maggie had come around to her point of view, especially after Tom talked to her and reminded her that everyone, no matter who they were, deserved a chance at the happiness love could bring.

He was a good man, her son-in-law.

Elaine hugged Teagan close and gave Maggie a smile. Then she saw Lance walking toward them, his gaze already intent on her.

They were going slow, and he allowed her plenty of space, but she loved spending time with him. She especially enjoyed being the recipient of his new dishes. Clearing out the taint of gossip seemed to have awoken his interest in experimenting with food again.

He climbed up the stands to join them, not settling for traditional air kisses, but kissing her full on the lips before taking her hand.

Joy flooded her heart.

They may not be in love yet, but they were definitely headed that way.

For the time being, she'd settle for happily ever now.

NEWLY DIVORCED, SHE'S ready for independence, family, and adventure ... until a chance meeting with her secret teenage crush threatens to derail her. Drop into your favorite online or local bookstore to get your print copy of Grown-Up Second Chance and start reading!

Diane O'Sullivan and her two sisters have hit the road in their 43-foot motorhome. With her ex far in the rearview mirror and only a few accounting clients left, Diane's looking forward to exploring the country.

When Joe Kelly shows up at their RV campsite outside Yellowstone, it's a charming coincidence. He's humorous and happy, reminding her of the girl she was. More than once he rescues her from the dangers of the park, and the tourists who visit it.

They could easily become involved.

But wait! That's exactly what she doesn't want. She has plans! After dumping her dull-as-dishwater ex, she's not ready to take on another project. And, isn't a man always a project?

Will Joe take the hint?

Grown-Up Second Chance is a later-in-life romantic comedy. It's the first in a series.

Drop into your favorite online or local bookstore to get your print copy of Grown-Up Second Chance mix your Cosmo or G & T, and get ready to embark on a road trip of laughter and love.

Author's Note

WHEN I WAS DOING THE research on New Orleans for *Away from Promise Cove*, I came across an article about the mayor and a high-ranking officer in the police force. Apparently, they were using a city-owned apartment to carry on an affair and were caught by surveillance camera. That little article spawned the relationship between Vince and Whitney.

I've been to New Orleans once on a business trip and found the French Quarter to be delightful. There was a store devoted to hot sauce. Bottles lined the walls. Making a choice was insanely difficult.

I'm sure things in the city remain the same as my memories, while other things are radically different. Some of the people I was with at the time have passed on.

This is how life goes. Reality no longer matches memories, and we lose people. But I've always thought it important to meet new ones and make new memories. Life in the present is so much richer than dwelling in the dimness of the past.

Things come to an end, and so it is with this series. This is the last Promise Cove book. I've enjoyed the people and the town, and I hope you did, too.

There's a new series brewing in my mind, but in the meantime, pick up a copy of Grown-Up Second Chance to go on a fun road trip with three sisters!

Casey

About the Author

CASEY DAWES WRITES non-steamy contemporary romance and inspirational women's fiction with romantic elements.

Her women's fiction series, Rocky Mountain Front, explores the five siblings from a ranching family living in Montana, the people who love them, and the characters in the small town in which they live. Previous to that she wrote a 5-book contemporary romance series about friends and family on the Central Coast. Her latest series features love between "seasoned" heroes and heroines in a small Montana town.

Currently, she and her husband are traveling the US in a small trailer with the cat who owns them. When not writing or editing, she is exploring national parks, haunting independent bookstores, and lurking in spinning and yarn stores trying not to get caught fondling the fiber!

Did you enjoy Promise Cove? Hop over to my website: www.caseydawes.com and pick up a free book of short stories. You will be added to my newsletter mailing list: On the Road to Your Next Read ...

Other Books by Casey Dawes

Promise Cove
Return to Promise Cove
Spring in Promise Cove
Hope in Promise Cove
Winter in Promise Cove
Promise Cove Wedding
Summer in Promise Cove
Away from Promise Cove
Beck Family Saga
This series revolves around a Montana ranching family—women's fiction with a touch of romance!
Home Is Where the Heart Is
Finding Home
Leaving Home
Coming Home
Starting for Home
Finally Home
RV Park Romance Series
Brand new romantic comedy series!
Grown-Up Second Chance
Her Son's Secret Father
Her Texas Cowboy

California Romance Series

Two mothers, two daughters, and one friend explore contemporary romance on the California coast.

California Sunset

California Wine

California Homecoming

California Thyme

California Sunrise

Montana Christmas Series

A new adult contemporary romance series set in Missoula Montana—just right for the holidays!

Sweet Montana Christmas

Montana Christmas Magic

Second Chance Christmas

www.ingramcontent.com/pod-product-compliance
Lightning Source LLC
Chambersburg PA
CBHW021157160726
47994CB00001B/245